A MURDER
IN MACEDON

To my sister Bridget and her husband Frank,
lovers of Greece!!

HISTORICAL NOTE

By 336 B.C. Philip of Macedon was leader of Greece. Macedon had become a great military power to the north of Greece and had brought under its sway the kingdom of Epirus on its western border and that of Thessaly on its east. Philip's army reforms and brilliant strategy had brought the independent Greek city-states, such as Athens and Thebes, to recognize his power and he had removed any threat from these by his great victory over the Athenian-Theban alliance at Chaeronea in 338 B.C. By 336 B.C. Philip had divorced his wife Olympias and married again. He had been hailed as captain general of Greece and was on the verge of launching a great military expedition against Persia. Despite the opposition of individuals such as Demosthenes of Athens, Philip's power had reached its zenith: In the summer of 336 B.C. he had summoned all the representatives of Greece to a great celebration at the old Macedonian capital of Aegae. Philip was on the verge of creating a new world: He had a new wife, a new baby son, the loyalty of the army, and the fealty of all Greece. The celebrations at Aegae were used to mark

the marriage of King Molossus of Epirus, Olympias's half-brother, to Cleopatra, Philip's daughter by another woman. They were also to emphasize Philip's power before he left to join his army, waiting beyond the Hellespont, under his two generals, Attalus and Parmenio. Philip knew others secretly fumed at what was happening: his kinsmen, the Lyncestrians; Demosthenes of Athens; Darius III of Persia, and, above all, his former wife Olympias and her son, the twenty-year-old Alexander. Philip ignored these and, in doing so, committed *hubris,* an arrogance that always provoked the anger of the gods. . . .

LIST OF HISTORICAL CHARACTERS

PHILIP OF MACEDON: king

OLYMPIAS: his divorced and rejected queen

ALEXANDER: son of Olympias, later Alexander the Great

EURYDICE: Philip's new wife

CARANUS: Eurydice's baby son

ARRIDHAEUS: half-wit, a son of Philip by one of his concu-
bines

LYNCESTRIANS: related to Philip with a claim to the throne
of Macedon

MOLOSSUS (or Alexander): king of Epirus, Olympias's
half-brother, bridegroom of Philip's daughter Cleopatra

ANTIPATER: chief of staff in Philip's army in Macedon. A veteran of Philip's campaigns

PARMENIO and ATTALUS: joint commanders in chief of the
Macedonian army in Asia. Attalus was uncle of Eurydice, Philip's new queen

PTOLEMY, NIARCHOS, HEPHAESTION: Alexander's companions

ARISTANDER: Olympias's sorcerer, later in the service of
   Alexander
DEMOSTHENES: Athenian orator
DARIUS III: new king of Persia, Alexander's great opponent
EURIPIDES: playwright who spent some time in Philip's court
ARISTOPHANES: playwright
PERDICCAS: a member of the royal bodyguard
PAUSANIAS: captain of the royal bodyguard
PERICLES: a great Athenian statesman of the fifth century B.C.
ARISTOTLE: Philosopher, tutor to Alexander.

It is very confusing when many of the historical characters
have the same name. E.g., I have called Philip's rivals the
Lyncestrians (their tribal name) to avoid repeating that one
of them was also called Alexander. The same name was also
used by the King of Molossus. According to textbooks
Philip's wife (who gave birth to Caranus) has been called
Eurydice, in other places Cleopatra. I have used Eurydice to
avoid any confusion with Alexander the Great's half-sister.

A MURDER
IN MACEDON

CHAPTER 1

PERSEPOLIS 336 B.C.

IN A SMALL, towered chamber off the Apanda, the great, pillared audience hall of his palace in Persepolis, Darius III, King of Kings, ruler of Persia and its empire, god's regent on earth and possessor of men's necks, ran his fingers through his oiled beard and smiled crookedly at the figure opposite. Darius shifted on the silk-clad cushions and, closing his eyes, savored the fragrant flavor of frankincense and myrrh. The slave girl, squatting between his thighs, one hand against his crotch, the other pushing a grape between the wet lips of her master, blinked and sighed softly.

"You may go," Darius whispered.

The girl disappeared. Darius sighed and rearranged his robes. His eyes wandered around, observing the gilt-topped pillars, the ceilings of gold and silver, the marble frescoed walls before returning to catch the sightless stare of Vizier Barses. Darius, born Cadoman, newly raised to the purple by this most subtle of viziers, quietly rejoiced at his own cunning. His gaze fell to the table in front of him and all the merriment died. A map was spread out: to its right, across the Hellespont, the empire of Persia, to its left the king-doms of Greece. Darius stabbed each of the names etched there: Athens with its fleet; Corinth with its wealth; Thebes and its soldiers; Delphi with its oracle. All the great cities and sacred places of Greece that his revered forebear Xerxes had tried to drag as low as Hades. Darius's finger moved north and stopped. He picked up the two small statues, one slightly larger than the other, each representing a Greek hoplite in full battle dress. The large, horsehair-plumed helmet, cuirass, leather skirt, rounded shield, and long pike or lance. Darius put them back so they covered the title MACEDON.

"The situation is quite clear, my dear Barses," he mur-mured. "Philip of Macedon is now master of Greece. He's defeated Athens and Thebes at Chaeronea. Soon he will be hailed as ruler of Greece, captain general of its armies." Dar-ius moved his finger. "And then he wishes to take what is mine. You see, my dear Barses, he's already despatched two generals, Attalus and Parmenio, across the Hellespont. They led a small force, two or three regiments, to hold the cross-ing till he arrives." Darius closed his eyes and gnawed on his lips. One-eyed, lame Philip! A Macedonian barbarian! Dar-ius opened his eyes. "A small army, Barses, but, we mustn't forget Xenephon, must we? He showed all the world that a Greek army can wander around Persia unscathed. So, what Xenephon did, Philip of Macedon can do. And, where Philip goes, his son Alexander will undoubtedly have to fol-low."

Darius paused at the faint cry from outside. He waggled a finger at Barses.

"Don't worry," he whispered. "Their pain will soon be over. I doubt if they'll be alive at dawn. My real worry is Philip. He has the impudence to proclaim himself a god." Darius rubbed a finger round his lips. If only he knew more about the politics of the Macedonian court! Philip was at war with his wife Olympias, that queen of snakes. Alexander was Olympias's boy and, when Olympias fought, Alexander would not stand aside. "I would have loved more time to meddle there," Darius declared. "Stirred up the hatred between father and son a little more. Nothing like a civil war, is there, Barses, to keep a tyrant occupied?"

Darius heard another cry. He rose and walked out onto the balcony and stared down. The huge parade ground below where the Immortals, the royal Persian guard, drilled and maneuvered, was now lit by a long row of bonfires stretching as far as the eye could see. In between each bonfire was a cross with a writhing figure nailed against it.

"How many live?" Darius's voice carried.

A captain of the guard stepped out of the shadows. He knelt and covered his face with his hands.

"Great king," he called, "only five survive. The rest—" The captain gestured with one hand. "They have choked."

Darius smelled the rottenness of the corpses that mingled with the exotic night odors from the imperial gardens.

"What is your wish, Great King?"

Darius stared up at the moonlit sky. He muttered a prayer to the Lord of Light. The moon was full and rounded, like a silver disc; the more he stared at it, the closer it came. Perhaps Philip was staring at that moon? Darius's hands balled into fists. He tapped these gently against the balustrade. Demosthenes, too, in his little house near the Agora in Athens, that great democrat, that fiery demogogue, that taker of Persian gold! Demosthenes would be dreaming his dreams. Of being a second Pericles, a man who could proclaim that he had saved Greece from tyranny. Well, Demosthenes could dream but he'd better earn the gold he'd taken.

"Great King?" the captain of the guard called.

Darius breathed in.

"Kill them!" he shouted, "but not with a lance. Break their legs. Let them choke like the rest!"

Darius watched his orders being carried out. Two guards ran across to a cross, a wooden board between their hands. The noble crucified there, naked, knew what was coming. He glimpsed the wooden board and screamed for pity. The two soldiers stopped on either side and, holding the board between them, brought it back and struck the man's legs just beneath the knee. Darius heard the crack and watched the body slide farther down the cross. As the soldiers moved to the next victim, he walked back into his small chamber and took a seat opposite the silent Barses. Darius poured himself a goblet of wine. He toasted his vizier silently and began to sip. A curtain was pulled back. A chamberlain entered this holy of holies and prostrated himself. Darius let him wait. It was good for all to know that he, king of kings, possessed their necks. Let them all know what it was like to press their faces against the cold marble floor of his palaces. Darius sipped again, putting his cup down; he clicked his fingers. The chamberlain approached, head down, face averted. He placed the scroll on a cushion beside Darius and withdrew into the darkness. Darius broke the seal and undid the scroll. It was a report from a Persian spy in Athens who, in turn, had received news from another in the old Macedonian capital of Aegae. Darius sighed long and noisily.

"It is done! It is done!" he repeated.

He snatched grapes from the bowl, placed one before Barses and chewed carefully. As he withdrew his hand, one of the rings on his finger caught the two Greek hoplites, knocking them both over. Darius saw this as a sign. He joined his hands in prayer and bowed.

"Good news, Barses! Within days, Philip of Macedon and his mongrel son will be no more!"

Darius studied his dead vizier. The embalmers had performed a most exquisite and delicate task. They had kept everything as it should be, except for the life in those dead eyes! Darius chuckled softly. Barses, the great vizier, stuffed like a cushion! A man who had helped him to the throne but dared offer him poison. However, Darius, by the lord of lights' intervention, had been saved from Barses's evil plotting. Indeed, in this very chamber, Darius had made Barses drink the same poison, drop by drop, watching the terror in his eyes and listening to that evil, old mouth beg for mercy. Outside, all those who had supported Barses had been crucified—a warning to those in Persia and abroad, not to lift their hands against the king of kings. Darius lay back on the cushions. Soon others would learn their lesson. Philip and his Macedonians. Darius puckered his lower lip between his fingers; perhaps, when he had finished with Macedon, he might visit Athens and demand that Demosthenes repay his gold.

THE PALACE OF AEGAE: JUNE 336 B.C.

OLYMPIAS, FORMERLY QUEEN of Philip of Macedon, sat in her small private chamber in a wing of the old royal palace. She, too, thought of death and plotted murder though she cleverly hid the seething hatred within her. She sat at her spinning wheel, one foot tapping the floor, flexing the thread, holding the shuttle as expertly as any weaver. She smiled across at the young woman who sat on cushions against the wall.

"You are well, Eurydice?"

"Oh yes!"

Olympias's soft, olive-skinned face broke into a smile. She

patted her auburn hair back beneath the dark veil that covered her head. She looked at Eurydice, then at the great, golden figure of the wine god, Dionysus, carved in the wall above her. Dionysus! Olympias's favorite, whose secret rites she celebrated in dark, lonely groves well away from the spies of her former husband. Olympias lowered her face. Men called her serene, her features perfectly sculptured: a slender nose, beautiful mouth, and light-green eyes that would glow with pleasure or gleam in anger.

"As beautiful as Aphrodite," one artist had dared to comment. "A figure that would be envied by Hera herself," another added.

Olympias watched the wheel spin. What did men know? What did they really think went on behind the mask she wore? Did they know the secret rites or the pact she had made? Or truly realize where she came from? She was the daughter of the King of Epirus. She was a descendant of Achilles who had fought and killed Hector of Troy in hand-to-hand combat. She had been visited by a god on the night her son Alexander was conceived! Zeus's thunder bolt had entered her womb and she had quickened. Zeus had then sealed her womb with his own special mark. Olympias gathered the flax in her hand. Now she had been displaced so brutally! A simple messenger had arrived in her quarters and announced:

"Philip of Macedon declares that Olympias is no longer his wife!"

Divorced! Supplanted by that soft-faced, mewling-mouthed girl who now squatted on the cushions holding her loathsome baby. Eurydice with her melonlike breasts, broad hips, and long legs; her stupid, foppish face, framed by lustrous black hair, showed all the intelligence of one of Philip's famous mares.

"Olympias?"

The former queen raised her head and smiled.

"Eurydice, my dear, what is it?"

Philip's new wife got up and brought across her baby swathed tightly in a purple, gold-fringed robe. Olympias noticed this and breathed in so noisily her nostrils flared. How dare she? How dare this bitch bring her brat into her presence swathed in royal purple?

"What is it, my dear?"

Eurydice, who adored Olympias and regarded her as her closest friend, pulled back the robe.

"Caranus is rather hot."

Olympias stopped her spinning and gently took the child. She pressed a finger against his dimpled cheek. The baby boy opened his eyes and cooed. Olympias rocked the infant, one finger snaking down the robe, pressing against his throat. If the gods are good Olympias thought, this brat will have a raging fever but the flesh was cool and silky soft. Olympias shook her head. She tucked Eurydice playfully under the chin.

"Caranus is well, a bouncing baby boy!"

"Will he grow up like Alexander?" Eurydice asked. "I saw him today on the drill ground. He was talking to his friends you know, the Jews Simeon and Miriam."

"Ah yes." Olympias smiled. "Simeon and Miriam Bartimaeus. Have you heard their story?"

Eurydice shook her head and stared lovingly into Olympias's light-green eyes. She adored this woman. Eurydice felt little regret at having supplanted her but, there again, that was Philip's fault not hers. Moreover, if Philip insisted on spilling his seed into her night afternight so Eurydice conceived a son whom he called Caranus, after the founder of his house, was that really her fault? Or, if Philip was even thinking of repudiating his own son Alexander, surely that was his right?

"You have been so kind," Eurydice broke in before Olympias could reply to her former question.

"Child, child." Olympias stretched out a hand, turning her fingers slightly so her nails wouldn't rake the young woman's cheek. "Any one who is married to Philip needs all the kindness in the world. He drinks until he can hardly move and he copulates with anything that will agree with him. Men, women." Olympias giggled behind her hand. "Sometimes even goats!"

Eurydice swallowed hard in embarrassment. She blushed and looked down at the baby. Philip was such an ardent lover. Drunk or sober he'd mount her like a stallion would a mare. If she wasn't available, due to her monthly courses or the last few weeks of her pregnancy, then one of her slave girls would do just as well. Philip with his one eye, his shattered leg, his bruised arm, his scheming mind.

"Don't worry," Olympias purred. "I know it all, Eurydice! If you need any advice, just come and see me."

"I came tonight," the new queen replied, "because Philip is drinking with his companions."

"Ah yes. Philip and his companions! You know, Eurydice, they have all the morals of a herd of mountain goats. They have taken more women and sacked more cities than Hercules did in his prime."

Eurydice caught the mockery in Olympias's voice, the veiled insult to Hercules, the god whom Philip claimed as one of his ancestors. Olympias touched the spinning wheel with her finger watching it move backward and forward.

"And is my son Alexander there?"

Eurydice shook her head. She squatted on the floor with her baby, rocking gently backward and forward.

"No, he's in his own quarters with the Jews, Miriam and Simeon."

"Ah yes," Olympias replied. "I was going to tell you

about them! They are twins you know? Their parents were slaves. Philip bought them from a Sidonian merchant. The mother was, I remember, small and dark. She did not have your child-bearing hips. Philip had to hire a special physician. Ah." Olympias tapped the side of her head. "I forget his name but he had to open the poor woman's womb and pluck the babes out."

"What happened to her?" Eurydice broke in, remembering her own labor pains.

"Oh she died," Olympias retorted. "There was nothing the physician could do except give her an opiate. The twins were a boy and girl joined at the elbow."

Eurydice stared back, open-mouthed. Stupid, Olympias thought, you are so stupid you don't deserve to live. She gave this girl, her rival, the queen who had supplanted her, a most dazzling smile.

"The physician cut them apart," she continued. "You can still see the mark on their elbows. I went down to inspect them—ugly, little creatures they were. Not," she added quickly, "like your beautiful Caranus."

Eurydice nodded solemnly. The man Simeon was square, thick-set, clean-shaven, like Alexander. Eurydice was frightened of the Jew's dark brooding eyes; his slightly pointed ears and hair that hung in ringlets, gave him an appearance of a satyr. The woman, Miriam, well, she was of medium height but rather angular, pretty in a sharp-featured way but no breasts or hips to talk about. Her quick eyes reminded Eurydice of a kestrel Philip kept in their bedchamber.

"Well, their father later died," Olympias continued. "I remember Philip going down to tell the children; they must have been about ten years old. Philip, as usual, was drunk. He pointed to the boy and said he could join Alexander's troop. They led him away and the girl started screaming. So Philip shouted, 'For goodness sake, shut her up!' "

Olympias tittered behind her hand. "Well, you know Antipater," she said, referring to Philip's one-eyed commander. "He drew his sword, thinking Philip wanted her dead."

Eurydice joined in the laughter. Antipater was a grizzled, old man with a smile like vinegar and a temper to match. He may be the bravest of Philip's companions but he was certainly not the brightest.

"Marched too long in the sun without his helmet on," Philip had once commented.

"What happened?" Eurydice asked.

"Oh, the boy became one of Philip's principal scribes; he carries the royal seal."

"And the girl?"

"I don't know." Olympias gathered the wool into her lap. "She's so thin and sharp-featured. She can't be my son's lover. Alexander doesn't like women too much. I wonder why? Anyway, Miriam was raised with the other boys. They say she can run like a gazelle and swim like a fish. But then?" Olympias was genuinely puzzled. She hadn't really thought about the Jews. They had posed no danger. Secretive, they worshipped an Unknown God whose name they dared not pronounce.

"Ah yes." Olympias leaned down and stroked Caranus gently on the brow. "They are also actors. They play stories from their people's history. Alexander is intrigued, as he is by anything strange." The words came out more waspish than Olympias intended so her smile widened. She licked her lips. "Would you like some wine, Eurydice?" She clicked her fingers.

The old man sitting on a stool in a shadowy corner rose. He shuffled forward, his small, pebblelike eyes caught those of Olympias. He held up his right hand showing the large ring on the middle finger. Olympias shook her head imperceptibly. Now was not the time, she thought, for Aristander of Telemesus, her seer, her necromancer, to open his ring so Eurydice could drink more than she intended. There would be a time and a place but this was not it. Aristander brought the cups across. Eurydice grabbed hers and slurped at it. Olympias lifted her eyes to the ceiling and muttered a prayer to Dionysus, the great god of the dark glade. Then, turning, she poured a little of the wine on the ground to the shades of her many victims.

"And what does Philip intend to do tomorrow?" Olympias asked.

Eurydice watched the old man shuffle back to his stool. She had forgotten he was there. Eurydice felt a chill and stared round the room. People whispered so many stories about Olympias. Eurydice nervously picked at the tassels of her baby's shawl. It was dark in here. Oil lamps glowed in their alcoves. The marble mosaic on the floor showing the head of Medea seemed to spring to life—its eyes caught the light and seemed to glare up at her. Perhaps it was time she went? She made to rise.

"No, no, stay!" Olympias stretched and touched her rival on the tip of her nose. "I am so lonely, Eurydice. No one ever comes to see me, not even Alexander. Growing old all alone!" she continued wistfully. "You were going to tell me about tomorrow?"

"Philip is going to walk into the amphitheater," Eurydice replied. "All the ambassadors from Greece and elsewhere will be there. He's had twelve great statues constructed, representing the Olympian gods. They will be pulled in first and each set above an altar specially dedicated to them."

"And then?"

"Philip has had a statue made of himself. That, too, will be wheeled into the amphitheater. Sacrifices will be made."

Olympias could have bitten her lip in fury.

"So," she snorted, "Philip now sees himself as one of the Olympians, does he?"

Eurydice's eyes narrowed. Olympias lowered her head and examined the wool in her lap. In the corner Aristander moved restlessly on his stool. Olympias cursed herself; she'd shown her temper and this girl had to be watched.

"It's only right," she murmured. Olympias picked up the flax, wrapping it round her hands, letting her fingers feel the texture. "I am making you something, Eurydice."

"Oh, what is it?"

"It's going to be a surprise," Olympias replied. "Something for you to wear but I won't give you it. Well, not for some time yet. So, tell me more about tomorrow?"

"Well." Eurydice was now becoming confused. Her baby was asleep in her arms but she felt uncomfortable. She had come here to hide from Philip's great feast. She felt lonely, Uncle Attalus was far away with Parmenio across the Hellespont.

"It will be a great day," Olympias urged. "Are you going to be there?"

"Oh yes, in the royal box," the young woman chattered on. "Caranus and I. Oh, and the Lyncestrians." Eurydice referred to the two brothers, distant kinsmen of Philip.

Olympias fingered the precious piece of jade round her neck. She must not forget the Lyncestrians! The "twin rats" she called them, with their furtive faces and darting eyes. Olympias's spies had informed her that they constantly grumbled how kinsman Philip was getting above himself and not acting like a true Macedonian prince. Were they a danger? She wondered? Could they threaten her son? No, not as long as Philip was alive, but that was the problem. How long should Philip live? That oracle from Delphi, when Philip had asked if he would vanquish the king of Persia, replied: "The bull is wreathed for sacrifice. All is ready. The slayer is at hand." Philip thought the oracle was referring to Persia, but was it?

Eurydice sipped at her wine. She could not understand these abrupt periods of silence. It was as if Olympias didn't really want her here, but then she'd smile, and all would be well.

"Philip is going to enter the amphitheater by himself," Eurydice offered.

"Is he now?"

"Oh yes. Only his son-in-law Molossus on one side and Alexander on the other. His bodyguards are going before him. Philip says he wants to show the envoys of Greece that he's not a tyrant."

"He's a fool!" Olympias snapped.

Aristander scraped back his stool. Eurydice nearly dropped her cup. Olympias's face had changed—skin tight, eyes blazing, mouth curled in the rictus of a smile. Olympias, however, acted concerned and angry.

"He's a fool," she repeated, "to walk by himself, with so many of his enemies present. He has one eye missing; the soldiers may call him a fox but he limps like an old goat!"

"Is he in danger?" Eurydice, now alarmed, scrambled to her feet, cradling the baby in the crook of her arm.

"I am sorry."

Olympias also rose. She embraced the girl, pulling her close. Her touch was so soft, her perfume so fragrant, Eurydice relaxed; Olympias was only concerned.

"I will see Philip." Olympias pushed her gently away. "I'll have words with your husband," she teased. "Now," she murmured, "go back to your chamber, girl. Philip will expect you there when he comes lumbering back from the feast, belly full of wine and loins full of lust. You can't disappoint him can you?"

The girl bowed and, as soon as the door closed behind her, Olympias tore the veil from her hair and threw it on the floor.

"I'll kill her!" she whispered hoarsely. Olympias picked up the flax lying around the great spinning wheel and raised it up as if in sacrifice. "I'll weave her a noose," she grated, "I'll put it round her pretty neck and watch those lovely legs kick. And, as for her son?"

Olympias walked over to where a small brazier of charcoal stood near the window. She stood, warming her fingers, listening to the distant sounds of revelry from elsewhere in the palace.

"I am Philip's wife!" she hissed. "Alexander is my son. Yet look at us, Aristander? I'm divorced and there are rumors that Alexander is a bastard, an illegitimate by-blow."

"Hush, Mistress," Aristander came shuffling out of the darkness, his stick rattling like the tap of a deathwatch beatle. "Hush now, Mistress."

Olympias turned, her hair fell down to her shoulders; her head was tilted, chin against her chest. Terrifying, Aristander thought, she is the Medea! He recalled the lines from Euripides' play.

" 'We are slaves of the gods,' " he quoted. " 'Whatever we be, we are their playthings!' "

"Not me."

Olympias walked slowly toward him. She moved languorously, flowing like a dancer beginning the first steps of some wild, exotic rite. Her hair billowed out, her hands came up.

"Aristander, we must walk again. I must prepare for the god."

Her hand caught his thin wrist. The seer winced at the pain that shot up his arm. Olympias's eyes now glowed. No longer green, they caught and reflected the blazing fire.

"Alexander," Aristander replied, not thinking; he just had to break this spell. "Alexander, you should make sure that all is well with him before we meet our spy."

"Not now!" Olympias snapped.

Yet Aristander's words had their effect. She closed her eyes and sat down on the small chair before her spinning wheel.

"I do not wish to meet Alexander. Not tonight of all nights. But there is a way; come with me!"

Olympias took her cloak from a peg on the wall and wrapped it round her. She pulled up the hood so it covered her head and most of her face. Aristander knew what she meant. When she swept out of the door along the long, vaulted gallery, he scampered along after her. "Olympias's dog" they called him but he didn't really care because Aristander had his own secret plans. The palace galleries were lit by oil lamps and burning torches. Every so often they would pass the Pezetairi, the royal bodyguards, hoplites in full armor, breastplates, leather skirts, greaves, horse-plumed helmets, rounded shields, and long pikes or lances. They snapped to attention as she passed, their shields clashing against the swords that hung in their leather scabbards. Olympias swept on by though, as always, she took careful note of their faces. They were the same ones she had passed earlier in the evening. Olympias relaxed. An unexpected change of guard, those she knew, being replaced by those she didn't, was always an augury of impending danger in the bloody, violent feuds of the Macedonian royal house.

Olympias turned a corner and went down some steps; here the air was colder, more stale. The passageway ahead of her led to a storeroom. Olympias went halfway down then stopped. Aristander searched for the concealed lever and the hidden door swung open. Aristander took a torch from an iron clasp in the wall. He ushered Olympias in and closed the door quietly behind them. The passageway was narrow, no more than a yard wide, just enough room for a man to draw his sword and defend himself. In the darkness Olympias smiled. This ancient palace of Macedon was a crumbling, old pile. Its maze of corridors, a relic from the bloody past, when princes had fought each other for control. Philip had been educated in such a terrible school. His mother had murdered his father and then tried to kill Philip and his brothers. Philip had fled to Thebes where he had learned the art of war as well as the important and only lesson in politics: seize your opponents and kill them. Philip had used this corridor in the destruction of his rivals and, shortly after his marriage to Olympias, when he had been full of passion and eager to show and tell her everything, he had taken her here. Philip had forgotten but Olympias hadn't.

They must have walked for some time when the narrow pathway began to climb. Aristander began to wheeze and, on one occasion, had to beg his mistress to stop. She did, snapping her fingers impatiently. A rat slithered across her sandaled feet but Olympias didn't flinch.

"You know where we are going, Aristander, and you know the reason why."

She turned and swept on. Her seer hurried behind her, cursing under his breath as a faint breeze caught the torch and showered him with sparks. At last the path leveled out. Olympias moved more slowly. Small shafts of light now began to appear in the wall. Olympias stopped at one of these and peered through. It took some time for her eyes to become accustomed to the light. The old palace hall lay before her, porticoed columns stretching down on either side. The room was full of men sprawled on couches, servants moving about with wine jugs. At the far end, by himself, lounging on the lion couch of Macedon, was her one-eyed, lecherous goat of a husband, Philip! Olympias, eyes half-closed, breathed in. Philip was sprawled, a laurel wreath tilted drunkenly on his head. He was feeling a slave girl while bawling across at Antipater who looked as though, if he drank another drop, he'd keel over like the pig he was. The wall was thick but Olympias caught the sound of music. Philip had hired special dancing and music troupes from all over Greece; these now competed desperately with the raucous revelry of Philip and his companions. Olympias let out her breath in a sigh of hatred. One day she'd have her vengeance. She walked on. She ignored the other small apertures in the wall but stopped at one and peered through at Eurydice, in her chamber, standing in a small tub of soapy water while slave girls bathed and sponged her with perfumed water and fragrant creams. Olympias passed on. She turned a corner, counting slowly to herself. She stopped and peered through an eyehole. Her face softened. Alexander was in his own private chamber, lounging on a couch, his guards standing in the shadows behind him.

"Oh Alexander!" Olympias breathed and scrabbled at the wall as if she wanted to break through and touch him.

CHAPTER 2

ALEXANDER, SON OF Philip of Macedon, stretched out on the small, silver-edged couch, fingers tapping the crater of wine before him. The other dishes of food he ignored. He could ask a slave to taste them as Olympias had whispered that he should be careful of poison. Alexander stared up at the ceiling, noticing the cracks and cobwebs. He raised his hand, snapped his fingers, and the two soldiers standing in the shadows behind went out through the side door.

"Now I'm truly alone."

Alexander stared across at the wall. The painting was cracked and fading but he made out the hunters, armed with clubs, bringing down a wild stag on some mythical mountainside.

"Why did Father bring us here?" Alexander murmured.

The palace of Aegae was old and crumbling, often disused. Philip, the great victor, had moved his capital to Pella and brought in the best sculptors, architects, and craftsmen to build him a city of marble that would be the envy of the Greek world. Alexander tweaked his nose. Father was like that. A barbarian who wanted to be an aesthete. A soldier who wanted to be a peacemaker. A tyrant who wanted to be a democrat. Alexander closed his eyes. And eyes, a father who owed his life to his son. However, Philip never spoke of that so neither would he. Each had given the other life: Philip on Olympias, Alexander at Chaeronea when he had led his cavalry in that mad, wild charge that had shattered the Theban phalanx.

Alexander couldn't keep his thoughts still. He was not concerned about tomorrow. The old proverb was correct, that would take care of itself. Philip could posture as captain general of the League of Corinth. He could wander around in saffron-edged white robes, pretend to be a god from Olympus, and have his feast and games, but then what? Philip had divorced Olympias and Alexander had heard the whispers circulating through the palace: how Philip now regarded him as a bastard, an illegitimate son. So what would happen now? Philip had a new wife, Eurydice, with her mewling infant. Babies grew to boys, boys to men. A wolf was a wolf even though it was a cub. Perhaps Olympias was right. Alexander's hand stretched out to the wine bowl but then he brought it away.

"Moderation in all things," he whispered.

He stretched out on the couch, tapping his sandaled feet together. He would like to go down and join his father and his companions in their revelry but Alexander had no stomach for it. Instead he would lie here on a couch, as befits a Macedonian who had killed both a boar in the hunt and a man in battle.

Alexander looked over the rim of the table; his pet tortoise had not yet crawled across the floor; it was barely halfway. Alexander, on the advice of his former tutor Aristotle, managed his brooding like he managed everything else. When the tortoise reached the far wall he would stop and call for Miriam. But what happened if it turned back half-way? Alexander smiled at the shuffling shell. Or came toward him? Or went around in circles? What would Aristotle advise then? Alexander lay back on the couch returning to more serious thoughts. His father was to be hailed as captain General of Greece and, after the feasting, he would march across the Hellespont to bring the Persian empire to its knees.

"And what will he do with me?" Alexander murmured. "Leave me here to plot revolt? Or take me with him? Give me the command of some regiment or brigade? All work no glory!" Alexander looked toward the far wall. He was sure he was not alone; Mother must be about. He'd heard rumors of secret passages in this old palace and Olympias never left him alone!

"I am well," he almost shouted. "I am well and I am happy. I have not yet touched a drop of wine so I am sober."

"You are brooding!"

Alexander swung his legs off the couch and sat up.

"Miriam Bartimaeus, you are snooping!" Alexander got to his feet. He clasped the young woman's hand and gestured for her to sit on the cushions at the other side of the table. "I was going to wait until that tortoise crossed the floor," he declared, sitting down, "and then I was going to call you."

"What tortoise?" Miriam swung around on the cushions.

"It's gone." Alexander laughed. "Back into the shadows."

Miriam pointed her fingers across the table. "Think, don't brood! Remember, Alexander, Aristotle taught us that in the Gardens of Midas."

"The Gardens of Midas!"

Alexander tapped his feet on the floor. Memories flooded back: beautiful vineyards around the Mieza, the country house where he and his companions had attended Aristotle's academy. The Greek philosopher and teacher had come to

Macedon just in time; a few weeks later the Persians had crucified his former protector Hermeias.

"Does Aristotle still write?" Miriam asked, her black eyes bright with merriment.

"Oh, he writes," Alexander replied, trying to keep his face straight, "letters full of advice!"

"Do you remember the way he used to walk?"

Miriam sprang to her feet. In the twinkling of an eye she ceased to be the rather angular, stiff-backed Jewess but became spindle-shanked Aristotle, with his dyed hair and beard, his be-ringed fingers, his effete way of walking; above all, his stare, eyebrows slightly raised, mouth half open, as he posed some brilliant question or trapped them in Logic. Alexander laughed as Miriam flounced back on the cushions.

"I miss him," she said softly. "I mock Aristotle behind his back but I do miss him."

"I miss them all," Alexander retorted, his face grim.

He studied Miriam as if memorizing her every feature: high cheekbones, those quick, darting eyes, narrow nose, thin lips. Her black hair was pulled back in an elegant curve to a bob on the back of her head covered with a net of threaded gold, kept in place by little silver clasps. Alexander liked Miriam, not because of her honesty and bluntness; the lack of makeup and kohl on her olive-skinned face; or the simple, graceful way she dressed—light underdress of olive-green and her yellow-red embroidered mantle clasped by a brooch carved in the shape of Medusa. Alexander noticed this and grinned. Probably a present from Mother? He offered a plate of sugared plums before Miriam could ask another question. Alexander liked the Jewess because he could talk to her, one of the few women who didn't frighten him. She had a sense of humor. She could put things in perspective and neither of his parents viewed her as a threat. In

Olympias's eyes she was an Amazon. Philip simply dismissed her as an ugly woman. Alexander was glad Miriam and her twin brother Simeon had not been exiled along with the rest of his friends, Hephaestion, Ptolemy, and Niarchos.

Miriam bit into a plum; with Alexander, she reasoned, you soon learned when to talk and when to keep quiet. She nibbled the sugared skin and idly wondered what would happen if it was poisoned.

"It isn't!" Alexander didn't shift his gaze from the wall behind her. "It isn't poisoned, if that's what you are thinking, I made them myself!"

"You are frightened of tomorow, aren't you?"

"No, I'm not."

"Do you remember?" Miriam persisted. "Do you remember when we were in the Gardens of Midas? I was about eleven and Aristotle had fallen ill. He'd climbed a tree and eaten grapes that weren't fully ripe. Anyway, we went swimming. You and Ptolemy led the rest. You turned back halfway. . . ."

"Aye, I remember." Alexander picked up a sugared plum and popped it into his mouth. "I said I was ashamed. I couldn't swim a river. You replied, 'So what? A water rat can do that.' " He pulled the stone out of his mouth and threw it into the dish. "What's that got to do with tomorrow?"

Miriam leaned her arms on the table. "Simeon and I have been talking," she whispered. "Philip can proclaim himself what he likes, Zeus or Apollo. I can call myself the high priest of Jerusalem; it doesn't mean that I am."

"I'm frightened," Alexander declared. He ran a finger around the wine bowl. "To do nothing, Miriam, except wait is the hardest thing I know."

Miriam studied his face. Alexander was only twenty, his red-gold hair was cut short and parted down the middle. A girlish, delicate face, except for the cleft chin and the furrows that were already appearing in his brow. It was his eyes that fascinated her, always had, one green the other brown, that and the way he slightly tilted his head when he was thinking or was perplexed. She would like to stretch her hand out, just to touch his rather flushed cheek but she dare not. That was the bond between her and Alexander. Not just childhood companions or friends who had snuggled up to each other beneath the blankets when they camped out in the dark woods and valleys of Macedon.

"Alexander," she whispered, "tell me."

"I am not frightened about tomorrow but the future."

"It's not that," she snapped. "What else?"

Alexander passed across a small piece of papyrus. Miriam unfolded it. At first she couldn't make out the writing; the ink was blurred, the letters cramped. Alexander got up and moved an oil lamp closer.

"They are quotations!" Miriam exclaimed. " 'Hard son of Peleus, your mother nursed you on deceit.' " She glanced up. "It's a quotation from the *Iliad!*"

"Read on!"

" 'They are lies,' " Miriam continued, " 'when they call you the issue of Zeus, since you fall short of the truth of those who were begotten by Zeus.' " Miriam fought back her tears.

"I found it pushed under my door," Alexander interrupted.

Miriam kept her head down. Whoever had written this had hit the mark. Alexander was proud that Olympias was descended from Achilles whose father was Peleus. The quotation was a bitter attack upon both Alexander and Olympias, alluding to the growing rumor that Alexander was not Philip's son and should not inherit the throne of Macedonia. Whoever had written this knew Alexander well. He had a love of Homer's *Iliad* and always kept a copy, with a dagger, under his pillow. Wherever Alexander went, Homer's *Iliad* went with him. He'd known it so well, and was able to recite it so clearly, even Philip's mockery had turned to admiration.

"They are just baiting you," Miriam replied.

"Who?" Alexander asked.

"I don't know." She shook her head.

"What happens if they are right?" Alexander's eyes now glowed. "What happens if I am not Philip's son?"

"That is nonsense." Miriam shook her head.

"No, I mean . . ." Alexander paused as if he dare not say the words, "What happens if the second quotation is only a mockery of the truth? That I was begotten by a god, by Zeus himself? You've heard the stories?"

"I've heard the legend," Miriam replied drily. "Don't let your mind wander down that path. You don't have to be a son of Philip or begotten by a god to be great. These troubles will pass!"

Alexander rolled up the piece of paper.

"Remember," Miriam continued, quoting from the *Iliad*, " 'You are an extraordinary young man. And you shall go on to extraordinary experiences. You shall achieve glory towering to heaven. . . .' "

" 'And usurp god's throne?' " Alexander teased, finishing the quotation. "You think such ambitions are blasphemy, don't you?"

" 'If they can't be realized,' " Miriam quoted from a play, this time by Aristophanes, " 'Then yes they are.' "

Alexander raised up his wine bowl toward the ceiling. " 'Oh, Dionysus,' " he whispered, " 'now action rests with you.' "

Miriam felt a shiver run down her spine for she recognized the quotation from Euripides' dark play the *Bacchae*.

" 'You are near,' " Alexander continued, still quoting the playwright. " 'Punish this man but first distract his wits. Bewilder him with madness.' "

He brought the bowl down, sipped from it, then handed it across to Miriam to do likewise. The harsh wine caught at the back of her throat and she coughed, yet she was glad to hide her confusion. Alexander was on the verge of losing his fiery temper. She wondered if he was cursing the person who'd sent that anonymous letter, or his father? Alexander drank again.

" 'Now, all promises are forgotten,' " he whispered, again quoting Homer. Alexander placed the wine bowl down. "Do you know what Father once said, Miriam?" He didn't wait for her reply. "He came, years ago, to visit us in the Gardens of Midas." Alexander fought to control his temper. "I wished to show him an experiment." He flailed his hands. "Something Aristotle had taught us. Philip called me a mooncalf and asked if I was a warrior or a maid?" Alexander ran his tongue around his lips. "I lost my temper. I took him to task about his women and the children he was begetting. What would happen to me, I asked, his heir, if those bastard children grew to manhood and challenged me for the crown? Do you know what he said?"

Miriam did but she kept silent.

"Philip replied, if I was fit to rule I would beat them and if I was not, I would die. How can a father say that to his son, Miriam?" Alexander straightened up at a knock on the door.

The young guards officer who entered was dressed in a cuirass, the ends of the red scarf tied around his neck, pushed beneath the breastplate. The white skirt that fell to his knees had leather, metal-studded straps sewn on to it. Greaves covered his legs, military sandals on his feet. A short stabbing sword swung in the belt hitched over his shoulder.

In one hand he carried his dark woollen cloak, in the other a ceremonial helmet. The room was dark and Miriam couldn't make out the man's features.

"Yes, who are you?" she asked.

Alexander's hand slipped beneath a cushion for the dagger concealed there.

"By Apollo, man, come into the light!"

The soldier walked forward. Alexander pushed the dagger away and, smiling, rose to his feet.

"Pausanias!" He clasped the captain of the guards' gauntleted wrists, then stepped back. "You look as if you are on parade, or intent on seduction."

Pausanias's sallow face broke into a grin.

"I'm on duty tonight and tomorrow morning. Philip wants me sober."

"And what does he want with me?" Alexander asked.

Pausanias's eyes, lizardlike, slid toward Miriam. She glared back. She didn't like Pausanias. A good soldier by all accounts but womanish in his ways, sly and secretive. One of Philip's creatures, a guard or spy, she wondered? Pausanias blinked and shrugged as if Miriam didn't matter.

"You can stare at the woman," Alexander remarked, "for as long as you like, Pausanias. What does my father want with me?"

"The procession begins at dawn," Pausanias replied. "Or, at least, that's when the gates to the amphitheater are to be opened. Representatives will take their seats and the ceremony commences."

"And?"

"Your father has commanded me and the bodyguard to go ahead of him, to stand just inside the amphitheater. You and Molossus, King of Epirus, will accompany your father through the gates. You are to wear no armor and neither will he."

"Philip should have been a playwright," Alexander declared. "Aristophanes and Euripides would have envied him. So, tomorrow morning he is going to play the great democrat is he?"

"It's your half-sister's wedding," Pausanias retorted. "Your father is also to be hailed as a captain general of Greece. Now is not the time for strife." Pausanias gave a lopsided grin.

"And tonight?" Alexander asked. "It's Philip the drunkard, Philip the lecher?"

Pausanias bowed stiffly and stepped back.

"You should not talk of your father the king that way," he murmured.

"Well at least you are one person in the palace who acknowledges he is my father," Alexander retorted.

"Your father has also asked you to join him."

"Tell my father," Alexander replied, "that, like you, I wish to be sober now and tomorrow."

Pausanias bowed and left the chamber.

"I don't like him much," Miriam declared. She got up from the cushions. Alexander was still staring at the door, head slightly sideways, drumming his fingers on his stomach.

"I know what you are saying, Miriam. I don't either. There are sordid stories about Pausanias." He glanced over his shoulder at her. "But not tonight." He went back to his couch. "I thought you and your brother were going to put on a play? Stage one of the scenes from your people's history?"

"David and Absalom," Miriam replied.

"David was your great warrior king?"

"He was touched by the Lord," Miriam answered.

"Do you ever want to go back there?" Alexander asked curiously, offering her the wine bowl; Miriam shook her head.

"No," she replied, "Jerusalem is a desert. Zion is desolate."

"But your people have returned. The great Cyrus released them."

"There's nothing there for us," Miriam replied. "What would Simeon and I do?" She held her voice steady. "To you we are Israelites, Jews, but to those in Jerusalem, we are strangers. Some would even regard us as apostates."

"But you don't sacrifice to our gods?"

" 'A pure heart create in me: put a steadfast spirit within me.' "

"What's that?" Alexander asked.

"It's from a poem, allegedly written by David."

"And Absalom?"

"Absalom was David's son," Miriam replied, "David's favorite, a brave warrior, a very handsome man with a head of hair that would have been the envy of any woman. Absalom rose in rebellion. He was defeated and fled through a forest but his hair became trapped in the overhanging branches of a tree. One of David's officers caught up with him. He thrust a spear straight through Absalom's heart."

"And what did David do?"

"David wept. He wrote a beautiful lament. 'Absalom, My Son: Absalom, My Son Absalom.' " Miriam found the memories of the story her father had taught her made her lip quiver. "Before he died," she continued, "David left secret instructions that the man who'd slain his son was to be killed."

Alexander was now staring moodily. You have a beautiful face, Miriam thought. She studied him carefully, wiping the sweat from her hands on her dress. A face she had seen on some of the statues, carved by the sculptors Philip had brought from Athens. Alexander was of medium stature, his body of pleasing proportion but it was his face that held her, like that of a young Apollo, not beautiful but grave and solemn, eyes ever watchful. But was he Philip's son? Miriam could see Olympias in him, the contours of his face, his complexion, hair, and lips; yet if she stared at him for eternity, she could see nothing of Philip. What happened, she wondered, if the rumors were true?

"I wonder," Alexander declared, "if Philip is going to kill me?"

"Alexander!"

"He killed his own brothers! He may regret it. But what if I am to die, Miriam? No more Olympias, no more Alexander."

"All of Greece would hate him," she replied but, as soon as the words were out of her mouth, Miriam knew it sounded lame and weak.

"What would the rest of Greece care?" Alexander exclaimed. "So Philip has killed his son. One Macedonian less. I can just hear Demosthenes in Athens chuckling with glee."

"Demosthenes," Miriam replied, "is a windbag. He ran away at Chaeronea!"

The door to the chamber was suddenly flung open. Alexander started, Miriam half-rose. A young man staggered in, his white robe food-stained; he almost ran toward them. The wine cup in his hand was held unsteadily so it slopped on the floor. In his other hand he held a small bunch of grapes that he thrust to his mouth and gobbled noisily.

"You are going to have a play, Alexander." The young man offered the grapes but Alexander shook his head.

"Arridhaeus, Arridhaeus!" Alexander said soothingly. He grasped his half-brother's arm and pulled him to the couch beside him.

Miriam stared with pity at this caricature of a Macedonian prince. Arridhaeus was an imbecile who staggered around the palace, a buffoon, the source of mockery. In some ways he looked like Philip, the curled hair, beard and moustache, the same nose, but the mouth was slack, the eyes vacant and watery.

"I want to see your play," Arridhaeus declared. He stared at Miriam and blinked. "I want a woman." He put the grapes down and scratched at his crotch. "It's becoming bigger again." His hands slid between the folds of his stained gown. "It always gets big when I drink. But you are not a slave girl, are you?" He sputtered wine and bits of grape to the edge of his mouth. "You are Miriam. I have just seen your brother." He turned and stared at Alexander. "Can I see the play?"

"Of course you can, Arridhaeus," Alexander replied. "Where have you been?"

"I went to see Father but he started laughing at me, throwing scraps of food. He said my thing was as big as a tent peg and told me to see a slave girl.

"And did you?"

"Yes, but she ran away laughing."

Alexander eased the wine cup out of his half-brother's hand.

"If you hadn't interfered," Arridhaeus continued, "if you hadn't interfered, I would have had a wife by now."

Miriam held her breath. Most times Arridhaeus was simple. They said he had been born a healthy child until Olympias went to visit him. Arridhaeus's mother had died of a fever within days while Arridhaeus lay in a coma and, when he recovered, his brain was gone. He was nothing more than a cretin, powerful testimony to Olympias's determination that no one would challenge her darling Alexander.

While Arridhaeus chattered on Alexander tried to soothe him. Miriam recalled how Olympias, the author of such misfortune, had questioned her, making her stand in a chamber with those dreadful snakes crawling all about her. No wonder Alexander was frightened of women with Olympias as his mother. Miriam half-listened to Arridhaeus's complaints; she knew that this imbecilic half-brother of Alexander was correct. Philip had tried to marry him off to the daughter of the satrap of Caria. Alexander, suffering one of his panic attacks, and believing his father was about to disown him, had opened his own secret negotiations with the satrap—a Persian governor, whose lands lay just beyond the Hellespont—of strategic importance when Philip marched east. Philip had heard about Alexander's plans and, in fury, had broken off all negotiations and sent Alexander's principal friends and advisers into exile. It was a wonder she and Simeon had not joined them.

"You wouldn't have liked her." Miriam decided to stop Arridhaeus's listing of complaints. "The woman had a terrible reputation. She would have frightened you."

Arridhaeus's hand went to his lips. "Would she?"

"A veritable Medusa." Miriam smiled sympathetically. "You are much safer here."

"Am I?" Arridhaeus grinned vacantly. "I could be a king you know? There are those who would like to make me king."

"Oh, I am sure there are," Alexander replied drily.

"Who would like to make you king?" Miriam asked curiously.

"Oh." Arridhaeus closed his eyes. "Oh, this person and that. I forget their names. If I was king," he continued, "I'd have every woman. Except you." He stared at Miriam. "I like you. I love your brother. I know where your brother is."

Before they could stop him, Arridhaeus got up and staggered out of the room.

"Your brother is kind," Alexander remarked. "Five minutes with Arridhaeus and you feel exhausted."

"Simeon says he is brighter than you think. Sometimes he

can be quite silly. Who," she added, "would want to make him king?"

"Oh, Arridhaeus is always saying that. The nobles mock and humor him. . . ."

"They should leave him alone."

Simeon came into the room. Under his arm he carried masks, gowns, and cloaks. He put these on the floor, came over, and kissed Miriam on her brow. He grinned at Alexander.

"You should join the party, Prince of Macedon; the wine is flowing like water." Simeon sighed and sat down beside his sister.

"Did you want to leave it?" Alexander asked sharply.

"I don't like being drunk," Simeon replied. He rubbed his stomach. I've already eaten something that doesn't agree with me." He glanced at his sister. "And our task this evening is to prevent Alexander of Macedon from falling into a black fit of despair. I think the story of Samson and Deliah—"

"Absalom," Alexander replied. "I want the story of David and Absalom." He smiled. "Nothing else or I will brood."

Arridhaeus came back into the room. He went and crouched like a dog beside Simeon who absentmindedly put his arm around his shoulder. Miriam studied Simeon closely. His usual jovial face looked a bit peakish but, there again, if he had been looking after Arridhaeus, no wonder. She'd never understood Simeon's care and concern for this imbecilic prince. She felt sorry for Arridhaeus but Simeon, ever since he was a boy, had always allowed Arridhaeus to trot behind him. He would sit and patiently explain things to him.

"I feel I have to," Simeon once declared. "He's Philip's son and we owe Philip a debt. Do you know, when Mother was about to give birth, he hired a special physician? Father said he was always kind and Arridhaeus is his son."

"I've lost my present!" Arridhaeus declared, getting to his feet.

"Oh, don't start that again!" Simeon snapped.

"What is it?" Miriam asked.

"Oh, it's a figure of Apollo," Simeon replied quickly. "Philip gave it as a present; now it's gone. Arridhaeus!" he exclaimed, "you know what you are like; the palace is littered with your possessions."

Simeon got to his feet. He was now holding his stomach, his clean-shaven face creased in pain.

"Are you well?" Alexander asked anxiously.

"I've eaten too much, that's my problem. No, Arridhaeus, you sit there."

But the prince was off, scuttling into the corner to fetch the tortoise he had seen.

"Can I have this?" he asked. "I've never," he lied, "had a pet."

"You can have it," Alexander said. "It's a most disobedient tortoise, mind you. It refuses to walk in a straight line." He grinned. "But the same can be said for most people in this palace." He glanced at Simeon. "If Philip conquers Persia," he asked abruptly, "what will be left for me?"

"The rest of the world," Simeon quipped back.

"Have you heard anything?" Alexander asked. "From Hephaestion, Ptolemy . . . ?"

"You know I haven't," Simeon shook his head. "Even if they wrote, Philip would intercept the letters."

"Come on!"

Miriam also got to her feet before Alexander lapsed deeper into his brooding. She bowed mockingly.

"Simeon and Miriam Bartimaeus present the story of David and Absalom."

"But there are only two of you!" Arridhaeus exclaimed.

"At the greater Dionysia," Simeon explained referring to

the great drama festival at Athens, "a playwright is only allowed three actors, that's why we have the masks. Miriam and I will play different people."

"You said three?" Arridhaeus said.

"Oh, you can take a part as well." Simeon took a mask and slipped it over Arridhaeus's head. "You are a soldier and so you must stand silently."

He and Miriam withdrew, put on the cloaks and masks and then, with dramatic flourishes, they began the story of David and his wayward son Absalom. Alexander watched intently. Miriam noticed he now pushed the wine bowl well away and was pleased. Whatever Alexander did, he did well, and that's what worried her now. He was brooding, turning something over and over in his mind, and she wondered what. Alexander was fearful. As a boy he used to have panic attacks and found the only way to combat these was through energetic and lightning action. Would he do that now, Miriam wondered, here in this dark, blood-stained palace of Macedon? Was Alexander's mind turning to murder? Would he strike against Philip before Philip struck against him? In this case would David be Alexander and Absalom Philip? And those lines he'd quoted from Euripides. Were they simply the bloody prologue to a murderous first act?

CHAPTER 3

OLYMPIAS MOVED THROUGH the disused and derelict cemetery that lay on the brow of a hill beyond the palace park; Aristander hobbled behind her. The moon was full, the stars glowed like lamps lowered from heaven. Olympias was dressed for the sacrifice, clothed in black from head to toe, her face covered in white paste, her lips a bright red. She and her necromancer moved to the appointed place, threading their way around the gabled top pillars and ornamental heads of the decaying gravestones. Here, that of a young cavalryman depicted on horseback striking down an enemy; the kindly father with his children at a meal; water pots on those of young women who had died unmarried. Athena's owls, which haunted such places, hooted mournfully; night-birds flew from branch to branch yet the evening was a balmy one. The air was rich with the sweet scent of silver firs, birch, and laurel. Somewhere in the woods beyond, a wolf welcomed the moon.

"Is he here?" Olympias turned to Aristander.

"He'll come!" the sorcerer replied.

They reached their appointed place in the middle of the cemetery. Aristander tapped Olympias on the elbow and pointed down an overgrown path. A figure was approaching them carrying a covered lantern; sandaled feet crunched on the pebble path. Olympias pulled the veil across her face so only her kohl-ringed eyes were visible. The man came on. Aristander took the purse of silver Darics and shook the coins out. The man came and crouched before them. There was no ceremony, no greeting. He simply counted the coins. He was about to put them in his purse but Olympias moved like a snake; her sandaled foot crushed his fingers.

"First!" she hissed, "we see what you have to sell!"

The man, one of Philip's scribes, looked up. He guessed who this was, but the least said the better.

"The king will go into the amphitheater alone tomorrow morning," he bleated. "King Molossus of Epirus will accompany him, as will his son Alexander."

The man stumbled on the words; the sandaled foot was hurting him and he'd nearly said "your son."

"We know that," Olympias hissed. "Come on, man. There is more to sell than that." She pressed her sandaled foot harder.

The scribe gazed up fearfully. Perhaps it was not the wisest thing to have come here to a cemetery in the dead of night but the royal palace was riddled with spy holes. There were many who'd go running to Philip reporting that his disused, discarded queen had been visited by a royal scribe. Yet the silver winked so invitingly.

"I have more," he stammered.

The sandaled foot was withdrawn. He moved to get up.

"Kneel!" Olympias hissed.

"There are movements among the guards—"

"The guards regiment?" Olympias broke in quickly.

"The same. They are being moved up from Pella. They are marching tonight; they'll be here by tomorrow evening."

Olympias narrowed her eyes. Soldiers were already bivouacked in the palace grounds so why was Philip bringing up a crack corps of phalanx men?

"Messengers have also been prepared."

"Messengers? To go where?"

"I don't know."

"Has a proclomation been issued?"

"Not that I know of."

Again the man made to rise but Olympias's clawlike hand stretched out and pressed his head down.

"Keep your eyes lowered," she whispered.

The man did so, unaware that Aristander had now slipped behind him.

"What else have you discovered?"

"Philip is angry with the Lyncestrians," the scribe declared, referring to the two brothers, sons of Europus, leader of a mountain tribe with as much claim to the throne of Macedon as Philip had.

"Why is that?" Olympias asked.

"They have brought more men here than they should have done." The fellow pointed across to the dark woods, their outline barely visible in the moonlight. "They are camped only a march away."

"Now why should they do that?" Olympias murmured. "My two Lyncestrian rats, aggressive troublemakers, ever watchful for the main chance."

"I don't know," the scribe hissed.

"And my brother Molossus, king of Epirus?"

"He is happy enough." The scribe now looked fearfully up.

Olympias smiled.

"I've just betrayed myself." She smiled behind the veil. "But you." Her hand went out. "You are a good and faithful servant. Look at me! What is your name?"

"Cleander."

"Cleander, kiss the hand of your queen!"

The scribe seized the soft, fragrant fingers; he closed his eyes and pressed them to his lips. The hand turned, stifling his mouth even as, behind him, Aristander drove the long Syrian dagger into his back just beneath the neck. Olympias freed her hand and stepped away. Cleander slouched forward, hands out, and then collapsed on all fours. Aristander struck again, and the scribe died, a pool of blood gushing out of his mouth. Aristander turned him over. In his early days the necromancer had been a soldier, a light-armed warrior used to the bloody work of battle. He drew his dagger across the man's throat and allowed the hot blood to splash into the small, metal bowl he carried. He handed this to Olympias.

She took a small phial from a pouch in the pocket of her cloak and poured a little in while Aristander dragged the corpse away. Olympias walked to the square tomb that housed her secrets and always served as an altar. She put the blood-filled bowl down and, throwing back her veil, lifted her hands in a short prayer to Dionysus. Olympias paused and then, with all her strength, mouthed a hymn of hate to Hecate, queen of the night. She prayed for vengeance. Vengeance on her enemies: Philip and Eurydice, the Lyncestrians, those who had humiliated her, those who threatened to bring her son to destruction. She paused halfway through and sipped the still warm blood before continuing. Olympias felt triumphant. She was a maenad. She had participated in the secret rites, and what was blood but the food and gift of the gods? After she had finished,

Olympias used the phial to sprinkle the four corners of the tomb and then threw it and the still wet bowl at Aristander.

"We have done enough," she whispered. "Tonight we sleep but tomorrow . . ."

The words sounded dramatic but Olympias really wondered what the future would bring. Tomorrow would belong to the men, the warriors, the shield, the sword, the phalanx; and what power did she have? Nothing except the powers of darkness; perhaps that would be enough.

"Bring the blood bowl," she commanded. "Let us examine Hecate's reply!"

Olympias and Aristander slipped back into the palace, through secret passageways, to her own chamber. She sat on cushions while Aristander knelt before her examining the bowl. He moved it slowly in the torchlight, to see what signs, what dangers the future held.

"I'm tired," Olympias snarled.

Aristander lifted his head. He peered anxiously around the room. He did not like being here alone with Olympias and her snakes. Would Philip, he wondered, keep his word? Beyond the gauze curtain Aristander could see Olympias's huge feather-filled mattress, lamps glowing on either side of the bed.

"I am waiting."

The seer finished his examination, lifted his head, stood up, and backed to the door.

"You want the truth, my lady?"

"As ever!"

"There is great danger for Philip and it is very close."

The queen smiled. Aristander now had his hand on the latch. Olympias's smile faded.

"And?"

"Great danger also for you, my lady, and for Alexander."

Then Aristander was gone leaving Olympias, knuckles to

her mouth, eyes rounded, fighting hard to control the terrors seething within her.

On the Pynx, the assembly hill overlooking the Parthenon in Athens, the orator Demosthenes also crouched and stared into the visions of the night. He could not sleep; his house was full of mourning over the death of his favorite daughter. Demosthenes stared at the statue of Athena glowing in the light of the myriad torches around it. The city slept; only the occasional noise of revelry from some supper party or the sound of horses neighing in their stables disturbed the quiet night. Demosthenes gazed around. This spot had witnessed some of his greatest victories as well as some of his most humiliating defeats. Demosthenes breathed in slowly, surely, remembering what he had been taught in the Academy.

"The control of breath," his teacher had declared, "is to control the moods of the mind. A great speaker must know how to breathe."

Demosthenes had been hailed as a great speaker, and why not? As a boy he had practiced with pebbles in his mouth. As a young man he had gone down to the seashore, training his voice to rise above the crash of the waves or the call of the seabirds. In Athens, in the marketplace, or the Pynx, or the council chamber it was no different. Demosthenes smiled bleakly. He remembered Aristophanes' play *The Birds;* that's what his fellow citizens were like, chattering birds who lived in Cuckoo Land or frogs who croaked beside their ponds, as Sophocles said, unaware of the great stork to the north, Philip of Macedon, ready to gobble them up. Demosthenes got to his feet. If it hadn't been for the silence or the danger that he might be seen and mocked, he would have launched into one of his famous speeches against Philip the tyrant. Yet, there was more to it than that. Demosthenes still squirmed with embarrassment when he remembered that incident, twelve years earlier, when he had headed a delegation to Philip in Pella. The Macedonian had invited him to speak. And what had happened? Demosthenes had stumbled, stammered, and eventually dried up. He'd returned embarrassed to Athens and put up with the sniggers and barbed comments, yet Philip had terrified him. When Athens and Thebes joined forces and met those of Philip at Chaeronea, Demosthenes had taken his spear and shield, inscribed with the words WITH FORTUNE, and marched with the rest. And what had happened? Philip had smashed the sacred band of Thebes, left the Athenian dead piled high like autumn leaves while he, the great Demosthenes, had fled like a shadow. Now Philip was master of Greece. Tomorrow he would be hailed as captain general and, by autumn, he would be marching into Persia with Athens' great fleet ready to do his every bidding.

Demosthenes heard a sound and whirled round. After all, if he was hunting Philip why shouldn't Philip be hunting him? He relaxed as his friend Pasocles came out through the portico.

"I saw you leave." Pasocles rubbed his red-rimmed eyes. "Demosthenes, you should sleep. The future will take care of itself."

"But will it?" Demosthenes asked. "Just think, Pasocles, Philip is ready to receive the golden crowns of Athens and other cities. They say he is calling himself a god. So, to be struck down at the very moment of his triumph! In the eyes of all Greece!" Demosthenes held his hand up, a favorite gesture as he warmed to his theme. "Like a play at the great Dionysia," he whispered. "A tyrant falling from the pinnacle of power for all to see. Does the future hold such promise?"

"When will we know?" Pasocles asked. He just wished Demosthenes would lower his voice. Philip had his spies here in Athens.

"We will know soon enough. The gold I received from Darius has been well spent. The same ship that took our delegates, will slip its mooring and be gone before the dust even settles. Riders will also bring their news."

Demosthenes walked toward the speaker's podium. He could feel the thrill within him whenever he came here to address his fellow citizens. Pasocles knew Demosthenes was already rehearsing his part. First he'd stand sideways, almost whispering so that the people had to strain to catch his words. Then, as Demosthenes got into his stride, he'd slowly turn, one hand moving like a magician weaving his spell until the people were no longer conscious of the man but only the voice, proclaiming what they wanted to hear. The tyrant was dead! Greece was free! Athens would be its own mistress! Pasocles chewed nervously on his thumbnail. He followed Demosthenes over to the podium.

"But what about the rest?" he urged. " 'Remem-ber,' " Pasocles quoted from Demosthenes' own speeches, " 'if Philip were to die tomorrow, there would be another Philip.' "

Demosthenes didn't turn but just waggled a finger.

"I heard you. I listen to what you say," Pasocles persisted. "You called Alexander a mooncalf. Yet—"

"And I also quoted the famous proverb," Demosthenes interrupted. " 'That a wolf is still a wolf even though its only a cub.' " Demosthenes spread his hands as if the citizens of Athens now stood before him. "The news will come," he declared. "Philip will die. The Macedonians will return to what they are good at, the only thing they are good at, Pasocles, killing each other! Why wait?" Demosthenes came over and grasped Pasocles' hand. "Why wait for the news to arrive before we celebrate? Philip will die. His best generals Attalus and Parmenio are stranded across the Hellespont along with ten thousand of their best troops. Olympias is divorced, a

recluse hidden away in her own chambers. And Alexander?"
Demosthenes snapped his fingers. "He may be a wolf cub
but he is also a mooncalf. He can quote his Homer and pretend to be Achilles." Demosthenes scratched his curled
beard and moustache. "Do you remember your *Iliad*?
Alexander certainly does. Achilles was killed by the man he
despised the most. Do you really think they'll allow such a
mooncalf to sit on Philip's throne? Alexander, a boy of
twenty years," Demosthenes spat the words out slowly,
"whose only triumph is the subjugation of some unruly hill-
top tribe? No, no, my friend, there are those in Macedon
who will take care of Alexander." He winked at Pasocles.
"We have a traitor, closer to the heart of things than Philip
and his mooncalf ever suspect."

"And Persia?" Pasocles asked. "The great king?"

"The great king has sent us gold," Demosthenes replied.
"Once he hears that Philip is dead, he'll regard the money
as well spent. Darius has troubles of his own. There are ten
thousand Macedonians in his territories. Moreover, if our
news is correct, he is still crucifying those who tried to kill
him. Everything will fall into the lap of Athens." Demosthenes now returned to the podium. He had forgotten
about Pasocles, about his own daughter's corpse stiffening
under her winding sheet. He was here, a man greater than
Pericles, come to hear the salutations and hails of the city he
loved.

Miriam and Simeon were describing the death of Absalom,
hanging by his hair "from a laurel tree," when Pausanias
reentered the chamber. Alexander made a sign for Miriam to
pause.

"It's Father again, isn't it?"

"He wishes to speak to the Israelites," Pausanias retorted.
"Sir, he did not ask for you."

"Then I'm coming, too," Arridhaeus spoke up. "Father won't hurt me if Simeon's there."

Alexander got to his feet. He raised his bowl and ostentatiously poured the wine onto the floor.

"I have drunk enough," he declared. "Miriam, Simeon, I'll see you tomorrow."

He left the room. Pausanias had to wait until Miriam and her brother put the masks away, Arridhaeus flapping around them like a gadfly. They made themselves presentable though it would not have been noticed because, by the time they entered the banqueting hall, Philip and his companions were too drunk to notice. Here and there a man lounged on a couch; others sprawled on the floor. Two were arguing noisily, shouting at each other and throwing food. Philip sat on the lion couch; the laurel wreath around his head gave his one-eyed, sardonic face the look of a satyr, a true follower of Dionysus. Philip waved Miriam and Simeon forward. He staggered to his feet, pushing those companions fast asleep on nearby couches onto the floor. Philip cleaned the couch with the hem of his robe. He grasped Arridhaeus by the hair and pushed him across to sit beside Antipater.

"Eat and drink there," Philip ordered his hapless son.

"If you want to pee or vomit, go outside." He belched and sat down.

Miriam just smiled. She knew Philip of old. He drank a lot and he acted drunk, but he never was. Philip leaned over and patted Simeon on the knee.

"You look peakish, boy. I can't have that in one of my scribes."

"A little stomach trouble, Sire."

"Like your father," Philip murmured. "Timaeus was a good man but he could not hold his cups."

He winked at Miriam who smiled shyly back. Try as she might, Miriam couldn't dislike this man. The soldiers called him the one-eyed fox and, because of his sexual proclivities, the mountain goat of Macedon. To her, however, he had always been kind, very generous, never once offering her insult or snub. Philip blew his cheeks out.

"Look at them!" he roared, gesturing down the hall. "They fight like lions, as relentlessly as a leopard in pursuit but they are only mad, drunken boys. They'll drink till they fall and tomorrow they'll be teasing each other about who did what to whom." He picked up his wine goblet and leered. "The buggers get so drunk they can't tell male from female. Thank the gods there aren't any sheep wandering the corridors; not even they would be safe."

Miriam followed his gaze. Philip's companions, his commanders, his kinsmen, those who stood with him in the shield war were all flush-faced, slobbery-mouthed, and bleary-eyed; they lunged at each other or tried to grasp the slave girls as they passed. Now and again one would stagger to his feet and toast the king. Philip would pledge them back because, among the Macedonians, not to pledge toast for toast was a deadly insult. Weapons were banned; if they weren't, the hall would be turned into a battleground as old grudges and grievances were settled. Philip smacked his knee and roared with laughter.

"Do you know what happened today?" He giggled behind his hand and swayed dangerously on the couch. "Do you know what happened today, Biriam?" His good eye blinked. "Biriam, Biriam?" He grinned at her. "Who's Biriam?"

"Miriam, Sire!"

"Of course you are. I'm only teasing you. Anyway, I tried a case today. Two thieves tried to steal a figurine. You've seen the one; it's somewhere around here, a statue of Hermes." Philip spread his hands out. "You know, it's . . . " he gestured at his grizzle-faced commander Antipater, who was sitting solemnly beside Arridhaeus, "it's as big as Antipater's cock!"

The veteran commander, his face covered in scars of old battles, slurped from his cup. Antipater was Philip's whipping boy, brave as a bear and as bad tempered. Antipater would allow Philip to insult him, he'd keep his face impassive and, when he'd had enough, he'd growl and Philip would shut up.

"Anyway," Philip continued, "Antipater here caught the two buggers. Now, stealing from the king, that's treason. These two lads thought they were going to be crucified." He got to his feet. "But I am Philip of Macedon! I am the son of Hercules, the father of my people!"

"In more ways than one," Antipater murmured.

"I am Philip, king!" His voice carried down the hall stifling the clamor.

Immediately his hearth companions seized their goblets and sprang to their feet. A few collapsed but the hall rang down with acclamations.

"Philip the king! Philip the king!"

Philip swayed dangerously.

"Tomorrow!" he shouted, "captain general of all Greece and, within the year, we'll all ride like kings through Persoppolis and sit on the peacock throne! Plunder by the cartload! Women as exquisite, as exquisite . . ." Philip raised his cup. "To beautiful women!" He slumped down on the couch, drained his cup, and held it out for a servant to refill.

"You are a liar and a boaster," Antipater growled. "Look at us, Philip! Only two good eyes between us and now we sit like old men—"

"Speak for yourself!" Philip retorted.

"You were telling a story," Antipater jibed. He turned to

steady Arridhaeus who was rocking himself gently backward and forward on the couch. "By Apollo, man, sit still!"

Philip looked at his half-witted son. Miriam glimpsed the pain and sorrow in his face.

"I'm sorry, Arridhaeus," Philip whispered.

He spoke so softly, so lucidly, Antipater's head came up with a start.

"I'm sorry," Philip repeated. He leaned across, seized Arridhaeus's face between his great hands, and squeezed gently. The prince gazed, bleary-eyed, back. "I could have saved you from the great bitch," Philip whispered. "But I didn't think she'd hurt you. Now there's nothing we can do." He closed his one good eye, shoulders hunched as if he were praying. " 'The bull is wreathed for sacrifice,' " he quoted the Delphic Oracle. " 'All is ready. The slayer is at hand.' " He let his hands go. "Where's Alexander?" he murmured. "Where's my boy?" A tear rolled down his cheek. He lifted the wine cup. "May the gods help us all!" He wiped some oil from his close-cut beard and stared at his hand. "I was telling a story, wasn't I? About the two thieves? Ah yes, they were brought before me and, do you know what? I ordered the first to run from Macedon and the second to chase him!"

Miriam laughed. Philip edged along the couch toward her.

"What do you think of that, Miriam, eh? You should have seen the relief on their faces. I have never seen anything so funny in my life! How is Alexander?" Philip suddenly became cold-hard sober. "Why isn't he here?"

"He thinks you are still in a temper with him," Miriam replied tactfully. "He doesn't want to incur your anger."

"You mean like last time?" Philip declared.

Miriam knew what he was talking about but kept silent.

"On my wedding night?" Philip turned and glared at Antipater. "You were there!"

The old man nodded. He, too, knew the story as did every one at the Macedonian court.

"Attalus didn't mean it," Philip continued, referring to his general now leading his troops across the Hellespont. "Attalus was drunk."

"He shouldn't have said it," Antipater broke in.

"All he did," Philip replied, measuring his words, "was get to his feet, toast me, his niece Eurydice, who is now my queen, and say that at last Macedon would have a legitimate heir."

"He shouldn't have said it," Antipater repeated. "It sounded as if he was implying Alexander was a bastard."

Philip laughed, a short sharp bark. "That's what Alexander said. First time the boy ever really lost his temper. Sprang to his feet he did, threw his cup at Attalus. 'Are you calling me a bastard?' he yelled." Philip stared into his wine cup. "I truly thought he was going to hurt Attalus. That's why I drew my sword. I wasn't going to hurt Alexander." He fell silent.

Miriam stiffened. They all knew what had happened next. Philip had drawn his sword and lunged at Alexander but he was so drunk he'd fallen flat on his face, shouting curses. Alexander simply walked down the hall, then turned at the door, pointing in disdain at his prostrate father.

"Look at him," Alexander had scoffed. "The man who wants to cross from Europe to Asia. Yet, he's that drunk, he can't even move from couch to couch!"

The deadly insults that had been exchanged, together with Philip's marriage to Eurydice, had led to an open rift between father and son. For a while Alexander and Olympias had gone into exile until Philip had begged them to return, not out of any family feeling, but more due to the influence of Antipater. The old general had repeated the rumor, allegedly started by Demosthenes, that if Philip couldn't control his own family how could he control Greece?

"Ah well—" Philip was going to continue speaking but he stopped, staring down the hallway. He felt uneasy, something was wrong. Were the gods displeased at what he intended? His great design? He scrutinized his guests.

"Come on!" Philip bawled at the poet, Neopotelemus. "Come on, Neopotelemus! Recite a poem. Catch the flavor of this marvelous evening!" Philip spread his arms expansively. "Let this be an occasion all Greece will remember. Games, banquets, and poetry!"

The hall fell silent as the straggly, gray-haired poet scrambled to his feet. He winked at the young man sharing his couch, rearranged his robes to hide the wine stains, and, taking a deep breath, walked to the center of the hall. He gazed at Philip, trying to catch the mood of his host, and began to recite a poem that extolled Philip's achievements but reminded his listeners that the glory of man always ends in death.

Miriam heard the last sombre sentence and stared narrow-eyed at Philip. It seemed inappropriate to mention death at this festive time. Or was Neopotelemus merely fulfilling the role of the prophet and reminding Philip that he was mortal? The king kept his head down, and then he began to clap and the rest of the assembly joined in. Neopotelemus bowed and walked back to his couch. Philip wiped a tear from his eye.

"Do you want some wine?" he abruptly asked Miriam.

"No, Sire."

"Would you like to go home?" Philip continued. "I bought your father as a slave but you are both free. You have the same rights and privileges as any here. There is no need for you to stay in Macedon. You may go whenever you wish."

Miriam looked at her brother Simeon, who shrugged one shoulder. The invitation had caught them by surprise. Miriam had never thought about it but she sensed some danger behind Philip's offer; something menacing was about to happen, as if different forces were converging on this ancient palace. Miriam smiled to hide her unease. She should be careful. If she spoke about such fears to her brother, he'd just dismiss her as a Cassandra.

"Ah, Sire." Miriam leaned across. "You are too gracious but Macedon is our home. There is no one in Israel."

Philip just turned away, leaning over to drunkenly stroke Arridhaeus's face.

"Ah well," he slurped. "I have made the offer. The rest is up to you." The king talked measuredly as if unaware of the growing clamor as his companions and kinsmen returned to their roistering. "You are not like the rest," he continued. "Alexander's friends. They can stay beyond our borders until Olympus melts, dog turds the lot of them." He waved his hand. "You may go!"

Miriam and Simeon rose.

"Oh, and you can take him with you!" Philip grasped Arridhaeus and pushed him toward them.

Once outside the chamber Miriam leaned against the wall breathing out noisily.

"What do you make of that?" Simeon asked.

Arridhaeus went and crouched down beside Miriam, squatting on his haunches, peering down the passageway.

"I don't know."

Miriam walked to a small window and gazed out. The night sky was changing. The day would soon be here. She felt tired and tomorrow the festivities would continue.

"Would you like to leave?" Simeon came up behind her.

"Would you?" she asked.

Simeon shook his head. "For good or bad, whatever we think of these people, Miriam, they are our own."

They walked down across the small atrium to the rear of the palace where they had been given quarters.

"Will you help me find it?" Arridhaeus came trotting up. "My Apollo. I mean it was my gift. I've lost it. I—"

"Oh shut up!" Simeon shouted crossly. "You're always losing things!"

Miriam slipped a snake ring from her finger.

"Take this Arridhaeus," she said wearily. "It's a better gift."

The prince seized this and held it up like a child with a bauble.

"When I am king," he said, "I'll make you one of my queens." And he scampered off.

Miriam watched him go. "What happens?" she asked. "What would happen, Simeon?" she paused.

"If what?"

"Here we are at Aegae; Philip sits in isolated splendor being toasted as the captain general of Greece and the future conqueror of Persia. Alexander broods by himself. Olympias," Miriam raised her eyebrows, "as always, Olympias stays in the dark, bending over her spinning wheel as if she was one of the Fates. Eurydice chatters about her newborn child. Alexander's friends and ours are exiles while Arridhaeus the idiot babbles about being a king. It's like a pot boiling isn't it? You see the water rise; you know it's only a matter of time before it spills over."

"You think that will happen here?" Simeon asked anxiously.

Miriam tapped him on the nose. "Don't say I've got the

second sight," she added quickly. "Olympias is divorced. Alexander is isolated. Philip rides in glory over everyone. Do you think this situation can go on for ever?"

"What can we do?" Simeon asked. He grasped his sister's arm. "Father always said you were the clever one."

"I care for you, Simeon, I care for myself, and I care for Alexander, as do you. When the pot boils over, and it will do soon, let's hope that our God intervenes to protect us." She half-listened to the distant sound of revelry. "There'll be a bloodbath," she whispered. "And this old palace, which has seen so many murders, will have more ghosts to house."

CHAPTER 4

T<small>RUMPETS BRAYED TO</small> the clash of armor. Soldiers from the guards brigade, only a token force—dressed in full armor, corselet, greaves, the horsehair plumes of their helmets nodding in the morning breeze—filed into the amphitheater. The sky above was reddening, the stars disappearing. Miriam sat in her seat facing the main gate of the amphitheater, which stood only a short distance from the old palace. She had risen early, bathed and dressed quickly in a fine, saffron-dyed, linen dress. Her mantle was fastened with a jewelled-flower brooch, a gift from Alexander; on her arms golden bracelets, around her head a fragrant wreath that the chamberlains had given her when they led her to her seat.

Miriam felt the cold stone beside her and moved restlessly on the tasseled cushion. Simeon had not come. He had lurched into her chamber, pasty-faced, clutched his stomach, shook his head, and hand across his mouth, had fled back down the passageway. On her right Arridhaeus scratched his genitals and looked vacantly around. He held the olive wooden doll Miriam had given him up against his cheek and rocked gently to and fro. Around them sat the envoys and representatives from all over Greece, many of them still showing the signs of last night's carousing. Nevertheless, every one was there: representatives from Thebes, dark-eyed, olive-skinned, their blue-black hair and beards rich with fragrant oil; Athenians, dressed elegantly, their faces discreetly painted; red-faced, wild-haired nobles of Macedon; emissaries from Crete and the other islands; only Sparta was absent. When Philip had written to them, telling of his great victory at Chaeronea, the Spartans had sent back a cryptic message: "Measure your shadow: Is it any longer since your victory?" They had refused his invitation.

Behind Miriam, on the upper tiers, were the charioteers, musicians, singers, athletes, and wrestlers. Once the great opening ceremony was finished, the day was to be given over to festivities, banquets, and festivals. Philip was determined to impress his status and power on all of Greece. The tribesmen from the hills of Macedon had also arrived, dressed in their sheep-skin rugs; the rank sweat from their unwashed bodies mingled with the sweet incense and the fragrant flowers strewn across the amphitheater floor.

"Is it going to begin yet?" Arridhaeus asked.

"Shush!" She patted his hand. "Soon it will!"

Miriam gazed down at the rounded orchestra where twelve great altars had been set up. Before each roared a fire where sweaty slaughterers waited, cleavers in hand, for the cattle, now lowing in their pens beyond the amphitheater, to be driven up for sacrifice. All around them flapped banners and pennants, depicting the different insignias of the gods or scenes from the labors of Hercules, proclaiming once again Philip's descent from this great man-god. To Miriam's right, on the stage, was a huge lion throne draped in purple. On either side of it two chairs, almost footstools, one for Molossus king of Epirus, the other for Alexander. Miriam bit her lip. She wondered if Alexander would accept the snub and hoped that the prince had kept his word and not spent the night brooding in his chamber over cups of wine. In the row below her Eurydice cradled her baby, Antipater next to her. There was no sign of Olympias.

The trumpets brayed again. The gates to the amphitheater were opened and the gods of Olympus were brought in on specially built floats: Zeus, looking remarkably like Philip of Macedon, seated on a lion throne, thunderbolts in his hand; Apollo the hunter; Poseidon with his trident and net; Artemis with her hunting bow; and, finally, a statue of Philip, clothed in purple and, on his head, a Persian crown. The crowd cheered. The gods were taken before their altars; then the cattle were driven in. The slaughter began. Throats were slashed, the bodies carefully dismembered, filling the air with the bittersweet smell of fresh blood. Once the sacrifices were completed the gates were closed again. A herald stepped forward; in a ringing voice he proclaimed that Philip of Macedon, captain general of Greece, was about to enter the amphitheater. Again the clapping broke out, but Miriam saw the scowls of the Thebans, the sardonic smiles of the Athenians, and, on the bench below, far to her right, the Lyncestrian brothers, heads together, sniggering like two clowns. Miriam closed her eyes and prayed to her own Unnamed God that Alexander would not resist or protest. She opened her eyes. The amphitheater was being cleaned, the fires doused; young girls, dressed gorgeously in the style of nymphs, were now sprinkling the ground with herbs and fragrant water.

Outside the amphitheater, Philip waited at the end of the long avenue leading up to the gates. He stamped his sandaled feet and once again arranged his purple, gold-edged cloak more closely around his shoulders. He had drunk too deeply the night before and, when his barber had asked how he wanted his hair cut, Philip had snapped, "In silence if you please!" Now all was ready. The amphitheater gates opened. Philip stared to his right. He bit back his annoyance at the sour look on Alexander's face, then smiled grimly to himself. Such things would not last for long. He looked over his shoulder at the blond-haired, pale-faced Molossus.

"You look exhausted!"

The king of Epirus smiled wanly back.

Philip drew closer and nudged him playfully in the ribs.

"Cleopatra's a lively girl?"

"She is most gracious, Sire."

"Dog's turds!" Philip scoffed. "She is my daughter and has the morals of an alley cat."

Philip looked away. He wished he hadn't said that. Molossus might begin to wonder about the secret life of his young bride. Philip, now he had got rid of Olympias, wanted the kingdom of Epirus on his side before he marched east. Molossus would keep an eye on Macedon's border and Cleopatra would keep an eye on Molossus.

"The Queen?" Molossus coughed. "Olympias is not here?"

Philip stared up at the sky. "No, she isn't! She's brooding in her chamber, playing with that bloody spinning wheel! What's that line from Homer? 'The only joys of a woman's heart are to have her sorrows ever on her tongue'? The poet must have been thinking of Olympias when he wrote that."

"Mother sends her regards."

Philip spun around. Alexander was standing, his purple cloak thrown casually over his arms, legs apart, staring defiantly at him.

"Good." Philip blinked his good eye. "And when you see her, give her mine!"

Alexander drew closer. "She should be here!"

"I invited her."

"To sit where? Among the tribesmen?"

Philip shrugged. "She'd be at her ease there."

Alexander's face flushed.

"Don't sulk!" Philip hissed. "This is my day. I want no impertinence or insults from you!" He clicked his fingers as a sign for Alexander to withdraw. His son refused to move. "What is it?" Philip snapped.

"When you march on Persia . . . ?"

"You will march with me."

"With a command?"

"You will march with me," Philip repeated.

"I commanded a cavalry wing at Chaeronea."

Philip felt his own anger boiling. He took a step closer. Alexander deliberately flinched at the gust of wine fumes from his father's mouth.

"You commanded the cavalry at Chaeronea," Philip mimicked. "And you are never going to let me forget it, are you?"

"I am your son. I am twenty years of age. I am heir to Macedon's throne!" Alexander let his temper loose. "I am not some baseborn son!"

"You mean like Arridhaeus?" Philip gibed. "I would have had two sons if that cruel bitch hadn't got her hands on him!"

Alexander took the laurel wreath from his head and tossed it into the dust.

"I want your answer," he declared. "And I want my friends recalled."

"I want! I want!" Philip jeered, stamping his foot. "Pick up that wreath! Put it on your head or I'll have you arrested and put in a place where you'll not bother me again!" Philip took a step forward, his face only a few inches from Alexander's. "Don't you humiliate me, boy!" he whispered hoarsely. He gazed over his shoulder to where Molossus,

Pausanias, and other members of his bodyguard were watching him curiously. "This is my day," Philip continued. "All of Greece watches. These matters," he added tactfully, "can be discussed later, I promise you."

Alexander stepped back, picked up the laurel wreath, and walked away. Philip sighed. He'd lost his son. But what did it matter? Was Alexander really his son? Philip stared down at his sandaled feet. He remembered the first time he had met Olympias in the great hall of Samothrace where they had both gone to celebrate the rites of Dionysus. Olympias, her hair flying wild, her naked body soaked in precious oils, Philip believed she had been touched by the gods. They had made passionate love in dark cypress groves, Olympias writhing like one of her snakes beneath him. Philip scraped the sand with his sandaled foot. Such passion had to cool but should it turn to hatred? Philip had always wondered if Olympias had been unfaithful. She undoubtedly was absorbed in secret rites. Philip himself had seen the snakes writhing over and around his wife's naked body while Olympias stood, eyes full of divine madness, lost in a mystical trance. So was Alexander his son? Quiet, bookish, with a violent temper, Philip knew about Alexander's panic attacks, his uncertainty, his desire to please and be accepted. That was not Philip. Nevertheless, at the same time, once committed, Alexander had proved to be a redoubtable fighter, a superb horseman, an excellent cavalry commander. His wild, mad charge at Chaeronea had shattered the sacred band of Thebes while Alexander had proved himself equally ruthless against mountain tribes in Thessaly. Philip breathed out noisily. But to be a king? Philip remembered his own savage fighting for the throne of Macedon. It had been sword against sword, brother against brother. No blood tie was sacred. No bond of friendship inviolable. What had to be done, had to be done and, if necessary, it would be done again.

"Sire, they are ready."

Philip glanced at Pausanias. The young guard comman-der's face was slightly pale, shimmering in a sheen of sweat.

"You are not frightened, are you?" Philip whispered.

Pausanias shook his head. Philip saw the wildness in Pau-sanias's eyes and wondered if he had chosen properly. He glanced over to his far right where the small temple of Dionysus stood surrounded by a vineyard that nestled up against the city wall. Pausanias followed his gaze.

" 'The bull is wreathed for sacrifice,' " Pausanias mur-mured.

" 'All is ready. The slayer is at hand.' "

" 'There is no god greater than Dionysus,' " Philip replied, quoting from Euripides and nodding toward the small temple.

Pausanias's jaw tightened. He was about to speak when there was another fanfare of trumpets from the amphithe-ater; the gates opened and the heralds came out.

"Yes," Philip declared, "everything is ready."

He hitched his robe around his shoulders. One hand held the mantle until he remembered Demosthenes stood like that. He grinned and his hand fell away. I wonder what that old hypocrite is doing, Philip thought. He snapped his fin-gers. A page boy ran forward carrying a golden wreath on a scarlet cushion. Philip put the wreath on his head.

"Well!" he barked, "let's not keep them waiting. I'm hun-gry and I want to drink!"

The royal bodyguard, not dressed in armor, but in white linen tunics and robes, formed ranks behind him. Twelve in all including Pausanias. All they carried was the sarissa, the long spear used by the phalanx men in the Macedonian army. They marched forward, going around Philip, heading toward the gate. Philip felt a pain in his shattered leg and rubbed his thigh.

I must walk straight, he thought, slowly, measuredly.

"You shouldn't have done that." Alexander was now standing on his right while Molossus, king of Epirus, took up his position on the other side. "You should have a proper bodyguard," Alexander continued heatedly.

"Nonsense!" Philip replied. "I want to show these delegates that Philip of Macedon fears no one man. I want to walk into that amphitheater like a Pericles, unaccompanied by anyone, certainly not soldiers clad in armor." He smiled at his son. "That's the way things are done in Greece," he whispered.

Alexander looked away. The guards, now twenty paces in front of them, passed through the gates of the amphitheater.

"Now!" Philip ordered.

He walked forward, head erect, his one good eye fixed on that gateway. This was the climax of his life! He, Philip of Macdeon, was to be hailed as a captain general of Greece. He would be its war leader, to punish Persia, to free the cities of Asia, to receive the acclamations of all. Philip the God! Philip a new Pericles! Statues of him already stood in Athens, Corinth, and soon in Persia. He ignored the pain in his leg. He didn't care about Molossus or Alexander walking by his side. He was above such things. He was a god touched by the gods. A few tribesmen unable to get into the amphitheater hurried up and stood on either side of the sacred way. Philip smiled and raised his hand. Macedonians, he thought, wild and savage; no one would dare approach the king so close, but these were his people. He was almost at the gateway. Inside, his guards were lining up on either side. Philip gazed across at the rounded orchestra. He saw the Jewess Miriam; she was holding Arridhaeus's arm. Philip smiled. He would remember that when this was all over. Such acts of kindness should never be forgotten. He noticed Miriam was leaving her seat, clutching Arridhaeus by the arm. She was skirting the orchestra, coming toward the gateway. Philip glanced quickly at Alexander. The king knew what the Jewish girl was doing. She would stand close to try and catch Alexander's eye, warn him to keep his temper in check. Well, the girl needn't worry. Pausanias was now coming back through the gateway, walking purposefully toward them. Philip's stomach tightened: images of Olympias, Alexander jumping on the back of his great black warhorse Bucephalus. Pausanias was now walking quickly toward Philip, a look of concern on his face. Had something gone wrong? Philip walked on. He expected Pausanias to slow down, to raise his hand and bow. Instead the guard commander, eyes dark in his pale face, came on at a run. Philip saw the flash of steel in his hand.

"No!" Philip roared, yet it was too late. Pausanias was on him, the knife going under his ribs. Philip screamed at the hot, searing pain. Philip's hand went out to grasp his murderer but Pausanias was already backing away, throwing his robe off, running like a hare through the gates, down the royal way, toward the small temple of Dionysus. Philip couldn't stand the pain; he turned. Alexander was staring gape-mouthed.

"My son!" Philip keeled to the ground. He had lost all feelings in his legs. He knew the wound was fatal. Images swirled through his tortured mind: Olympias grinning; Demosthenes, his hands held high above the Agora in Athens; one-eyed Antipater. A roaring filled Philip's ears, like that of his troops as the Thebans and Athenians broke at Chaeronea. Philip squirmed on the ground. He saw the hilt of the dagger, carved in the shape of a chariot, and recalled the words of the seer, "Beware the rider in the chariot!" Too late now. Philip lifted his head. People were thronging around.

"I am a god," he murmured. "Immortal. Mortal no longer!" And closed his eyes.

All around the king's corpse people milled. Miriam seized Alexander's arm. Arridhaeus was screaming, his mouth a rounded *O*. Behind them the news had swept the amphitheater. People were leaving their seats. In their haste, altars were knocked over, banners and pennants pulled down. The Athenian envoys were already leaving, not even bothering to pay their respects. Alexander appeared rooted to the spot. The Lyncestrians were also shoving their way through, and one threw a hateful glance in Alexander's direction. This was no surprise assassination, Miriam thought. Philip's murder was planned. She grasped Alexander's arm and, staring across, could see Pausanias already losing himself among the vine groves.

"Alexander! Alexander!" she cried.

He, as in a dream, took the wreath from his head, placed it on his father's corpse and crouched down. Miriam grasped his hair.

"Alexander!" Miriam hissed. "You must not stay here!"

She glanced up at the shadow that blocked out the sun. One-eyed Antipater was gazing coolly down at them.

"Antipater!" Miriam yelled but her voice faltered.

The grizzled veteran was studying Alexander, a strange look on his cruel face.

Molossus, however, had recovered his wits. He turned and shouted at the royal bodyguard screaming that they should follow Pausanias. Three of them, well distant from the rest, hurried in pursuit. Miriam looked at Molossus.

"Take the princes," she whispered. "Take them and the king's corpse to the palace. Bar the doors. Seek out Olympias."

Gathering up her dress and kicking off her sandals, Miriam followed Pausanias's pursuers around the white pillared temple into the dark coolness of the grove. She stopped and looked around. Alexander was now on his feet. He appeared to have recovered and was shouting orders. Royal bodyguards were picking up the king's corpse. Miriam ran on; the path was long and winding. She rounded a corner; the path to the vineyard ran like an arrow in front of her. She glimpsed the gate at the far end. A rider was waiting with horses. Pausanias was almost there. The three bodyguards were closing in when, suddenly, Pausanias's arms went up in the air, like an athlete at the games crossing the finishing line. He stumbled over something and fell. The rider galloped away.

"No!" Miriam screamed. "No!"

But the bodyguards took no heed. Time and again javelins rose and fell. By the time Miriam reached them, the assassin was dead, sprawled in a bloody tangle of robes, eyes open, face twisted in its last agony. Miriam knelt down beside the blood-soaked corpse. The guards drew away.

"You should have taken him!" she snapped.

They were leaning on the javelins, mouths open gasping for breath.

"He killed the King!"

"What are your names?" Miriam asked.

"What bloody business is it of yours?" One of the bodyguards squatted down on the other side of the corpse.

"I am the king's friend," Miriam replied tartly.

"The king's dead!"

"Then Alexander is king," Miriam retorted.

The guardsman blinked and grinned. "My name is Perdiccas." He pointed to the other two now wiping the sweat from their necks. One of them had gone to the gate and come back.

"No sign of the horses," he grumbled.

"I asked your names!" Miriam declared.

"Hush now, girl," Perdiccas replied. "You've got mine, the other two are Leonatus and Xenephon. So don't sit in judgment on us." He grasped his javelin. "This is all we were armed with." He pulled back Pausanias's blood-soaked robe. "He could have been armed and the bugger on the horse could have come to his help. Strange isn't it?" Perdiccas mused. "A few minutes ago this was our captain. Now he's Philip's assassin. We've killed him and, all he is, is a blood-soaked corpse." He looked up at the sun-filled sky. "No wonder they say the gods laugh at us." He glanced at his companions. "Philip should never have made Pausanias captain of the guard. He should never have let him within spear-throwing distance. Not if the gossip is true."

"What gossip?" Miriam asked.

Perdiccas got to his feet. "It's only camp gossip, not meant for a young maid's ears." Perdiccas screwed his eyes up. "You are the Jewess aren't you? Your brother is the royal scribe who looks after that idiot Arridhaeus?" He snapped his fingers at his companions. "Let's take the corpse back to the palace."

His companions hastened to obey. Perdiccas stretched out a hand, still blood-streaked, and helped Miriam to her feet. She studied the soldier closely. Perdiccas had a long, narrow face, a bit like a monkey; the eyes were bright and intelligent; the moustache and beard were close-clipped and smeared in oil.

"By tonight," Perdiccas whispered, watching Miriam study him, "you'll not know me from the rest. We'll be in full armor, but I'll give you a word of advice. Don't take things as they are. Do you understand me, girl? Philip's dead and you say Alexander will be king. Well, others think differently." He nodded with his head. "Did you see what happened back there? Young Molossus kept his nerve; Antipater's as cunning as a serpent. There are also the Lyncestrians. What I am saying, Jewess, is that Philip's dead and the crown of Macedon is up for grabs. It will be worn by he who commands the army. You see everyone leave? Heading for their houses or their horses? The Athenians will be crowing with laughter, the Thebans smirking behind their hands. In a week all Greece will know. Within two weeks Macedonian garrisons will be thrown out of every city and town. So, don't think Alexander's king. And, if he falls, all who are with him, all who are close to him, fall with him." He touched Miriam's neck gently. "May Apollo guide you. I hope I don't have to wring that pretty neck or chop at it with a sword or dagger."

He glanced at his companions who had now hoisted Pausanias's corpse, putting one of his arms around each of their necks—a grisly sight, as if he were some drunken comrade. Miriam felt a tremor of fear but she bit her lip. She had lived long enough in the company of these men to know that, in their eyes, cowardice was the only sin.

"Alexander will be king!" she declared defiantly. She stared at the gate. "Did you see who the horseman was?"

"A mere shadow," Perdiccas replied. "Nothing but a shadow!"

"Pausanias should have gotten away." Miriam realized she had left her sandals and her feet were beginning to ache.

Perdiccas pointed back along the path. Miriam glimpsed the vine shoots and tendrils that snaked out across it. One, in particular, was thick and black like a piece of rope.

"He tripped on that," Perdiccas declared. He went to join his companions but then looked round. "Strange isn't it? Philip always said there was no greater god than Dionysus. If Pausanias hadn't tripped on that vine shoot he would have gotten away." Perdiccas held his hand up, palm front, in a gesture of peace. "Take care, Jewess. Remember what I have said."

"Where will you take the corpse?"

"To the palace," Perdiccas shouted. "I am sure Olympias will wish to grieve over it. More important, that's where our wages are kept."

Miriam watched them go. She went to the gate and gazed along the pathway in the direction the horseman had fled, a narrow, winding track that ran between the trees and the temple wall. She went back in: Pausanias's blood was already soaking the sandy trackway. She crouched and studied the vine shoot over which the assassin had stumbled. It came from the tangle of vines across the pathway, snaking in among the trees to the other side. Miriam tugged and found it was loose. She went among the vines, following the shoot until she found its end, thin and tapering, in a small gap between two vines. She crouched down and studied the ground. She was sure the soil had been disturbed, as if someone had hastily covered his footprints. Miriam was also mystified by the large specks of soft, green lichen or moss, common enough in a graveyard, but not in a vineyard.

Miriam stared up through the tangled branches at the sky. Had someone been here, she wondered? Standing among the vines, waiting for Pausanias to run down that trackway, and plucking up the shoot like a rope? Pausanias would never have expected that. But, if that was the case, the murder must have been planned. Pausanias was only the cat's-paw, and who would do that? She tried to recall details about Pausanias but she knew very little. There was some connection between him and Epirus, the kingdom from which Olympias had come. Had that mad queen wreaked her vengeance at last? And, if Olympias was involved, was Alexander guilty of patricide? Miriam recalled the prince brooding the night before, his well-known resentments against his father, but then she remembered Alexander's face, his shock at his father's assassination. Alexander could be an actor. He could dissimulate and play the role, depending on the circumstances or the people he was talking to. Yet, in this case, that didn't make sense. If the murder was planned, how could Alexander persuade a man like Pausanias to kill the king? And those three guards led by Perdiccas? True, Molossus had to shout at them, but . . . Miriam closed her eyes; if she remembered rightly, Perdiccas and his two companions were already preparing to set off in pursuit. They'd come out of the gate, away from the rest. And who would know that Pausanias would flee this way? Why had the guards killed him? Pausanias could have been taken back for questioning.

Miriam opened her eyes. She knocked away the wasp buzzing in front of her face. She was hot and tired and she grimaced in annoyance. She was doing what her brother always accused her of, daydreaming. And what was the use? She let the vine go and hurried back onto the pathway. When she reached the amphitheater it was almost deserted. A few priests, hands flapping, faces wreathed in sorrow, loudly lamented at what had happened. Miriam went into the gateway. A few people sat about but the place had lost its glory. The statues of the gods stood neglected; some of the altars were overturned. The golden crowns placed on a table in front of Philip's throne had disappeared, as had the purple, gold-fringed cloth that covered the throne.

"What's the matter, girl?"

Miriam turned. A man sat on one of the lower tiers, dressed in a dark-blue tunic. Miriam noticed the wrist guard on his hand, elbows resting on his knees, hands cupped before his mouth; he was staring across at the throne, a wistful look in his eyes. He turned his head again.

"You look concerned!"

"The King is dead." Miriam walked across the soft, flower-strewn sand.

"So he is," the man replied, drumming his fingers against his mouth. "And all this is over."

"Do you know what's happening?" Miriam asked, curious at this man's coolness.

"They have taken the king's corpse back to the palace. Everything is in chaos. The envoys have fled. They say there will be fighting before nightfall but that's the way of the world, isn't it, girl?" He pointed to the figure of Philip still seated like a god on his throne. "The gods decide and they have now." When he glanced back the girl had gone.

The man, a Cretan, known to his friends as Cephalus the Archer, gazed around the amphitheater. He had to wait, arouse no suspicion. Cephalus, in fact, was as bewildered as the rest. At his feet, hidden beneath a cloak, was a short Cretan bow and a quiver of arrows. He'd been paid in good silver Darics to come here and shoot Philip as he sat on the throne. Cephalus had accepted the payment, slipping into the amphitheater, bow and arrows carefully concealed. He was to wait till the appointed time. It would have been an easy shot. The king, sitting on his throne, resplendent in white against a purple background. Cephalus could have loosed at least two arrows. But that was the way of things! Everyone would have been looking at the king. Cephalus, who'd been seated up at the top, with no one who knew him, would have loosed and walked away, as he had so many times when he'd killed his victim. Cephalus was a Cretan, an assassin. Sometimes he'd fought for this army, sometimes for that. On special occasions he would carry out private agreements, killing with a bow or a knife or poison. This would have been no different. Now Cephalus was annoyed. He did not know who had hired him; that had been done secretly in a city tavern. He'd been told who to kill, how to flee the amphitheater, and where to go. Cephalus, however, was now bewildered. He struggled to contain his anger. Didn't they trust him, he wondered, that they had to hire someone else? Cephalus had decided to stay, certainly till any soldiers were out of sight, and he could take his weapons and slip away unobserved. He was supposed to meet someone at a wayside tavern between here and Pella. However, if he stayed here, they might at least come to do the decent thing and pay him what they owed. After all, it wasn't his fault that someone else had killed the king.

"Ah well!" Cephalus sighed.

He picked up his cloak carefully, folding the stout horn bow and narrow quiver of arrows. He walked down the steps and was in the shadow of the gateway when he heard his name called. He turned round and smiled at the young fop whom he'd glimpsed earlier dozing on a seat behind him.

"Cephalus?"

The Cretan's face hardened.

"Cephalus."

The young fop's face broke into a smile. He stopped, swaying on his feet, and came closer. He placed one hand on Cephalus's shoulder and swayed tipsily.

"What is it?"

"I have something for you."

"What?"

The fop leaned forward and, as he did so, thrust his dagger deep into Cephalus's heart.

CHAPTER 5

MIRIAM FOUND THE palace in total confusion. A few guards stood on duty but there was no officer or commander around. The soldiers were not from the crack regiments but raw recruits who looked nervously through the eyelets of their heavy hoplite helmets. Servants were fleeing. Some carried goods they had plundered from the storerooms and chambers. In the main atrium, guarded by a few of Philip's companions, the dead king's corpse lay on a bier, a purple sheet tossed over it. Miriam espied a sandaled foot jutting out; Philip's hand lolled down but all rings had been removed. A young page ran up and tugged at her arm, beckoning her to follow. She did so and the boy led her to the back of the palace, which overlooked the gardens, to the cavernous chambers where Philip had relegated his divorced wife. In one curtain-draped room, Olympias sat on a small stool, Alexander on the couch to her right. Simeon, looking pale-faced and sweaty, stood in the far corner. On the balcony beyond, Molossus nervously fidgeted.

"Just in time, girl!" Olympias snapped. She beckoned to the stool beside her. "You saw it all?"

Miriam nodded.

"Pausanias?" Alexander lifted his head.

"He's dead," Miriam declared.

"The fool!" Olympias snarled.

"Mother," Alexander scratched his head.

Face slightly to one side, Alexander was blinking, lips moving soundlessly. Miriam recognized the signs. Alexander was experiencing one of those intense panic attacks that always afflicted him in a crisis. He'd either become tired and listless or frenetically determined to ruthlessly carry out what he had decided.

He'll either swim across the river or turn back, Miriam thought. And if he turns back, we are all dead. Olympias was staring at her son, eyes hard; her face was freshly painted. She had a small tiara, or clasp-comb, dug deeply into her lustrous hair. She was dressed in a pure white gown with a purple shawl over her shoulders.

"You were going to say?" Olympias's eyes held those of Miriam. "Alexander, you were going to say something?"

"You hardly look the grieving widow!" Alexander snapped.

"I'm not Philip's widow," she retorted. "Don't forget, he divorced me!"

"They'll lay the murder at my door," Alexander declared. "How can a patricide be accepted as king?"

"I don't give an asp's wing," Olympias snarled, "what the Macedonians think!" She grasped Alexander's arm. "You must act and act now!" She made a chopping movement with her hands. "You must be ruthless!"

"They'll say I killed Father!"

"Even if they do," Olympias riposted, "even if you did kill

him, you are not guilty of patricide." She seized Alexander's face between her hands. "You are the son of a god, Alexander. Remember the line from the *Iliad*? Achilles was born of an immortal god?"

Alexander's lips no longer moved.

"What can be done?" He breathed in so long and violently, the nostrils of his nose flared like that of a horse.

"Philip's corpse lies out in the atrium," Olympias declared. "As for Pausanias's murder, only the gods know."

"Where's the nearest regiment?" Alexander asked.

"About an hour's march between here and Pella," Simeon declared.

"More important," Olympias's voice was now silky. "Where's that one-eyed cyclops Antipater?" She sat rocking on a stool, staring at her splayed, painted finger nails. "You have Philip's rings and seals?"

Alexander stooped between his feet and picked up a small, leather pouch.

"Molossus!" he called.

The young king came in off the balcony. He looked frightened. He had been drinking and some of the wine stained his gown. The young page who had brought Miriam in, burst into the chamber.

"The Lyncestrians!" he gasped. "They are bringing their tribesmen into Aegae!"

"How many?" Olympias snapped.

"They say four to five hundred!"

"This was planned, this was planned!" Olympias got to her feet. "Alexander, are you going to sit there like a mooncalf?"

"Father's companions, the guards?" Alexander replied.

"They'll stand aside."

Olympias now looked like a veritable Medea. Yet, for the first time ever, Miriam saw fear in her eyes. The queen knew what would happen: the Lyncestrians would sweep into the palace grounds, the guards would break out, those who remained would be massacred. Alexander would be killed. The Lyncestrians would accuse him of Philip's murder and, within a week, there would be a new dynasty of kings in Macedon.

"You are king!" Miriam declared softly. She grasped Alexander's hand. "But, if you don't act like one, you'll end the day a corpse and take us all with you!"

"What do you want me for?" Molossus exclaimed.

Alexander, rubbing his hands, got to his feet.

"How close are your men?"

"I've got two hundred outside the palace walls," Molossus replied. "They are well armed."

Alexander walked to a chest and opened it. He took out a large sack and thrust it into Molossus's hands.

"Tell them there is more. They must stand and fight. Can you do that?"

Molossus swallowed hard.

"Do it!" Olympias screamed.

"Just hold them," Alexander whispered. He grasped Molossus by the shoulder. "Don't jump the wrong way," he continued. "If I die, do you think they'll let Olympias's brother live?"

"And if they die?" Molossus's eyes now took on a more calculating look.

"You are my friend and my brother," Alexander replied calmly. "You and yours will be kings of Epirus as long as mine are of Macedon. Eternal friendship!"

Molossus weighed the bag in his hands. "I don't need this," he countered.

"Yes you do," Alexander replied. "Men fight better for gold. Ask yours this question. Do they want this? Because, if they let the Lyncestrians through, it will all go to them."

Molossus hurried out. Alexander went to the pouch and took out a ring, which he thrust into the page's hand.

"Where's Antipater?"

"With the guards, your father's companions. They are drinking in the hall."

"That's it." Alexander glanced at his mother. "They are waiting. They are waiting to see which way I'll jump. Fetch Antipater!"

The page hurried off. Alexander sat down.

"We'll know in a matter of hours," he declared, "if the worst is about to happen!"

"I have poison and a dagger," Olympias retorted. "I'll drink it myself and, when a Lyncestrian leans over to kiss my lips, I'll slash him in the groin!"

Alexander threw his head back and laughed. "You should have been a warrior, Mother."

"Like you?" Olympias spat back.

Alexander's face blushed. There were footsteps outside. Antipater strode into the chamber. Alexander didn't rise from his couch. He moved slightly sideways and patted the cushions beside him. The one-eyed commander, much the worse for drink, but still steady on his feet, came and sat down, breathing noisily.

"You are commander of the guard," Alexander began. "Where are my soldiers, Antipater?"

"You've not been hailed as king," Antipater retorted. "You have no authority!"

"I have the seals."

"You have no authority!" Antipater repeated. "The men say you killed your father."

"Pausanias did that."

"They say Pausanias held the knife but you helped Pausanias." Antipater's one good eye slid to Olympias. "You and your mother."

"Antipater, Antipater." Olympias leaned across. "Like my husband you are one-eyed but you haven't a tenth of his brain. You think you are back in time, don't you? Antipater the kingmaker? The Lyncestrians and Alexander will fight to the death and Antipater and the army will back the winner. You stupid fool!" she gibed.

Antipater drew back from her venom, his face flushed.

"Do you think the Lyncestrians will let you live?" Olympias continued. "Philip's boon companion in his drunkenness, in his killing and his lechery? You'll be dead by spring! A rotting cadaver. You and your young wife!"

"You were always a foul-mouthed bitch," Antipater retorted. He drew himself up. "The troops have not hailed your son."

Miriam watched, wondering what would happen. Antipater was crucial. If he lifted a finger the regiments would move.

"The Lyncestrians won't get here," Alexander broke in. "Molossus and his Epirotes will block them. My companions," he lied, "those whom Philip exiled, are on their way home. The regiment outside Pella has declared for me."

Antipater's good eye blinked. He swallowed hard. Miriam's heart glowed. This old veteran had thought he could stride in here and play the kingmaker but, like everyone else, had underestimated Alexander. Olympias would rage while Alexander would plot. Alexander clapped Antipater on the shoulder, then with his other hand, brought up the knife he had concealed under the cushion. He dug the point into Antipater's neck.

"What are you going to do, threaten me?" The old soldier kept his head very still.

"No, Antipater. I have been sitting here, thinking carefully. I'm going to kill you. Then," Alexander chewed the corner of his lips, "then I'm going to cut my arm and claim you came in here and tried to murder me. I'll announce to my father's companions and officers that you were involved in Pausanias's death plot. That's why the man was killed!"

"They won't believe you!"

"Oh yes they will." Alexander smiled. "After all, you were responsible for my father's well-being. Who gave the order for Philip to walk into that amphitheater unarmed, unprotected? Who recommended that Pausanias be made a commander? Who arranged for him to be on duty today? Why didn't you do anything to stop him?"

"I had nothing to do with it." Antipater lifted his hands. "I swear on my wife, on my children. Philip arranged it all."

"But Philip isn't here, is he?" Alexander replied. "Not everyone will believe me but I'll sow doubts, cause confusion, create enough time to act." Alexander took the knife away but he motioned with his hand for Simeon to stand in the doorway. "On the other hand, Antipater, you are my father's closest friend and my greatest ally. I intend to take my father's armies across the Hellespont. I will need a regent in Macedon." Alexander ignored his mother's indrawn hiss of breath. "You don't have to go campaigning," Alexander continued sweetly, "you'll be king for me in Macedon. Stay here with your young wife. Watch the house while I am gone." Alexander clasped Antipater's hand. He withdrew the blood-red ruby ring from his finger and tossed it to the page boy. "Your wife, your kinfolk?" Alexander asked.

"They are in the palace."

"The boy will fetch them, he has my token. They'll be safe here with me."

"Wait!"

The page turned at the door as Antipater beckoned him back.

"Go to Perdiccas," he rasped. "Collect him and the other officers; tell him to meet me here."

The page ran off. Alexander now embraced Antipater, kissing him gently on the side of the temple.

"You know what has to be done," he whispered. "Do it, and do it ruthlessly, no mistakes!"

For a while all was confusion. Antipater's wife and children came hurrying along, pale-faced, round-eyed, their meagre possessions wrapped in a bundle. Antipater kissed them but told them to wait in an antechamber. A short while later Antipater's officers arrived. Miriam recognized the leading men from Philip's circle of companions. Alexander made them stand until he rose, gesturing them to sit where they could.

"I had no hand in my father's murder," he began. "I swear that by all the gods. Pausanias the assassin is dead but others now threaten our throne. Antipater and I . . ." Alexander stood, one hand on Antipater's shoulder, "have decided to take the appropriate action. Molossus, king of Epirus, and those troops he has have now blocked the way against the traitorous and treasonable Lyncestrians. A regiment of guards is now moving toward Aegae. Antipater and I have decided to bring all regiments here, not only for my father's funeral, but for the acclamation of me as king."

The officers stared impassively back.

"Now these are my orders. Any servant who leaves the palace is to be killed on sight. Anyone who plunders and breaks the king's peace is to be cut down. All officials are confirmed in their posts. Every officer will receive remuneration, an increase in pay, a cut in taxes, and the same goes for the rest of the army."

Miriam watched the grins appear on the soldiers' faces.

"Anyone who disobeys," Antipater broke in, "is to be killed immediately. I want every one of the guards in full battle armor on parade outside. Well," Antipater barked, "don't sit there getting your arses cold!"

The officers left. Antipater gave Alexander a rather mocking bow.

"My wife and children will stay with you, I suppose?"

"Of course," Olympias purred. "They'll be safe here."

"You'll keep your word, Alexander?" Antipater didn't even bother to glance in Olympias's direction.

"If you keep yours," Alexander replied. "Every man has a second chance and you've had yours, Antipater. So I'll tell you this." He got to his feet. "I promise you, Antipater, by all that you hold holy, if you flinch, if you veer from your loyalty, either now or in the future, I'll take your head and those of all your kin."

Antipater's face broke into a smile. "You are Philip's heir," he replied softly. "Only those who deserve to be king become king. You will never doubt me again."

Olympias hurried to the door after him.

"And that bitch, Eurydice!" she screamed. "I want her under arrest, her and that puking babe!" She walked back into the room, put her hands on the small of her back, and breathed in deeply. She gazed under heavy-lidded eyes at Alexander. "Eurydice is mine," she hissed. "Never forget that, Alexander." And picking up her mantle, Olympias walked out of the chamber.

Alexander listened to her sandaled footsteps fade, then getting up, closed the olive-wood doors. He beckoned Simeon and Miriam closer.

"I have done what I can," he declared. "At least for the moment. How is your stomach, Simeon?"

"Better." He rubbed his side and glanced quickly at his sister. "Grapes never agree with me."

"Pausanias would agree with that," Alexander joked, then his face became serious. "You followed the guards, Miriam. Do you think they killed Pausanias deliberately? I mean, they could have taken him prisoner."

"Yes and no," Miriam replied. "Pausanias was heading toward the gate at the far side of the vineyard. Another man was waiting with a spare horse."

"And?" Alexander asked.

"Pausanias tripped on a vine. The guards said they killed him because they feared resistance."

"Was he armed?"

"Not that I could see," Miriam replied. "Nor was he carrying anything." Miriam flicked some dust from her gown. "There was someone else in the vineyard," she continued. "You know how the vine shoots run the path, like trip ropes. Someone was hiding among the trees. Pausanias was a warrior, a soldier, he would take care as he ran."

"Someone pulled the vine shoot up?" Alexander asked.

"Yes they did."

"Aren't you worried?" Simeon broke in, listening to sounds in different parts of the palace, men shouting, the clash of armor.

"I have done what I can," Alexander insisted. "Antipater will hold the officers and the guards loyal. Molossus and his Epirotes will check the Lyncestrians. I will crush any revolt here. I am the king's heir. The soldiers will remember that. The real trouble will come in the next few weeks, in Thebes, Athens, and elsewhere. They'll try their luck, expel our garrisons, teach the *mooncalf* a lesson." Alexander bitterly recalled Demosthenes' public insult.

Alexander's jaw was now tense; his eyes lifeless, hard as glass. He reminded Miriam of Olympias.

"What is more important," he continued, "is that they will try to depict me as my father's murderer. Pausanias wielded the dagger but who controlled Pausanias? They'll lay the blame at my door and that of mother."

Alexander got to his feet. He walked to a small chest in the corner, opened it, and brought back a leather pouch. He undid the string around the neck and shook the assassin's dagger onto the table. It was still streaked and dirty. Alexander picked it up, gingerly balancing it between his hands. He turned it carefully so it caught the light from the oil lamps. The handle was carved in the shape of Apollo's charioteer. The blade was long, seven or eight inches; the metal had a bluish glint.

"This is new," Alexander declared. "It's of Scythian design. There was an old warning my father used to joke about: 'Beware the chariot and the charioteer.' He always thought it was a reference to some battle. He'd never dreamed it was a dagger." He handed this to Miriam.

She balanced it in her hand. It was light, easy to wield.

"Pausanias must have hidden it in the folds of his cloak."

"You hold it well," Alexander murmured. He leaned across and squeezed Miriam's lips gently between his forefinger and thumb. "You were brave today, wasn't she Simeon? I saw you run. You reminded me of the way you used to race like a deer when we trained in the Gardens of Midas." He took the dagger from her hand. "I have a task for you. You are my friends, my companions. You are also actors and therefore enjoy the same sacred status as envoys. I want you to find out who was behind my father's murder. Who controlled Pausanias? I want to be able to swear to all of Greece that I am no patricide."

"But the Lyncestrians, surely?" Simeon broke in, his good-humored face now pale and anxious. "They must have hired Pausanias. And, once Philip was dead, decided to strike?"

"I don't think so," Alexander replied. "Pausanias was from Epirus." He paused and stared up at the metal embossments in the wooden ceiling. "Isn't it strange," he wondered, "so are the three guards who killed him." He wagged a finger at Miriam, his head slightly to one side. "Remember that." He caught her strange look. "I know what you are thinking, Miriam: that I am going to send you on a wild-goose chase; that I am responsible for my father's murder. I swear, by my mother's womb, I had good cause for griev-ance. At times I hated Philip." He joined his hands together as a king would before he took some solemn oath. "I swear, by any god and your unknown one, I am innocent of Philip's blood. Oh, by the way, where is Arridhaeus?"

"He's with the soldiers," Simeon declared. "I saw him playing counters. He'll be safe. Why, you don't think some-one will put him forward?"

"Antipater may have done," Alexander replied. "He might have waited until the Lyncestrians and I destroyed each other, killed whomever remained and then used Arrid-haeus as a puppet."

"Could Antipater be guilty?" Miriam asked.

"Yes and no," Alexander replied. "No in the sense that he wouldn't plot against Philip, but yes, once Philip was gone, Antipater would do what he liked."

"You paid a heavy price for his loyalty," Simeon declared.

Alexander threw his head back and laughed so much, his shoulders shook and the tears rolled down his cheeks. He glanced at Simeon again, at the way he was gaping at him, and he bellowed with laughter, his face transformed, boyish, full of impish mischief. He leaned over, put one hand on Miriam's shoulder and the other on Simeon's, and squeezed gently. He smiled at them. Miriam's heart lurched. When Alexander of Macedon was charming, when he smiled, when he touched, no one could oppose him. It was Alexander at his best, care-fully courageous, ever ready to see the joke, either against himself or everybody else. Alexander withdrew his hands.

"Can you imagine?" he whispered, like a boy planning some mischief. "Can you just imagine when I leave Mace-don under Antipater, what Olympias will think? They hate each other. They'll fight from morning till night. One will obstruct, ridicule, and plot against the other. Each will send me letters blaming the other. Macedon will be safer under those two than it would be if I remained. If Olympias plots, Antipater will tell me and vice versa so over that I'll lose no sleep."

"What about your mother?" Miriam asked. "Was she involved in Philip's death?"

Alexander's smile disappeared. "Yes, dear mother," he breathed. "Sometimes, Miriam, she charges me a heavy rent for my nine-months stay in her womb." He joined his hands and pressed them against his mouth, resting his elbows on his knees. "Let's start from the beginning. Pausanias was captain of my father's guard. Father was showing off. He wanted to walk into that amphitheater as if he was the great Pericles of Athens. No armor, no guards. My father was neither stupid nor arrogant. But what he did was stupid and arrogant, and he paid the price. Now, Pausanias walked back toward him. He killed the king and fled. According to you, Miriam, someone was waiting in the vineyard; they pulled up that shoot, Pausanias fell, and the guards killed him." He paused before continuing. "So, question one: Why did Philip trust Pausanias so much? Question two: Who was waiting for Pausanias and where was he fleeing to? Question three: Who made him trip? Question four: Why did those guards pursue and kill him so quickly? Oh, I know Molossus shouted at them but why did they spear him?"

"They made a reference," Miriam recalled. "Something about Pausanias and your father?"

"There's a story," Alexander replied, looking at a cut on his hand. "About four or five years ago, Pausanias and Philip were lovers. You know father; age or sex made no difference. He wasn't called the mountain goat of Macedon for nothing. He'd mount anything, even a pig, when he was drunk.

Now Philip and Pausanias had a lover's quarrel. Pausanias was sent to Attalus."

"The same general who's commanding the troops across the Hellespont?" Simeon asked.

"The same," Alexander replied. "Uncle to Eurydice, a man not very popular with mother. Attalus acted worse than my father. He invited Pausanias to a banquet where he listened to the young man's grievances but made him so drunk that Pausanias could hardly stand. Now, according to what I have heard, Attalus then raped him, mounting him like one dog upon another. When he had finished, he invited his other guests, not to mention the grooms from the stables, to do the same."

Miriam flinched at the cruelty Alexander was describing. She had heard rumors of similar practices, of Macedonians humiliating each other, but never with such viciousness.

"You can imagine," Alexander continued, "Pausanias's distress the next morning. He had been raped and publicly mocked. He returned to my father, demanding justice and vengeance against Attalus."

"But, of course, Attalus was Eurydice's uncle?"

"Yes, and you know Father. Sometimes he wished to upset no one. You've heard the story about when he took the city of Olympus?" Alexander smiled. "Well, after the assault, Philip had drunk deeply and was drinking more. The captives were paraded before him. A young man shouted out, 'Eh Philip, I knew your father!' Philip ordered him to come closer. When he did, the young man whispered, 'Sire, I did not know your father at all but, the way you are sitting, you can see your crotch.' Philip laughed and had the man freed." Alexander paused. He closed his eyes for a while. "Philip was like that." He continued thickly. "Generous to a fault. He wouldn't upset Attalus but, at the same time, he'd want to keep Pausanias sweet."

"So he made him captain of the guard?"

"Yes." Alexander tapped the nail of his thumb against his teeth.

"But if Pausanias should murder anyone," Miriam declared, "it should be Attalus not Philip. Unless, of course Pausanias regarded Philip as responsible, either for the rape or for refusing to do anything about it." Miriam swallowed and realized how thirsty and tired she was.

"Wait there a moment." Alexander got up and walked out of the chamber.

Miriam followed. She noticed soldiers from the guards regiment now lined the passageways. Alexander summoned two of them and whispered. Both men, horse-hair-plumed helmets tucked beneath their arms, listened carefully, then hurried off. Alexander stood in the passageway tapping his foot. He came back, winked at Miriam, and walked farther into the royal quarters. Miriam heard a child laugh and realized Alexander was ensuring that Antipater's family was still there. Straining her ears, Miriam now thought the palace was quiet. A servant appeared. He looked as if he had been crying. He brought a tray of food into the room and put it down. He was about to walk away when Miriam seized his arm.

"Taste it!" she ordered.

The fellow did so. He picked up a piece of toasted cheese, some of the small balls of ground meat and happily popped them into his mouth while he half-filled a goblet and quickly swallowed the watered wine.

"Thank you." Miriam smiled.

"I know." The man's tired eyes held hers. "All the to-ing and fro-ing, Mistress, but it's quiet now. The soldiers are everywhere. All the servants are back except two. The soldiers killed them at the gates, caught them smuggling plunder from the palace." He scurried off, his sandals slapping against the marble.

Miriam went back. Simeon was sitting, staring at a mosaic on the wall that showed Hercules cleaning the stables of King Augeus.

"You are quiet, brother?"

"Sister, I'm nervous." Simeon laughed, a short harsh sound; he refused to meet her eye. "We are Jews and we are actors, Miriam. Palace politics—"

"Nonsense," she interrupted, sitting down.

Miriam filled the wine cups, adding generous portions of water. Hadn't Philip remarked on that, she thought, only the night before? That they were Jews and free to go back to their native land? Had he been hinting that something was about to happen? But surely he didn't know his own murder was being planned? So what?

Alexander strode back into the room, slamming the door behind him.

"Antipater has seen to my father's corpse, Pausanias's, too. They have brought a third one in, a man found stabbed in the amphitheater just within the entrance way. Ah well, we'll see."

Alexander sat down and ate quickly. It was as if nothing had happened and they were back in the gardens of Midas, hurrying their food before Aristotle returned to give them a lecture.

"Did Pausanias have any family here?" Miriam asked.

Alexander jumped up and walked to the door. He threw it open and shouted down the corridor.

"Hermanocrates!" he yelled. "Pausanias's tutor. He's somewhere in this palace hiding like the little mouse he is. Find him, arrest him, and keep him until he has been questioned!"

Miriam heard the clatter of armor. Alexander came back into the chamber grinning from ear to ear.

"I had forgotten about Hermanocrates," he said, picking up his wine cup. "He's a self-styled philosopher, a sophist. He loved Pausanias beyond all telling. He's the only family Pausanias had."

"Wouldn't he have fled?"

"Not Hermanocrates," Alexander retorted. "He's got a clubfoot, he hates horses, and where would he flee to? But come, we've stayed long enough in the shadows."

He went across and opened a chest, took out a small short stabbing sword, threw the scabbard on the ground, finished his wine, and walked out of the chamber. Miriam and Simeon followed. Alexander walked quickly, with a swagger that reminded them of Philip. Every so often he would stop, snap his fingers, and tell one of the soldiers to follow him. By the time they reached the atrium, a squad of at least ten protected them. Antipater sat behind a desk. There was no sign of Philip's body; messengers, two or three cavalry men, lounged about. Scribes sat on stools busily writing out messages that Antipater would imprint with a seal, calling a man forward and hurrying him off.

"The guards are loyal, to a man." Antipater got to his feet. "By nightfall there will be two regiments within the palace grounds."

"And the Lyncestrians?"

"No news at present but there's been a bloody fray about two miles outside the city, or so a peddler told us."

"And my father's corpse?"

Antipater nodded at a door leading into the courtyard. "Olympias has taken care of that."

CHAPTER 6

ALEXANDER, FOLLOWED BY Miriam and Simeon, walked out and stood on the steep steps that looked out over the great parade ground in front of the old palace. Miriam gaped in astonishment. Alexander kept his face impassive. A great funeral pyre had been built, fashioned out of logs, about nine feet high. It had been covered in purple-gold drapes. On the top lay Philip's corpse beneath a black and silver burial pall that covered everything except the dead man's face. On each side of the pyre hung trophies of Philip's victories: a Scythian suit of armor, banners from captured cities, Thessalian horse gear, the armor of Athenian hoplites stripped from corpses at Chaeronea. The pyre was surrounded by braziers full of glowing coals. Beyond these stood a circle of phalanx men dressed in full ceremonial armor. To the right of the pyre, ringed by burning pitch torches driven into the ground, a huge cross had been erected on which Pausanias's corpse had been nailed. The cadaver had been stripped, the great open spear wounds turning blue-black. Miriam flinched and stared up at the darkening sky. She caught the smell

of perfumes from the pyre as well as the resin and sandalwood mingling with the pungent stench of pitch and
charcoal.

"Mother has been busy," Alexander whispered, "and she
was always one for drama. If she hadn't been queen, she
would have made a marvellous priestess."

Alexander went down the steps and stood before his father's corpse. He took handfuls of incense from a bowl and
sprinkled it on the pyre. Miriam stared over at the cross.
The corpse hung limply. In the darkness beyond the cross,
she glimpsed other corpses laid out.

"They must be servants?" Simeon whispered. "Those
whom the guards killed?"

Alexander walked back up the steps where Antipater and
other officers had assembled.

"Your mother wouldn't be checked," Antipater whispered. "She demanded this was how it was to be done."

Alexander turned and spread his hands.

"By Zeus," he called. "By Apollo, by all the gods of
Olympus, by all that is sacred, I, Alexander, swear first that
I am innocent of my father's blood. Secondly, those who are
guilty will pay for this terrible crime!"

In answer the phalanx men began to beat their spears
against their shields. The noise grew to a crescendo accompanied by a chanting: "Alexander! Alexander! Alexander!"

The object of this veneration just stood, one foot slightly
forward, staring sorrowfully down at his father's bier. He
raised his hand for silence. Olympias, Miriam reflected, was
not the only actor in the family. Alexander's opening words,
however, were drowned out by the shrill bray of trumpets.
Two heralds came around the corner, dressed in black from
head to toe. They blew on the trumpets again and stood
aside to allow the chariot through: a simple wickerwork,

light-weight affair drawn by two black horses. Olympias stood in it, next to the charioteer, clothed in black and silver, a cypress wreath around her head, the upper part of her face covered by a golden mask. Miriam recognized it as that worn by Medea in Europides' play the *Bacchae*. The chariot stopped. Olympias got down. In her hand she carried a cushion. On it lay a gold-plated wreath, like the crowns bestowed upon victorious athletes at the games.

"Oh no!" Alexander whispered.

Miriam thought Olympias was going to take the crown to the funeral pyre; instead, she walked slowly toward the crucified Pausanias. She stopped before the cross. The charioteer ran forward with a cushioned stool. Olympias stood on this. She kissed the cheek of the crucified man, then lifting the wreath, placed it gently on the dead man's head. This time Olympias kissed the gaping, blood-caked lips, stepped down from the stool, and walked slowly back to the chariot.

Her actions caused a stir and muted protests from the troops. Antipater cursed under his breath but Alexander didn't move. Once the chariot was gone, he turned to Antipater.

"The other corpses?" he asked, as if Olympias's actions had never occurred.

"Some are servants," the commander replied, "guilty of looting. They were killed on the spot. Another's a drunken officer, misguided enough to declare for the Lyncestrians. One, however, is more interesting."

He walked briskly down the steps, Alexander and his party following. Miriam averted her eyes from the naked man so barbarously nailed to the cross, now more macabre with that wreath on his straggly, dusty hair. Antipater grasped a pitch torch.

"Olympias wanted these corpses brought here," he announced. "She says they can be burned on her husband's funeral pyre, companions on his journey down to Hades." He winked at Alexander. "Or slaves when he goes up to Olympus?"

"The interesting corpse?" Alexander queried.

Antipater pulled back a cloak and lowered the torch. Miriam glimpsed the narrow, sharp features, the neatly trimmed moustache and beard.

"I saw him!" she declared. "On my return to the palace. He was in the gateway to the amphitheater."

"That's where he was found," Antipater replied, pointing to a great stain in the man's left side. "Stabbed through the heart, a good clean thrust."

Alexander crouched down and tapped the man's face with his middle finger.

"Does anyone know who he is?"

"Cephalus," Antipater replied. "He's a Cretan, a master bowman. A quiver of arrows and bow were found near him. That's what I've been told."

"And what else have you been told?" Miriam asked.

The one-eyed commander looked up at the sky.

"Attalus," he replied. "Cephalus was supposed to be serving with Attalus."

"So why isn't he across the Hellespont?" Alexander asked. "With the rest of the troops?"

Antipater refused to look up. "I don't know, perhaps he came here to pay his respects?"

Alexander rose, spun on his heel, and walked back into the palace. For a while he just walked the corridors and passageways checking on the guards. He avoided the women's quarters.

"I do not want to visit Mother," Alexander declared once he, Simeon, and Miriam had returned to his chamber. He took a wine jug and filled their silver goblets. "Why did she do that, Miriam? Why crown the body of her husband's murderer with a wreath?"

"Your mother," Miriam replied, "is being honest. Philip had divorced and repudiated her. Olympias, in her heart, must have murdered him on many an occasion."

"But?"

"But I don't think it's only that," Miriam continued. "Alexander, your mother will do anything to protect you. By crowning Pausanias, she has publicly taken the guilt of your father's death to herself, diverting any suspicion from you."

"Then why not leave it at that?" Simeon broke in.

"I can't." Alexander turned, his face flushed with fury. "Mother can play Medea, Cassandra, Helen of Troy, whatever she wants, but I want to know who really murdered my father. I only wish Mother would think before she acts. If Olympias was involved, tongues will wag, so was Alexander. I know they call me 'Mother's Boy.' " He took a deep breath. "But I shall deal with Mother later."

For a while Alexander sat, tapping his foot against the floor.

"I am sorry, Simeon. I didn't mean to be angry." He glanced around. "It's getting dark," he continued. "I'd like more lamps to be lit. I should be out among the troops."

"Well, why aren't you?" Simeon declared, eager to mend bridges.

"That's the hardest part," Alexander replied. "Father said, never rush around. If I go out, chatting to the troops, running hither and thither, I'll appear what they think I am, a boy eager to please. I must wait here until the Lyncestrians are crushed. Soon the royal council will meet—Philip's generals, the leaders of the clans—they must confirm me as king and the army must hail me. Only then, and I mean only then, will I be seen to act." He glanced at Miriam. "You look tired."

"I'm thinking of that archer," Miriam replied. "The one I saw in the amphitheater. Ceph—"

"Cephalus," Alexander completed the name.

"We know he wasn't here for the festivities," Miriam declared. "He must have slipped back here last night, then gotten into the amphitheater, sitting there with his bow and arrows."

"You think he came to kill Philip?"

"Possibly," Miriam replied, "but, when someone else finished the task, Cephalus had to be murdered."

"How many plots are there?" Simeon asked.

"I don't know," Miriam replied; her eyes held Alexander's. "What is more important, who were the intended victims?"

Alexander leaned back on the couch, his back against the rest, stretching out his legs.

"I would love to go down to the stables," he murmured, "take Bucephalus and ride, charge my enemies."

"And get your throat cut," Miriam interposed.

"I wish Aristotle was here," Alexander added. "I'd get him into some debate on the nature of things."

Miriam could see that the prince was on the verge of giving way to his panic and anxiety.

"Sleep," she said, "and, if you can't sleep, occupy your mind. Philip's murder has been committed. You have the funeral to arrange, people to reward as well as punish."

"And that includes Attalus," Alexander declared. He got to his feet. "What will you do?"

"Pausanias had a chamber?"

"Yes, at the other end of the palace, near the guard-house."

"And there's his tutor," Miriam said.

"Ah yes, Hermanocrates, he'll either be drunk or so agitated he'll be beating his head against the wall. You are going to search Pausanias's chamber aren't you?"

"Yes," Miriam replied.

"Then have a word with his tutor!"

Alexander, lips moving as he talked to himself, abruptly walked out of the chamber as if he had forgotten they were there. Miriam made a face and followed. Alexander fell deep into conversation with the guardsmen. Simeon walked into the atrium and searched out one of the chamberlains who led them around to the south side of the palace, which faced the amphitheater. Here were the storerooms and guards chambers. Pausanias's room was locked, but the chamberlain had a key that opened it. Inside, the chamber looked as if it hadn't been disturbed: a cot stood in the corner, a large amphora full of water, some linen cloths hanging on a peg, and an empty leather chest.

"What did you expect to find?" Simeon asked. He was not too sure whether he liked this new purposeful sister. "You are enjoying this, aren't you Miriam?"

She glanced over her shoulder.

"It keeps me busy," she replied. "Useful."

"It's not that is it?" Simeon, who had been leaning against the closed door, now walked toward her.

"You like being near Alexander, don't you?"

Miriam wondered if her brother was jealous of her or of Alexander.

"You don't have to be here," she replied. "You are a scribe, Simeon, and a good one. I owe my life to Philip. I also feel honored by Alexander's flattery, his companionship."

"You are one of the few women he allows so close."

Miriam grinned. "Now you do sound jealous."

Simeon blushed and shuffled his feet. "What did you hope to find here?"

Miriam walked across and pulled back the blankets from the military style bed.

"Nothing," she replied. "I expected to find nothing and I haven't been disappointed. Pausanias did not expect to come back here. Everything he owned, everything he possessed is gone, but he was a guards officer, Simeon. Where are his armor, sword, shield, and sarissa? You know what they are like? Where they go, their armor follows. Let's visit Hermanocrates."

They walked out into the corridor, which was silent.

"I told the chamberlain to stay here."

They walked outside onto the steps and down. It was growing dark. This part of the palace was deserted, quiet. Miriam shivered. Simeon went out into the courtyard calling for the chamberlain but Miriam backed away, wary of the shadows.

"Simeon!"

She heard her brother curse and exclaim. She ran forward and almost crashed into him because he was crouching. The chamberlain lay there, throat slashed from ear to ear, the front of his gown a soggy mess. Miriam felt the man's face; it was still warm.

"He wouldn't answer any questions." The voice was foppish and came down from the darkness somewhere in front of them.

Simeon gripped her arm.

"What are you going to do, Jews, run away? No one can run faster than an arrow."

"What do you want?" Miriam called. "Why did you kill this man?"

"I wanted to speak to him, ask him what you were doing in Pausanias's quarters."

Miriam caught the lisp on the letter *s*.

"What is it to you?" she called back.

"Only a task for which I am well paid." The voice took on a humorous tone. "Things are not going according to plan, but there again, that's scarcely my fault is it?"

"Then whose?" Simeon called.

No answer came. Miriam heard a scuffling. She rose and walked forward.

"Are you here?" she called. Her voice echoed through the darkness. Miriam suddenly felt weak, her stomach heaving; her legs couldn't stop trembling.

"I think we should go back," Simeon called.

They returned to the palace. Simeon sent two soldiers out to collect the chamberlain's corpse. They then asked directions and found Hermanocrates seated in a small guard chamber just off the atrium. A soldier lounged outside. There was no sign of Antipater and the rest, and Miriam guessed some news must have arrived.

The self-proclaimed sophist looked utterly woebegone. A small, fat, middle-aged man with thinning hair, quivering jowl, pudgy nose, and nervous furtive eyes. He was sitting, face in hands, on a stool in the corner. He didn't even bother to lift his head when Miriam and Simeon closed the door behind them.

"What am I to do?" he wailed, taking his hands away from his face. "I am a philosopher, a student of the world, a teacher, a pedagogue."

"If you are a philosopher," Miriam broke in, "then you should see this as part of your training."

"Who are you?" Hermanocrates' head went forward like that of a little bird. "Who are you?"

"Hush now." Miriam waved him back onto the stool. "We are brother and sister. Miriam and Simeon Bartimaeus; we are friends of Alexander."

The old philosopher's hands now fluttered like the wings of a trapped bird.

"I've heard of you," His voice rose to a screech. "You are the Jews, Israelites out of Egypt. I am innocent of anything and everything."

"Who said you weren't?" Simeon asked.

"It was a terrible thing he did," Hermanocrates gabbled on. "Terrible indeed."

"Why are you here?" Miriam asked. "No, I mean why were you with Pausanias here in Aegae?"

The old philosopher dropped his hands and picked at a stain on his threadbare gown.

"Because Pausanias let me," he mumbled. "I was his tutor. When he was a youth." He lifted his tear-stained face and Miriam felt sorry for this funny, old man who probably loved Pausanias to distraction. "He let me stay with him. He promised that, one day, when he married, I could tutor his children."

"Would he have married?" Miriam asked.

"He was comely and well thought of," Hermanocrates replied. "But . . ."

"He didn't like women, did he?"

Hermoncrates shook his head. "He was Philip's lover. He loved Philip with all his mind, heart, and soul. I was allowed to pick up the crumbs of what was left."

"Why did Attalus abuse him?" Miriam asked.

Hermanocrates' mouth formed into a rounded *O;* for a while he sat, shaking his head.

"Philip and Attalus were lovers. Pausanias and Philip were lovers." He paused. "By what authority do you ask me this?"

"We can fetch Antipater and some of his soldiers!" Simeon interrupted.

The philosopher's face creased into a smile. "There's no

need for that," he murmured. "I cannot stand violence. I wish to be gone."

"And you will be," Miriam replied, "if you answer our questions. We were talking about Attalus?"

"Pausanias went to a feast," Hermoncrates chattered on, glancing fearfully at Simeon. "Pausanias boasted about his standing with Philip so Attalus got him drunk and had him raped."

"And Pausanias wanted vengeance?"

"What do you think?"

"Why did Philip refuse?"

"It's obvious," Hermanocrates scoffed. "Attalus is one of Macedon's leading generals and Philip wanted his niece Eurydice's long legs wrapped around him. Pausanias said Philip was besotted by her."

"So what did Philip do?"

"He gave Pausanias silver, promoted him in the guards. Philip also made Attalus swear that he would never reveal what had happened. Philip took a similar oath. I couldn't understand all the fuss. I mean, these Macedonians," Hermanocrates sniffed haughtily, "they climb onto each other like dogs in heat." He coughed. "Well, apart from Alexander. But, yes, before you ask, Pausanias was more concerned that others did not know what had happened. In the main he was satisfied they didn't. Oh, there were rumors, gossip, but nothing out in the open."

"Did Pausanias ever," Miriam asked, "intimate that he was plotting to kill the king?"

"No," Hermanocrates answered quickly. "But there again, you'd expect me to say that wouldn't you? The only thing he ever said was, one day when he was in his cups, how he could be famous. I joked back, 'By doing something notable or killing someone famous.' But," he gabbled on, "I don't think Pausanias was listening."

"Whom did he meet?" Miriam asked.

"Oh, he was very secretive." Hermanocrates shook his head. "Going hither and thither, but he never told me. The only thing I did notice," Hermanocrates' legs began to shake, "was that he owned more money than I expected."

"And you don't know where that came from?"

Hermanocrates shook his head.

"Did you ever see his dagger?" Simeon asked.

The philosopher jumped to his feet. "I must go!" he wailed.

"Not yet," Miriam replied softly.

"No, I mean I must relieve myself. My stomach, my bladder."

Simeon escorted him out of the chamber. They returned a short while later. Hermanocrates was carrying a cup of wine that Simeon must have taken from somewhere.

"You are very kind." The philosopher sat down on a stool. "Are you sure I can go when you are finished with me?"

"If you satisfy us," Miriam said, "you have my word. You can go where you want, when we say, with a few coins to help you on your way."

"Pausanias did say one thing," Hermanocrates confessed. "A few days ago, we were out watching the delegates arrive for the king's festivities. Pausanias and I were standing by a window. He muttered something about hubris, about pride, which would be the downfall of many."

"We were talking about Pausanias's dagger?"

"Yes, I saw it, no different from anyone else's."

"You never saw one with a wooden handle carved in the shape of a chariot?"

Hermanocrates shook his head.

"And did he visit anyone?"

The philosopher gnawed at his lip, then scratched his unshaven chin. "I told you he was secretive."

"But he did visit people, didn't he?" Miriam insisted.

"Do you really want to know? He visited Alexander; once he went to the prince late at night. When he came back to his chamber, Pausanias was all indignant. He mentioned the attack on him by Attalus, how people were talking about it. He had gone to ask Alexander's help but the prince refused, saying it was nothing to do with him."

"Who else?" Miriam asked.

"That woman!" The words were spat out. "I've heard what she's done," Hermanocrates' voice shook. "Put a gold wreath on poor Pausanias's head!"

"Olympias?"

"I wouldn't put anything past that witch woman. Pausanias went to see her. Oh, it must have been ten or twelve days ago. He came back stinking of her perfume."

Miriam glanced at Simeon. "You are sure of that?"

"Oh yes, he strutted in here with her smell all about him, eyes half-closed, smiling. He had a bangle on his wrist. I knew what he had been up to."

"Tell us?" Simeon asked.

"Pausanias was of Epirote blood," Hermanocrates gabbled on. "He claimed a distant kinship with Olympias, but he couldn't fool me."

"By all that is holy!" Simeon breathed, "would you tell us what you know?"

"Pausanias had the body of a man," Hermanocrates stared at the floor, "but the mind of a woman. Sometimes he used to dress as one. Philip used to make him do that, hence Attalus's taunts. If he wanted to be a woman, then they'd treat him like one."

"And Olympias?" Miriam asked.

"Pausanias told me that she held the secret rites, those of the god Dionysus. Only women can attend. They go out in the groves, woods, and dark, secretive places. However, Olympias is no respecter of persons. She used those rites to allow men into her company, but they had to act and dress like women. You've heard the stories about the conception of Alexander? That Philip may not have been his father?" Hermanocrates now lowered his voice. "If he wasn't, that's how Olympias became pregnant. One of those mad, feverish rite dances where the women become men and the men become women; the women ride men as if bestriding a horse. Oh, Pausanias was full of it!"

"Did Philip know this?" Miriam asked.

"No, I think very few people did."

"Do you think Olympias persuaded Pausanias to kill Philip?"

"I am not sure. The rites were her way of getting revenge, of making sure she learned what Philip's close counselors were saying. Men like Pausanias would tell."

Miriam stared at this grubby, frightened, little man.

"But why should Olympias invite Pausanias?" she asked.

"I told you," he stammered. "Pausanias was like that."

"She also gave him money, didn't she?"

"I think so," he confessed.

"Oh, come on Hermanocrates!" Miriam urged. "You were close to Pausanias. I knew him as well, you know," she lied. "He spoke most favorably of you; Pausanias described you as a great teacher."

"Did he really?" Hermanocrates' face wreathed in smiles. "Did he really say that?"

"Oh yes, that's why we asked to see you. If anyone knew what was going on in Pausanias's mind, it would be his former tutor."

"But I knew nothing about the murder," Hermanocrates added anxiously. "I swear, by everything holy, I knew nothing of that. All Pausanias told me," he continued, "was that Olympias had a heart as black as night. She wanted Pausanias to kill someone but he didn't say who; that would be told at a later time. I remember Pausanias laughing. Olympias said he was well placed and when she told him the plan he could not and would not refuse."

"When Pausanias was killed, he was running through the small vineyard near the Temple of Dionysus," Miriam said. "There were horses there, another man waiting. You said Pausanias was a lonely man? But he must have, well, he must have had a friend, someone he could confide in?"

"There was no one." Hermanocrates shook his head. "I swear there was no one else." He ran a finger around his lips.

Miriam sensed he was lying but didn't want to frighten this furtive, little man.

"And last night?" she asked.

"He was on guard duty," Hermanocrates answered quickly. "When I met him, he was quiet, talking about the banquet, how drunk everyone had become."

"Met him?" Miriam got up and went and stood over Hermanocrates. "But I've just been to his chamber. He didn't sleep in his bed last night. You will tell the truth, won't you?"

Hermanocrates swallowed hard.

"He had a room."

"Where?"

"In the city, above a cobbler's shop, on the street called Straight, a short distance from the amphitheater."

"In which case, sir, you can take us there now!"

"But it's dark. There are soldiers on the streets!"

"Don't worry about them." Miriam took the man by his arm. "You'll be safe."

In the end, Antipater, who met them in the atrium, gave them a pass to leave. When they left the palace precincts, they discovered that the crumbling, old capital was more like a ghost city. Houses and shops were boarded up. The wine booths were closed; even the whores, who flocked to such occasions looking for custom, had fled. Soldiers stood on street corners and patrolled the alleyways. Now and again they were stopped, but when Miriam showed her pass, the soldiers let her proceed. They crossed the marketplace; as they did so a messenger, his horse lathered in sweat, pounded across shouting at the soldiers to stand aside. An officer caught the bridle, making the horse rear. The messenger cursed and struck out with his whip but the soldier, agile as a monkey, dodged it.

"What news?" the officer cried.

"It is for Antipater and the king!" The messenger replied.

He pulled back his cloak to show the small shield worn on his left arm, the symbol of a royal messenger. Miriam and Simeon, who also had been stopped by the soldiers, waited to see what would happen.

"Oh come on, lad," one of the soldiers shouted. "We are as ignorant as anyone else."

"The Lyncestrians have been annihilated," the messenger replied, pulling back the reins. "Their followers are either dead or in flight. The brothers are captured and, on the roads, every available soldier in Macedon is on the march."

His words were greeted by a cheer and he was allowed to go on. Miriam and Simeon, with Hermanocrates between them, hurried across the square, down a narrow alleyway and into the street called Straight. Simeon stopped.

"You go ahead!"

"Why?" Miriam asked.

Simeon looked back along the street.

"I don't know," he murmured. "I think we're being watched."

Miriam shrugged and followed Hermanocrates. The cobbler's shop stood halfway along. Its owner was most reluctant to answer Hermanocrates' pounding on the door, but at last he flung it open, grumbling and muttering. He held up the lantern, glimpsed Hermanocrates, and smirked.

"Your friend's not here," he gibed. "What's happening in the city?"

"Haven't you heard?" Miriam asked curiously.

"Well, the old king's dead. Killed by a thunderbolt wasn't he? Pretending to be Zeus. We in Macedon don't like that sort of thing." He shook his head. "I told young Pausanias that myself."

Miriam gathered the old man knew nothing about what had happened to his former tenant.

"We need to see his room," she declared.

"He'll object."

"No he won't," Hermanocrates replied, before Miriam could stop him. "He's dead!"

The old man stood aside, fingering his beard.

"There's only me and my wife and she—"

"Show us the room," Miriam interrupted.

The cobbler waved them inside. The small shop, and the room beyond, stank of leather, grease, sour cheese, and burned oil. He took them up a rickety staircase. The chamber above was nothing special, a bed and some furniture. Miriam shooed the old cobbler out and immediately opened the small chest. She took out a leather bag. Inside, neatly folded, was a nondescript tunic, a heavy military cloak, a dagger, a heavy purse full of coins, and a small scroll. The old man had lit one of the oil lamps. Miriam took the papyrus across and examined it carefully. At first she couldn't believe it.

"That's impossible!"

"What is?" Hermanocrates asked.

"It's a pass," she replied, "given under the king's personal seal only yesterday; it calls Pausanias Philip's close friend and would have allowed him to travel wherever he wished."

CHAPTER 7

MIRIAM SAT BACK on her heels and stared in disbelief at the parchment. Here was Philip's assassin who, only the day before, had been provided with a pass, money, and riding clothes to go wherever he wished. Had Philip gone mad? Had he planned his own murder? Miriam smiled. If Philip had had his way, he would have lived for ever and conquered the world. She told Hermanocrates to stand outside while she went around the rest of the chamber. She found women's clothes, some makeup, an expensive wig, clear testimony to Pausanias's secret life. There were also knives, a sword—and she wondered why Pausanias had used that dagger. Miriam was about to close the coffee lid when she threw it back. If Pausanias was going to flee, if a man had been waiting for him with a horse, then what were these items doing here? Pausanias would hardly kill Philip and then wander back through the streets of Aegae to collect his belongings; that didn't make sense. Miriam went across to the open window and looked out. The night was growing cold, the wind chilled the sweat on the side of her face. Miriam closed the shutters and sat down with her back to the wall. Her neck was hurting, her thighs were sore as if she had stood tense for too long.

"I wish I knew who you were," she whispered, as if talking to Pausanias's shade. "A friend of Philip, a friend of Olympias? What were you doing? What did you intend?"

She heard a knock on the door and the old cobbler came in. Miriam studied him closely. She noticed he moved his head sideways as if he couldn't hear very well.

"The young soldier who lived here. Did he have visitors?"

"Oh yes. Sometimes other soldiers, mostly that old snob standing outside, but I never asked questions. Pausanias always paid well." He scratched his face. "Is he coming back?" The cobbler smacked the back of his hand playfully. "Of course he's not, he's dead. Can I have his possessions?"

"In due time," Miriam replied. "Did Pausanias return here last night? If you help me," she offered, "you can keep his things."

The cobbler grinned. "For a short while he came back, early this morning with his friend outside; then he left."

"And?"

"Nothing!"

"Did anyone else visit the shop later?"

"No, not that I saw. But, there again, I have a sleep in the afternoon and neither my eyesight nor that of my wife is very good. She's as deaf as a post and I'm not much better."

"Thank you." Miriam, clutching the piece of parchment, got to her feet. She went outside and patted Hermanocrates on the shoulder. "Stay here for a while," she said. "If I haven't sent for you in the next three days, you are free to go wherever you wish."

She walked downstairs and out into the street. Simeon was waiting, hidden in the doorway of a house farther up.

"I was wrong," he confessed. "No one's following us. Did you find anything interesting?"

Miriam lifted the piece of parchment. "It's hard to believe, but Pausanias had a royal pass, signed by Philip himself, allowing him to go wherever he wished."

In the dark she couldn't make out Simeon's face, but she heard his gasp of surprise. They walked back toward the palace.

"It doesn't make sense." Miriam paused at a corner and stared up at the dark mass of the palace; pinpricks of light glowed from different windows. "Here we have Pausanias, a man of many talents, known to Philip, as well as Olympias," she added caustically, "in more ways than one. Pausanias was both a homosexual and transvestite. He's raped by Attalus and his cronies at a banquet. Philip compensates him by promoting him to commander of the palace guard. In the last few days Pausanias acts in a mysterious manner. We know Olympias wanted him to kill someone, probably Philip, but Pausanias seems to have had no motive for killing Philip. True, the king did not avenge the insult from Attalus, but at least he didn't send our young guards officer packing."

"Aren't you forgetting the Lyncestrians?"

Miriam rubbed her eyes. "No, I'll come to them in a while. Anyway, Pausanias kills Philip. Three guards set off in pursuit, as if they knew what was going to happen. Pausanias is tripped and killed, and the waiting horseman flees. Pausanias has no possessions on him and I find this pass, the money, as well as travel clothes in Pausanias's chamber above the cobbler's shop."

Miriam started as an officer called from across the street asking them to identify themselves. They did so and walked back into the palace. More soldiers had arrived, setting up camp in the grounds. Guards had been doubled along the colonnades and porticoed walks. Officers—some covered in dust, a few with minor wounds—thronged the corridors and atrium. Slaves were distributing wine. Miriam glimpsed Alexander moving among the soldiers, shaking hands, clapping them on the shoulder. He glanced at them, smiled shyly, and waved his hand.

He's a king, Miriam thought, he's victorious; now what will happen?

She and Simeon slipped around the crowd to their chamber. Simeon said he hadn't recovered and was going to bed. Miriam watched him go, then called out.

"Simeon!"

He turned. She pointed at his feet.

"You're wearing new sandals."

"Arridhaeus," he groaned. "He got his hands on some paint." He smiled thinly. "Good night, little sister."

Miriam went to her own chamber. She stared at the seven-branched candelabra painted on the wall; the drawing was exquisite, so accurate, a constant reminder of Jerusalem, of her own faith. Miriam crouched on the floor and covered her head with her prayer shawl. She closed her eyes and whispered one of the songs of David her father had taught her. Yet she was distracted; faces, images, scenes from the day pricked and caught her attention. Always Alexander! His different moods, that soul-freezing panic, the restless, frenetic activity, moving from a gentle, confused, young man to a hardened soldier, a bloodthirsty Macedonian prince. She realized the deep attraction; Alexander asked to be watched, and you never knew what his mood would be. Miriam thought of other young men, such as Perdiccas, the guardsman she had met in the vineyard. She tried to imagine being kissed by him, her clothes being removed, but she felt no excitement. Then she imagined Alexander and felt guilt at such a distraction.

Miriam opened her eyes and stared at the golden candelabra painted above a cedar tree of Lebanon. Alexander's
companions would soon be back: dark-haired Hephaestion,
tall, slender, serious-faced with a mordant wit; gentle-
mouthed, but his eyes full of cynicism, Hephaestion played
the role of Patroclus to Alexander's Achilles. Niarchos, the
short, stocky Cretan who loved gold and seemed intent on
amassing a fortune. Ptolemy, supposedly one of Philip's bastard sons, with his clever face and gangly body, sharp and
witty, cutting with his tongue. Ptolemy had once tried to
climb into Miriam's bed to find, as he put it, the secret place
between her thighs. They had been camping out in the forest around the grove of Midas. She had screamed and yelled.
Simeon had pulled his knife, Ptolemy had drawn his. She
had been terrified; Simeon was no warrior and Ptolemy was
a killer. Alexander had intervened and the following morning made them all swear that they would leave her alone.
Now they would all come back. Ptolemy would arrive, gal-
loping into the courtyard, shouting abuse. He'd immediately go to the stables to inspect the horseflesh. Miriam's
hand went to her lips: if Pausanias was going to flee, he'd
need a fast mount surely? Something fleet-footed. Miriam
got to her feet, her tiredness forgotten. She recalled the cobbler's shop, the open window, Pausanias's clothes in the
leather sack. She slipped her sandals on, threw her cloak
about her shoulders, and hurried down through one of the
passageways. A guards officer, rather drunk, tried to accost
her, but his more sober companions whispered in his ear
and the man jumped back as if he had been slapped.

Miriam ran down the stairs, into the grounds, and across
to the stables—long, barnlike structures built around a cobbled yard. It was a scene of frenetic activity. Torches were lit,
horses were being led in and out of boxes, and grooms hurried about carrying fodder or taking harness to be oiled or

repaired. Miriam searched out the keeper, a small, bald-headed former soldier whose limp reminded Miriam of Philip. He was drinking heavily, shouting orders, lashing out now and again with a cane at a groom or boy who didn't move fast enough. He saw Miriam waiting to speak. For a while he ignored her, then gestured her over.

"What's the matter?" He moved her into the torchlight and studied her face. "I know you. You're with Alexander, aren't you? You should be in bed. Preferably with someone else."

Miriam smiled. Such lewd comments were common; they were rarely given to offend.

"This morning," Miriam asked, "did anyone leave the stables? A rider who took a fresh mount with him?"

The stable master shook his head. "No, very few horses were needed for the ceremony."

Miriam turned away.

"Mind you, there was Philobetas."

"Who?"

"One of Philip's personal grooms. He took two horses out last night."

Miriam's heart skipped a beat.

"As I said, he took two horses last night and came back with them this afternoon; the horses looked as if they had really been lathered."

"Where had he been?"

"He was acting on the king's authority. I don't ask questions. I simply slip the harness on the horses and make sure they are fed, watered, rubbed down, not stolen, and well treated. When the army marches, I march with them, me and the grooms, the stable boys, the fodder men, the farriers—"

"Thank you, yes," Miriam interrupted. "Can I speak to this Philobetas?"

"He's over there." The stable master indicated with his head to a young man leading a horse around, cooling it off.

Miriam walked over.

"Philobetas?"

The man paused, letting the horse nuzzle him. He looked from under thick brows, a threatening glare, but Miriam could see he was frightened.

"Where have you been today?"

"None of your business."

Miriam smiled. This was her man; he might threaten, but he kept his voice low and didn't protest.

"I'll tell you what, Philobetas." Miriam indicated a small outhouse with the door open. "You can put that horse away and come and talk to me over there. Or I can scream and say I saw you near the gates at the far end of the vineyard."

Philobetas backed the horse into the stable. Miriam walked across the thronging yard and waited for him.

"I didn't know what to expect." He came and stood close, fearful that people might overhear them. "Yesterday the king told me to take two mounts, the best the stables had. I was to leave immediately. I was to stay out in the countryside, which I did, and then, just after dawn, take up station at the gateway, the one where Pausanias was killed."

Miriam glimpsed the terror in the young groom's eyes.

"I don't know anything," he whispered through tightened lips. "I am a messenger boy. Anyway, what is this to you?" He peered closer. "You're the woman, aren't you? The one I saw running down—"

"Alexander has sent me. No, there's no need to worry. I believe you. Just tell me what happened."

"I took the horses and waited in that trackway outside the vineyard. I was there just before dawn. Up and down, up and down, I rode and walked, exercising the horses. I was lonely, I was hungry, I wanted to be back with the feasting.

Suddenly I see a man running toward me. I recognized him as Pausanias; he kept his own horse here at the stable. Three other men were chasing him. I knew something terrible had happened but the king's orders were quite explicit. I was to take the horses and stay there. Once the man had mounted I was to lead him out into the countryside and return to the palace."

"Were there any saddlebags?"

"None! Just the horses."

"And then?"

"Pausanias tripped, he rolled, and his pursuers were on him. No questions asked, the first spear thrust must have taken him in the heart." He shrugged. "Something had gone wrong so I rode the horses for a while and came back to the stables."

"You saw no one else?"

"No one except you."

"And Philip gave no indication of where Pausanias was going to flee?"

"None whatsoever, Mistress, but it must have been far. They were the best horses we've got, fast as shot leaving a sling. I suppose Pausanias would have ridden one until it was blown, and then continued on the other." Philobetas shuffled his feet. "I'm a groom. I look after the royal mounts. I tend sick horses. If Philip had told me to climb to the top of the palace, I would have done it. Yes, it's a mystery what he told me to do, and until my dying day I'll wonder why." He took a step closer. "And as I don't want my dying day to be tomorrow, I'll keep my mouth shut."

"You have nothing to fear," Miriam replied and, leaving the stables, walked back to the palace.

Simeon woke her the next morning by rapping on the door, shouting her name. Miriam clambered out of bed and crossly told him to wait. She felt thickheaded, heavy limbed and she persisted in washing and changing her gown before sweeping her hair back with a clasp to the back of her head. She found Simeon waiting at the end of the passageway. He gestured fretfully and grasped her arm.

"Little sister, the king is waiting!"

As soon as they reached the foot of the stairs, Miriam realized something had happened during the night. The different courtyards they crossed were thronged with soldiers drinking or eating, their armor piled beside them. Guards had been doubled on doorways and all entrances.

Alexander was in the main hall of the palace, the same room where Philip had feasted and drunk the night before he died. Antipater sat on his right, Olympias to his left. Alexander was eating some bread and sipping at watered wine; he looked drawn and haggard as if he hadn't slept all night. Slaves moved around, bringing cooked food from the kitchens, which they placed on the table before him. Antipater, like any old soldier, was busy filling his mouth but Alexander seemed more determined to question the two individuals who knelt before him, hands lashed behind their backs. He gestured Miriam over and pointed to a stool beside his mother. Olympias sat dressed in a dark mantle; her face was painted white, and her eyes, dark pools of hatred, glared at the two prisoners who had dared challenge her darling son. The Lyncestrians had lost their sneering arrogance; their hair was blood-matted, their faces a mass of bruises; blood trickled out of their noses and the corners of their mouths, and their tunics were holed and rent.

"Our kinsmen." Alexander gestured with his hand. "The Lyncestrian brothers: traitors, rebels, and murderers."

One of the Lyncestrians lifted his head.

"We have more right to sit on the throne of Macedon than you baseborn!"

"Well, we've settled that once and for all," Olympias retorted. "You challenged by force and you were defeated by force. Now you will die."

"There speaks the whore queen!" The elder Lyncestrian spat back.

Alexander would have started forward but Olympias held him back.

"You killed my father!"

"Yes, yes, we did." The Lyncestrian smirked. He glanced at his brother, who seemed unconscious, shoulders bowed, head sagging. "It was easy to turn Pausanias, one of your father's bugger boys. Philip was impolitic; he should have thought twice before discarding his catamites to Attalus."

"And you supplied the dagger?" Miriam asked. "The Scythian knife? We recognized it as one of yours."

The Lyncestrian turned. "There speaks the Jewess, Alexander's little friend. Yes, we gave Pausanias the dagger for Philip's belly.

"You are lying," Miriam replied, pleased to see Olympias start and stare quizzically at her. "Whatever you did, you did not kill Philip. You might try and take the glory now, but all you've proved is that you are liars as well as traitors."

"We've questioned them already," Antipater gruffly interrupted. "It's the same old story. They persuaded Pausanias to kill Philip and, in the chaos, planned to seize the palace, murder the rest of Alexander's kin, and declare themselves king. That is all they will say."

"I'd have killed you." The Lyncestrian turned and smiled at Olympias. "I'd have let my tribesmen use you. They would have ridden you like the old mare you are! Queen!" He spat. "You surround yourself with mystery but you are no better than a whore!"

Alexander sprang to his feet and smashed his boot into

the man's stomach; the Lyncestrian collapsed, retching and coughing on the floor.

"Guilty!" Alexander proclaimed. "Whatever they have done, they are guilty. Let them die the ancient way."

"Everything is ready," Antipater replied. "The regiments wait outside."

The Lyncestrians were bundled to their feet. Their guards lashed ropes around them and dragged them out of the chamber. For a while Alexander sat, chest heaving. Antipater mumbled some excuse and left. Olympias sat as if carved out of stone. Alexander drank some more wine but then suddenly turned and spat the mouthful back into a bowl beside the couch.

"It's too early to drink," Olympias murmured. "Alexander, the revolt is finished, there's other business to do." She turned. If her painted face would have allowed, she would have smiled. "A clever question, little Jewess; whatever the Lyncestrians did, they didn't kill Philip."

"Did you?" Alexander snarled, turning on his mother. "Did you kill Father?"

"In my mind many times," Olympias replied.

"And why, last night?" Alexander asked.

"It is an ancient custom," Olympias retorted. She beat one fist against her chest. "I was Philip's wife. I was his queen. I am your mother." Her lower lip quivered. "To be rejected for the niece of Attalus, discarded like some old cloak. Pausanias, whether he knew it or not, avenged me. It is only fitting that I honor him."

"We are ready." Antipater stood in the doorway. "Alexander, now is the time!"

They left the hall and walked out onto the steps above the great parade ground. Philip's body still lay on his high pyre. Pausanias's corpse, the gold crown askew, had sagged, so a rope had been wrapped around his neck to hoist him back up. Other crosses now ran on either side of it; to each was nailed the corpse of a Lyncestrian commander, those elders of the clan who had joined their leaders in their ill-fated revolt. They had apparently died before crucifixion, their corpses lashed to these grisly gibbets. On three sides of the square were Philip's principal regiments, his veterans and companions who formed the core of the Macedonian phalanx. They stood, six lines deep, all dressed in full armor, shields on their arms, plumed helmets on their heads, their eighteen-foot sarrisas or pikes pointing to the sky.

Olympias, Miriam, and Simeon stood with Antipater in the shadows of the portico. Alexander went to the top step and lifted his hands. He began to address the soldiers in short, clipped sentences. Alexander reminded them of the glories his father had brought to Macedon. How Philip had made them masters of Greece, that he was Philip's rightful heir, and that the kingship had changed only in name.

"Henceforth," Alexander's voice rose, "no Macedonian will pay any duty or tax except the service of war, for we will show our vengeance over Philip's death in a way the world will never forget."

His words were greeted by a roar of approval and the clash of spears against shields. Alexander again held his hands up for silence.

"But there are others," he cried, "those who are traitors."

The Lyncestrians were brought out of the shadows, hustled down the steps, and made to kneel a few yards away from Philip's funeral bier. Their appearance was greeted by catcalls and yells. As this happened, carts trundled into the yard; before the first rank of soldiers, piles of stones were laid out. The carts creaked slowly around the square. The Lyncestrians, realizing what was going to happen, began to moan; one tried to struggle to his feet, but a soldier clubbed him to the ground.

"Soldiers of Macedon!" Alexander shouted. "Avenge me! Avenge Philip!"

Every second soldier in the first rank of each phalanx handed their spear and shield to their companions and stepped forward. The Lyncestrians, their legs bound, tried to crawl away, hide from the hail of stones hurled by the soldiers. Some missed, but soon the Lyncestrians were knocked senseless. The soldiers then closed in, pounding the bodies until every rock was thrown and the Lyncestrians, their heads and faces smashed, their corpses soaked in blood that spread out in pools around them, lay dead. An officer stepped forward and sliced off the heads of both Lyncestrians. These were tied to one of the poles on Philip's bier while the decapitated corpses were pushed up alongside the pyre.

Alexander went down and stood before his father's funeral bier. He covered his head with his cloak, spread his hands out, and prayed quietly. He then sprinkled the corpse with incense and other spices, took a torch from Antipater, and thrust it into the funeral pyre. Olympias and Antipater followed suit as did the other principal commanders. The flames caught hold, whipped up by the early morning breeze, and the great parade ground became transformed by the flames roaring up to the sky. Pausanias's corpse was taken down from the cross. When the flames reached the top of the pyre, it was thrown on, followed by the mangled bodies of the Lyncestrians as well as the corpses from the other gibbets. The funeral pyre had been soaked in incense and special spices, yet these couldn't hide the terrible stench of burning flesh. Miriam turned away while Simeon, murmuring some excuse, retreated back into the palace. Olympias hid in the shadows and watched. Farther down the steps

Alexander again raised his hands in a gesture of prayer. Eventually all sight of the king's corpse disappeared beneath a sheet of flame. Alexander took more fistfuls of incense and tossed these onto the pyre before walking back up the steps and into the palace.

Inside the atrium Alexander washed his hands and face and drank some wine. He beckoned Miriam and her brother closer.

"Soon I meet the clan elders," he murmured. "Tomorrow morning, probably in the square below, the army will hail me as king and commander in chief." He placed a hand on Miriam's and Simeon's shoulders. "You are going to have to act for me in this matter," he continued. "Already news is coming in that our garrisons are being expelled from key cities. Later this evening couriers will be despatched to Attalus and Parmenio, our generals across the Hellespont, telling them to stay where they are and wait for me to join them. The gods only know when that will take place!" Alexander smiled dazzlingly at Miriam. "But you've been busy on my behalf, haven't you?"

"Pausanias seemed to be trusted by Philip," Miriam declared.

"I know. I know. I know." Alexander ruffled his hair. "I've checked the treasury and seen the accounts. Days before his death, Philip apparently gave Pausanias rather generous amounts."

"Did the Lyncestrians confess anything?" Miriam asked.

"Oh, they admitted rebellion. They claimed Pausanias was their creature, but nothing substantial." Alexander drew a small scroll from the pocket of his tunic and thrust it into Miriam's hand. "That gives you the power to question whomever you want and do whatever you want. Look, I must hurry. I have to thank Molossus; he is leaving for Epirus."

Alexander strode off. Miriam and Simeon went down to

the kitchens and begged some food and wine from the servants. Afterward, Simeon went looking for Arridhaeus.

"He's probably hiding," he declared. "That's what Arridhaeus does when things become confusing."

Miriam went back through the palace. She found the people she was looking for, Philip's guards, sunning themselves in a small courtyard. They had taken off their helmets, breastplates, and the leather shirts underneath. Their weapons were piled in a corner and they sat, with their backs to the wall, sharing a goblet of wine and watching a fountain splash colored water high in the air. As Miriam approached, Perdiccas shaded his eyes and grinned.

"I wondered when you'd come back, little mouse." He patted his sweat-soaked thighs. Miriam noticed the cuts on his hands and arms. "Come on, girl. Sit down here and squirm. Every soldier needs a little pleasure."

"If I did," Miriam replied tartly, "you would only be too surprised by what might happen!"

Perdiccas guffawed with laughter, his companions joined in.

"You are not frightened," he retorted, as Miriam crouched down in front of him. "For a little mouse you are very brave."

"Why do you call me mouse?"

"Because you scurry about hither and thither, asking questions, little nose twitching." He looked closer. "But, there again, your nose isn't so little, is it?"

"It's bigger than certain parts of your anatomy!" Miriam retorted, tiring of his badinage.

Again guffaws of laughter. Perdiccas offered her his wine goblet; Miriam shook her head.

"You were involved in the fighting?" she asked.

His smile faded.

"Yes," Perdiccas replied. "Molossus's troops held the

rebels. They were doing a satisfactory job. We came up from behind in true Macedonian fashion." He grinned. "The Lyncestrians were desperate. They tried to break out; that's when we caught their leaders. So what do you want, little mouse?"

"On the day Philip was killed," Miriam replied, "something very strange happened. Pausanias stabbed Philip, then fled. The rest of the bodyguard stayed within the amphitheater or thronged at the gate, but you three came out, almost as if you knew something was going to happen."

"Well we saw the king fall. We didn't know what to do."

"That," Miriam retorted, "is a lie. You were disconcerted, puzzled. I think you had been given secret instructions, but became confused. Who gave you those instructions? Philip?"

Perdiccas bit the quick of his thumb and, turning his head, spat the piece of skin away.

"It was Philip, wasn't it?" Miriam insisted. "I mean, we can talk here in this sun-filled courtyard or we can meet the king and Antipater." Miriam tapped the small scroll Alexander had given her against the side of her face.

"All right, little mouse. We knew something might happen but, no, it wasn't Philip."

Miriam stared at him in disbelief.

"It was Pausanias."

"What?" Miriam was so surprised she almost rocked backward.

"Steady there." Perdiccas caught her arm, squeezed it, and winked. "Oh, a good week ago," Perdiccas rubbed a finger in his ear, "Pausanias gave me and my two companions quite explicit instructions: if anything untoward happened, we were to guard the king and not accept what appeared to have happened."

"But that doesn't make sense!" Miriam snapped.

"I know it doesn't." The soldier grinned. "But now you

know why we, er, as you say, were *disconcerted,* little mouse."

"Stop calling me that! Did you know why Pausanias issued such an instruction?"

"We've been talking about that ever since," one of his companions broke in. "We just thought Pausanias was taking special precautions, fearful of the king walking, unprotected, into an amphitheater full of enemies."

"When I met you in the vineyard, you made a reference to Pausanias's secret life. I have heard the story," she added quickly, "about what happened to Pausanias at Attalus's feast, but was it a secret among the guards?"

"At first it was," Perdiccas replied, "but about two weeks ago, the story began to circulate in all its gory details. We knew Pausanias could be a strange one, that he had been a lover of Philip's. However, the story of Attalus raised a few eyebrows and not a few sniggers."

Perdiccas got to his feet and towered over her.

"Strange isn't it?" he murmured. "I mean, Pausanias being raped months ago, but the story only surfacing in the last few days. It seems almost as if someone was spreading the story deliberately, doesn't it?"

CHAPTER 8

THE MACEDONIAN ARMY had now massed in the great parade ground in front of the old palace of Aegae. The sun had yet to rise. The sky was a dark blue; some of the stars had still not vanished. All during the previous night, phalanx after phalanx of troops had arrived in the capital: squadrons of cavalry, Cretan archers, spearmen, hoplites, the different parts of Philip's great war machine. They had marched onto the great open grasslands to the west of the palace before moving into the city. Now, the ceremony was to begin, the priests had made a sacrifice and, in the time-honored tradition of Macedon, two dogs had been cut up and their steaming flesh put on either side of the road that swept up to the palace. The regiments would march between these, take the oath, and hail Alexander as king of Macedon.

Miriam stood on the steps; in front of her Alexander and Olympias sat on two thrones. On a stool to Alexander's left, sat Antipater. Miriam had seen no sign of Eurydice. Philip's young wife appeared to have disappeared, either in hiding or in flight; Miriam had yet to summon up the courage to find out which. After her meeting with Perdiccas the previous day, Miriam had gone back to her chamber. She'd felt light-headed, rather sick, and had spent the day in her bed. Simeon, concerned, had summoned a physician who pronounced her fit enough.

"Not enough food, not enough sleep," the old man had announced. "If you get both, you'll feel better."

Miriam had. She had taken the sleeping potion, fallen asleep before sunset, and awakened early in the morning, hungry but refreshed.

Miriam breathed in the morning air. All around her Alexander's advisers and principal councillors thronged. So far, none of his friends had returned but the rumor was that, by evening, they would be back to assume their places of honor. Miriam leaned against a pillar and watched as the soldiers marched by, corselets, helmets, and greaves gleaming in the morning light. The neigh of horses and the shouts of officers filled the square. The principal regiments marched by; the rest would stay outside. The square had been cleaned of the funeral and the executions that had taken place there the previous day. The steps were washed and scrubbed, fresh pebbles laid out to cover where the funeral bier and crosses had stood.

At length all was ready. Alexander was hailed as king. Antipater, standing halfway down the steps, led the chorus, fist raised. Every time he shouted Alexander's name, the soldiers replied with a roar:

"King of Macedon! King of Macedon!"

Spears were clashed against shields. The officers, hands raised, took the oath, and Alexander replied, making the same promise he had before: abolition of taxes, prosperity at home, glory abroad. The troops loved it and the cheering would have gone on and on, rippling around the great concourse, if Alexander had not lifted his hands and announced certain changes: Antipater would be leader of the Macedon council; his mother Olympias, specifically referred to as Queen, would also have a role in government; Parmenio and Attalus would remain with the troops in Asia.

"Where," Alexander boasted, "we shall soon join them."

Alexander lowered his hands and, accompanied by his mother, swept back into the palace.

Miriam followed and stayed for a while in an antechamber until summoned. Alexander's room was now full of clerks and scribes, Simeon included. For a while she waited just within the doorway as Alexander, speaking fast, dictated a letter to this city or that commander. He wouldn't finish one letter but go on to another. In the main his message was the same: Philip was dead; Alexander, his legitimate heir and successor, had been hailed as king by both the council and the army; he expected and depended on their loyalty; all opposition was to be crushed, traitors like the Lyncestrians, ruthlessly dealt with. Alexander paused and beckoned Miriam over to stand next to where Simeon sat at a small table.

"I need Simeon here." Alexander's face was flushed, his eyes glittering. Miriam could smell the rich scent of wine on his breath. "Mother, however, is a problem. I can't find Eurydice, while Olympias needs to be questioned. Antipater and some of the officers still believe, rightly or wrongly, that she had a hand in Philip's death. They've reminded me that she is not Macedonian. They will only accept Olympias if I take a solemn oath that she is innocent of Philip's blood."

"Why don't you confront her yourself?" Miriam replied tartly.

She feared the witch queen and memories of her childhood, when Olympias, with her snakes, would come down to the Gardens of Midas. Sometimes Olympias would seek Miriam out.

"You shouldn't be frightened of Mother," Alexander grinned. "She likes you. If I visit her, I won't be out before dusk." Alexander gripped Miriam's fingers. "Please," he said, "for my sake, do this. My hands are full. . . ."

Miriam left Alexander and walked to the far end of the palace. Olympias's quarters were self-contained, at the end of a long passageway. No one went there, except by invitation. Miriam entered the queen mother's antechamber; Aristander was crouched on the floor, studying the shape of certain bones he'd thrown.

"Divining the future?" Miriam teased.

Olympias's sorcerer got to his feet, a sour smile on his thin lips.

"Nothing of the sort, Jewess, just seeing what the day might bring. You wish to see the queen?"

Miriam nodded.

"Then see her you shall. We expected you." Aristander clicked the bones in his hand. "I can tell the future."

Miriam was ushered into a small, gloomy chamber; oil lamps glowed weakly along a window ledge. Olympias sat at her spinning wheel. She was dressed in the same widow's weeds. She looked up, a piece of wool between her fingers.

"Ah, Miriam." She gestured at a quilted stool. "Come and tell your queen how things are. Wasn't it a grand sight? The soldiers marching in and out. The priests invoking the gods. The clash of armor and the roar of approval. Alexander will make a great king." She spun the wheel, deliberately allowing its clatter to break the silence. "He shall be a great king. He is god-given."

"Is he?" Miriam asked boldly, sitting down on the stool. "Madam, is Alexander god-given or the true son of Philip?"

Olympias clapped her hands and crowed with laughter.

"Wouldn't everyone like to know that?" She pulled the dark mantle over her hair and watched the wheel spin. "His soul is of the king of the gods, Ammon Ra." Olympias narrowed her eyes. "When Alexander marches into Egypt, he must visit Ammon Ra's temple at the Oasis of Siwah where the truth of his paternity will be revealed."

Miriam stared across at where the necromancer now stood in the shadows. What was Olympias implying? She thought. Why not just say that Alexander was a son of Dionysus, Apollo, or Zeus? Why choose an Egyptian god?

"I know what's going on in that teeming, little brain of yours," Olympias broke in. "My son wants answers to certain questions, doesn't he? Well, answers he will get, all in due time."

"Why did you crown Pausanias?" Miriam asked abruptly. She felt the atmosphere oppressive, as if Olympias, using some secret power from Aristander, was trying to seize her soul, bend her mind.

"I have explained that!" Olympias snapped. "Pausanias, whether he intended it or not, avenged me."

"But so publicly?" Miriam retorted.

Olympias shrugged, a sensuous movement of her shoulders. She clucked her tongue and raised one eyebrow.

"You are a clever girl, Miriam, you know why I did it. Philip hated me, I hated Philip. If people think that I murdered Philip, it diverts suspicion from Alexander."

"But it doesn't," Miriam replied. "Some people might say that mother and son were involved together, conspirators?"

"I know, I know, we both have a lot to lose." Olympias sighed. "I was divorced, rejected. Alexander was overlooked, rumor swirled about him being illegitimate, his friends were exiled. . . ."

"Did you have a hand in Philip's death?" Miriam insisted.

"Have you heard the story?" Olympias turned to face her. "They say that in the days before Philip was killed, I kept quoting a line from Euripides: 'Vengeance upon the father, upon the bride, upon the husband.'" It's a very good line but I didn't say it. So no, Miriam, if the truth be told, I did not have a hand in Philip of Macedon's murder." She licked a thread. "More's the pity!"

"But Pausanias visited you here?"

Olympias threw her head back and laughed. "Oh yes, he did. Pausanias was a man who wanted to be a woman. There's quite a few of them around, Miriam. All those brave soldiers in their armor and horse-hair plumes, they are more of womenkind than I."

"And Pausanias was one of these?"

"Pausanias certainly was."

"But you wanted him to kill someone?"

"My, my, you have been busy! Yes, I certainly did. Attalus had Pausanias raped. I wondered if Pausanias would do me a favor of invoking the blood feud and killing Eurydice."

"And?"

"He said he would think about it."

"So you had no knowledge that Pausanias was contemplating Philip's death?"

"No, not at all."

"And you had no hand in it?"

"Tell my son I have answered that question for the last time." Olympias's face became imperious. "I know what that one-eyed fox Antipater is up to; trying to discredit me in the council, isn't he? I've always hated that old bastard and I always will. If I have one ambition left in life, it's to make Antipater look forward to death. I am going to enjoy being co-regent with him."

"And the Lyncestrians?"

"Myself," Olympias airily replied, "I think there were a number of plots to kill Philip, possibly three or four. The Lyncestrians were one. I suspect they hired that archer. Oh

yes, I've heard about him—Cephalus. But who else was involved, I don't know." She paused at a knock on the door.

Arridhaeus shuffled into the room. He was clean shaven,
his hair washed and oiled, and he was dressed in fresh robes.
Miriam had glimpsed him during the parade ceremony, the
imbecilic young man seemed lost in his own world.

"I still can't find my Apollo."

"Come in my dear." Olympias smiled. "What is it you've
lost?"

"My Apollo." He wandered over and sat on top of a
chest. "It was a present from Father. It was very sharp."

Miriam glanced over her shoulder at him. "What do you
mean, Arridhaeus?"

"It was a knife," Arridhaeus smiled. "A knife," Arridhaeus
repeated. "Father said it was a Scythian one. The handle was
wooden, carved in the shape of a chariot with a man in it."

Aristander, standing in the shadows, shuffled uneasily.
Miriam's fingers flew to her lips.

"So that's what you've lost." Miriam came over and sat
beside him.

Even Olympias had stopped her playacting and was staring in disbelief at this half-witted young man.

"It was his knife," Olympias murmured. "I've heard comments that Pausanias was never seen to carry a knife like that."

"I had that knife," Arridhaeus went on, impervious to
the surprise he had created, "about two or three days before
Father's banquet. I lost it. I called it my Apollo."

"Do you know where you lost it?" Miriam asked.

"No, it was in a chest in my room, then one morning
after I got dressed, it was gone. I called it Apollo, but no
one, not even Simeon, wants to listen to me."

Miriam seized the young man's slack hand.

"I have found your dagger!"

Arridhaeus's face creased into a smile.

"I have found your dagger!" Miriam whispered. "But I will get it back for you on one condition, that you tell no one about it."

Arridhaeus got to his feet.

"Promise me," Miriam urged.

Arridhaeus made to go across the doorway that led deeper into the queen mother's quarters.

"Don't go there!" Olympias snapped. "On no account go in there, Arridhaeus. Wait outside for Miriam!"

Arridhaeus shuffled out.

"I thought that boy would never surprise me." Olympias declared. "But why did the assassin use his knife? Did Pausanias take it? Or was it given to him?"

Miriam studied this witch queen, this horror in female flesh. Memories flooded back to when, as a girl of eleven or twelve summers, she was interviewed by Olympias while, all around her, the queen's pet snakes hissed and curled. Miriam had liked Philip with his bluff, hearty ways and coarse humor, but she truly believed that Alexander's mother was either mad, possessed of a demon, or both. Olympias sat there, clothed in a costly black gown with a face as beautiful as Helen of Troy and a heart as cruel as Hecate, queen of the night.

"What are you thinking, Miriam?" Olympias's voice was low and sweet.

"How many years, my lady, were you married to Philip?"

Olympias blinked, the question had caught her off guard.

"Why, dear girl, about twenty." Olympias's gaze slipped to Aristander. "Why do you ask that?"

"You often proclaimed, my lady, that Philip had the morals of a mountain goat."

"And the physique to go with it."

"Perhaps so," Miriam hurried on, "but my question, my lady . . . Before his death Philip had publicly divorced and humiliated you. There were also rumors, growing by the day, that he believed Alexander was not his son." Miriam ignored Aristander's hiss of breath.

"What are you implying, Jewess?"

"My lady, I imply nothing. Why didn't Philip just take Eurydice into his household? What was the real cause of Philip's drastic actions toward you? After all, you are a queen, a princess of Epirus, a descendant of Achilles. Alexander is a warrior of twenty years. Philip must have known that both of you would not just stand aside and allow this to happen."

"Eurydice is a witch," Olympias riposted. "With her long legs and beautiful, sinuous body, a man would do anything when he was in bed with a whore like her."

"My lady, Eurydice is only a child in both body and mind. She hasn't the subtlety."

"You mean she's not me." Olympias laughed.

"If you say so, my lady."

Olympias leaned closer. "I know nothing of that," she whispered, "and tell my son I don't care. Alexander is one of two things: either the son of Philip or the son of a god. Whatever, he is divinely chosen, divinely touched."

"Where is Eurydice?" Miriam asked.

"She's in her chambers, I suppose." Olympias laughed. "With her mewling little infant. Strange girl! I've invited her here but she's too frightened. You are right, Miriam, she's certainly not me; all her magic was in her tits and bum." Olympias stifled a yawn. "But now I am tired. I have things to do while you have the answers my son wants."

Miriam took the hint and withdrew. Arridhaeus was sitting in an alcove farther along the passageway. He had plucked a flower and was examining it curiously. As Miriam approached, he put the flower in his hair and gestured that she sit next to him.

"Have you found my dagger?"

"Hush now!" Miriam seized his hand and stared pityingly into the lifeless eyes. "Arridhaeus, I am going to buy you a new one. It will be better than the other, but on one condition: you tell no one else. You ask no one about Apollo. Promise me that! If you do you might get hurt."

Arridhaeus gnawed on his lip. "Will I really? What will happen to me now Father has gone?"

"Nothing," Miriam replied. "Now, tell me, Arridhaeus, do you know who took your dagger?"

"No I don't." He shook his head.

Miriam looked around; the nearest guard stood at the end of the passageway, well out of earshot.

"Arridhaeus, do you remember when we put the play on?"

"Oh yes, about David and Absalom. I really enjoyed that. Can we do it again?"

"Soon," Miriam replied. "But, do you remember, Arridhaeus, claiming that one day you might be king?"

"Of course I do!"

"Who told you that? Who said you might be king?"

Arridhaeus blinked and grinned. "It's a secret!" He rocked backward and forward. "It's a secret! It's a secret!"

"But, you'll tell me your secret, won't you?"

"Can I kiss you? You always kiss people before you tell them a secret."

Miriam agreed. Arridhaeus gently pressed his lips against hers, eyes wide open. Miriam did not resist. Arridhaeus sat back and sighed.

"Antipater!"

"No, no, you were going to tell me the secret," Miriam coaxed.

"I've told you, Antipater. About five days ago, Antipater was in the hall drinking. He was by himself; because he'd killed a boar in the hunt, he's allowed to lounge on the couch. I expected him to drive me away, but he didn't. He invited me over and let me sit next to him. 'Arridhaeus,' he said, 'Do you like me?' I said I did, though, really, I am very frightened of him. Antipater said that if anything happened I was to stay close to him. I said why? He said, 'If you do, Arridhaeus, who knows, you might even be king.' "

"And that's all?" Miriam tried to hide her disappointment.

"Oh no." Arridhaeus's eyes became sly. "Do you know the guards who stand round the palace? Well, the ones near my chamber were always Antipater's men. And the day Father was killed, do you remember? When we were sitting in the amphitheater? Didn't you know those people behind us? They were also Antipater's men!"

Miriam stared at a fresco on the far wall of Achilles dragging Hector's body around the walls of Troy. Crudely done, the painting had a vigorous life of its own: the prancing horses, the huge wheels of the chariot, Hector's stripped corpse, his gaping mouth and blood-filled eyes, as if the artist were implying that Hector had not been dead when this humiliation took place.

"I must go now," Arridhaeus said. "I'm going to collect some more flowers for myself."

And he was up and away before Miriam could stop him.

She sat there for a while. Nothing makes sense, Miriam reflected: Olympias wanted Eurydice dead and asked Pausanias to do it but the queen was guilty of no involvement in Philip's murder. Philip had trusted Pausanias, the very man who was going to kill him. The king had given him gold, licence to travel, the best horses from the royal stable. But why? Perdiccas and the other two guards had been told by

Pausanias to guard the king, but again, why? Now Antipater, Philip's chosen and boon companion, seemed to know something about Philip's murder with his hint to that poor half-wit.

Miriam rose and went back to her own chamber. She took a piece of charcoal and a slate and drew faces: Pausanias, Olympias, Alexander, Philip. She went and sat with her back against the wall and stared at the faces she'd drawn. Alexander, she thought? Was he totally innocent? He'd resented his father and been fearful of the future but there was nothing to connect him to the Lyncestrians, to Pausanias, or to Cephalus the assassin. And Olympias? She was a murderess, full of anger and hate. She may have contemplated killing Philip but her real malice was centered on Eurydice. She had entertained Pausanias, pandered to his lusts and strange ways. Olympias had exploited Pausanias's hatred for Attalus in the hope that he would kill Eurydice. And Pausanias himself? A homosexual and transvestite, Philip's lover, he may have even had sex with Olympias. A disturbed young man, Pausanias had been full of hatred for Attalus and his family, had refused Olympias's offer to slay Eurydice but had killed Philip. He'd then tried to escape. According to the evidence, the king had agreed to provide him the wherewithal for an escape. However, those guards had caught up with him. Why had Pausanias told them to stay near the king? And who had been waiting in the vineyard to trip him up?

Miriam realized she was trapped in a circle of deceit. She got to her feet, went and stood by the window. Her chamber overlooked the royal gardens. Slaves were trimming the flower beds and sprinkling water. A child ran across, shrieking with delight as another chased it. Two soldiers came into view, sentries carrying out their duties in a half-hearted manner. The sun had grown strong and the heat was oppressive. Miriam closed her eyes. Philip used to like the gardens. He always boasted that, at heart, he was a farmer. But what was his role in this? On the night before he died, he had been acting the drunken lord. Yet Miriam had caught a sadness. Why had he made that strange offer to her and Simeon, that they could go back to their native country? Why had he trusted Pausanias so much? And the Lyncestrians? Miriam believed she was on firmer ground here. Cephalus was an assassin. He should have been across the Hellespont. Miriam was sure that Cephalus had been hired by the Lyncestrians to kill both Philip and Alexander. When Cephalus had been unable to do so, because of Pausanias, he had been killed. Cephalus's assassin was probably still in the palace; she and Simeon must have disturbed him near Pausanias's chamber, which is why that chamberlain had been murdered. The poor fellow had probably run into the assassin in the dark and had had to be silenced. Miriam breathed in and splashed some water to cool her cheeks. She recalled Olympias's words.

"How many plots were there?" she whispered.

Were the Lyncestrians in alliance with someone else, such as Attalus? Was there a conspiracy to remove Philip and Alexander from the scene? But what would have happened then? Who would have ruled Macedon? Attalus had no claim, though his niece Eurydice's baby son, Caranus, would be in direct line to the throne. Would there have been a division of spoils? The Lyncestrians acting as regent while Attalus became commander in chief of the Macedonian army? And Antipater, that grizzled, old fox? He seemed to know more than he'd ever admitted. Miriam splashed more water on her face, combed her hair, and left her chamber.

She stopped for a while in the hall for something to eat. She glimpsed Simeon sitting with the other clerks but there was no sign of Alexander or the man she was looking for. She wandered the palace and went out into one of the parade courtyards. Antipater was sitting on a bench cradling a cup of watered wine. He was watching soldiers drill under the harsh commands of their officers. He didn't even look up as she approached.

"You shouldn't be here, girl!"

"You mean I should sit in a chamber and spin?"

Antipater snorted with laughter. "One Olympias is enough. What do you want? You are creating quite a stir, scurrying around asking your questions!"

"I've one for you. Why did you promise Arridhaeus that, one day, he might be king?"

Antipater laughed, but he turned his face away and drank rather quickly from the goblet.

"You are going to say, aren't you," Miriam continued, "that it was only a joke! That you often jested with him, but that's a lie, Antipater; you don't joke!"

"I should have throttled him," Antipater murmured.

"You knew, didn't you? You knew something was going to happen?"

"Yes and no," Antipater replied. "I grew up with Philip," he continued. "I was by his side, me and Parmenio, back to back, shield against shield. Philip lost an eye and so did I. He said it made no difference." Antipater weaved his fingers together. "We were so close, we still had two good eyes between us." Antipater licked his lips. "I loved Philip. I always have. I always will. Whatever he asked I did. Just the three of us. Philip, Parmenio, Antipater."

"And then?"

"Attalus rises in the ranks. You've seen Attalus, haven't you, with his scrawny blond hair and pale face? A brave soldier, a brilliant commander, sly and cunning. He loved Philip but he hated Olympias. I mean, really hated her! Not like we all do, openly, ever ready to clash. Attalus was the soul of discretion, ever smiling, ever gracious; he and Olympias deserved each other, two snakes together. Anyway, he captured Philip's heart." Antipater's voice shook with emotion. "It was Attalus this and Attalus that. Promotion after promotion; then, one night, the army was coming back to Pella. Philip had organized one of his great drinking contests and Attalus brings his long-legged niece into Philip's tent. She was a veritable Aphrodite. Philip was so excited he almost knocked the table over until Attalus intervened. Eurydice was not some slave girl to be tumbled. She was a kinswoman. Attalus lured both Philip's heart and cock; Eurydice was the silken net. Now, I didn't mind that. Philip's heart was like a bee, moving from one flower to another. Olympias knew that he never stayed in one place or with one woman for long. Then something happened, I don't know what. Attalus began smirking, you know that constant smile, as if he had suddenly found the source of all wisdom. This was about fourteen or fifteen months ago, just before Philip married Eurydice. The king was sombre, withdrawn. He wouldn't tell us what was the matter but apparently Attalus knew. After that Attalus seemed unstoppable. He was created commander in chief with Pausanias, Philip married Eurydice, Olympias was divorced."

"Did Philip ever say why he rejected Olympias after so long?"

Antipater shook his head. "Never. But remember, Miriam, Attalus's taunt to Alexander at Philip's wedding feast, that Macedon would, at last, get a legitimate heir. I think three people know the real reason: Philip, and he's dead; Olympias; and that creature of hers, Aristander. Only one thing I did notice. Philip destroyed certain letters and records. Oh yes, and something else."

"What?"

"He said that if he ever invaded Egypt he would burn the shrine of Siwah that stands in an oasis farther down the Nile.

He would destroy it so it would seem to have never existed."

"What has an Egyptian shrine got to do with Olympias?"

"I don't know," Antipater retorted. "I'm telling you this." He sighed. "Well, it's up to you whether you tell Alexander."

"And Philip's death?" Miriam interrupted.

"I knew something was wrong. Attalus had to be watched. I have spies, too, Miriam. I might be a gruff old soldier but I knew the Persian gold was flowing into Demosthenes' pocket in Athens." He held up a finger. "I also suspect there has been correspondence between Demosthenes and Attalus." He smiled sourly at the surprise on Miriam's face. "Oh yes. And now, to complete the circle, we have Cephalus, the Cretan archer, found dead in the amphitheater where Philip was going to sit in glory. Yes, I suspected something was going to happen. No, I am not a traitor. I tried to warn Philip but he wouldn't listen; he thought I was jealous of Attalus. However, if Persia is writing to Demosthenes and Demosthenes is writing to Attalus and Attalus is staying in Asia with ten thousand hoplites, . . ." He slurped from the wine cup. "I could see what was going to happen! So, why shouldn't I prepare for the evil day?"

CHAPTER 9

MIRIAM HAD TO wait for a while in an antechamber before Alexander would see her; the room was now cleared of clerks and scribes.

"I've moved them elsewhere," Alexander smiled. He pointed to the great round table covered in maps and letters. "Rumor spreads as quickly as the wind, doesn't it? Our garrisons have been expelled from the Cadmea in Thebes; Athens has hailed Demosthenes as a great prophet and savior. Apparently," Alexander added bitterly, "he knew about my father's death within hours. Well." He gestured to a couch. "You had best sit down, Miriam. I've had complaints about your snooping." He winked. "Mother doesn't like it. So, whom have you been upsetting?"

Miriam told him exactly what had happened. Alexander sat forward, hands clasped; now and again he'd nod or tug at his hair.

"So, what you are saying," he concluded, "is that two plots converged. Pausanias, who apparently acted by himself, and, if Antipater is to be believed, and I think he is, that there was a second plot, which came to nothing. This was financed by Persian gold, supported by Demosthenes, and aided and abetted by traitors in Macedon—the Lyncestrians and Attalus our beloved general in Asia." He bent down and pulled out a casket from beneath the couch. "Now I've got something to show you."

Alexander drew out a scroll of parchment and tossed it into Miriam's lap. She unrolled the firm and glossy papyrus; the handwriting was neat, cursive, the letters clearly formed. All bore the signature of Demosthenes of Athens. One was to Cephalus the assassin archer, in which Demosthenes promised that he would be hailed as a savior of Greece for what he was about to do.

"The slaying of a tyrant is a holy and pious act." The letter concluded, "No one will blame you and you have the support of one who sits close in Philip's council." The second letter was much longer. It was addressed to "A friend and lover of liberty." Again Demosthenes, in his cogent, precise way, put forward reasons for Philip's murder. It would be an act revered by all men and would bring glory to those who carried it out. "Have no worries," the letter ran on, "those responsible for such an act will find refuge in any city in Greece or the territories of the great king. A life of honor and wealth for himself and his family. He will be given the title of "liberator," statues and altars will be erected to him. Like those who killed the tyrants of old, he will be regarded as a demigod." The letter ended urging his correspondent to stay firm and carry out what would be decided. The final letter was much more explicit. It was again addressed to "A": Demosthenes urged him to seize the opportunity presented by Philip's murder, and in the ensuing chaos, to seize the throne and crown of Macedon for himself.

Miriam glanced up. "So we know that Persia and Demosthenes plotted your father's destruction?"

"And mine," Alexander added sourly, "though not in so many words."

"Who is the "A?" Miriam asked.

"It must be Attalus," Alexander replied. He was watching Miriam intently.

"But there's a catch, isn't there?" Miriam asked.

"Yes there is. We found nothing on Pausanias, nothing on the Lyncestrians; like all good traitors, they destroyed any evidence as quickly as they could. These were found on my father's corpse."

Miriam gaped. Alexander laughed.

"I don't believe this!" Miriam gasped. "Philip was actually carrying these letters in his pocket?"

"Yes, one cleverly sewn in the inside of his mantle. When his corpse was brought back to the palace, no one dreamed of searching it. I did make sure that there were no seals or rings. I came across these."

"So Philip knew that on the day of his great triumph there was a plot against him involving Attalus, Demosthenes, and Persia, but did nothing about it? You are sure they are not forgeries?"

Alexander shook his head. "No, they are originals; that's Demosthenes' style and his signature. I have another piece of information," Alexander added. "You have heard of a man called Hecaetus?"

Miriam grimaced. "Yes, he's a Scythian?"

"Half Scythian, half Greek," Alexander replied. "A man of the shadows is our Hecaetus. Father's assassin, not like Cephalus, who hired out his services. Oh no. If Philip wanted something done, Hecaetus would carry it out. Do you remember the story about Demosthenes being invited to speak in front of my father at Pella?"

Miriam nodded. "Yes, Demosthenes stumbled, dried up, made himself look a fool."

"What you don't know," Alexander replied, "is that Demosthenes glimpsed Hecaetus standing behind my father. He thought he was looking at his own death. Now, Hecaetus and his select little group, ostensibly royal messengers, kept to their quarters following Father's death. Late yesterday I sent for Hecaetus. Do you know, he walks and acts like a girl, fingers dancing, a wiggle any courtesan would envy, light blond hair and watery blue eyes. He asked if he could be of service. I asked him if he knew anything about my father's death? He, of course, just laughed. 'Philip told me what to do,' Hecaetus declared, 'but he never discussed state secrets with me.' "

"Where was he on the morning Philip died?" Miriam asked.

"Now, that is the mystery." Alexander smoothed the skin of his face. He cocked his head sideways, his different-colored eyes screwed up against the sunlight streaming through a window. "Hecaetus said that five of his lovely boys . . ." Alexander drummed his fingers against his mouth. ". . . He calls them that; I call them assassins . . . were told to take up position in the palace and stay there until Philip's orders arrived."

"But they never did?"

"No, Hecaetus's companions sat in a palace courtyard fully armed, as Father had ordered. When the news came through of Philip's death, they returned to their quarters just near the stables."

Miriam studied the papyrus. Hecaetus, she knew by reputation, Philip's silent shadow. She also recalled that dandified, foppish voice that had spoken to her out of the darkness.

"I would like to meet this Hecaetus," she said.

"For the moment, that's impossible," Alexander replied. "He left last night. He and his companions, armed with letters and warrants, riding our swiftest horses. They are to arrange a meeting with Parmenio and Attalus across the Hellespont." He looked bleakly at Miriam. She repressed a shiver.

"You are going to kill Attalus, aren't you?"

"I have no choice," Alexander replied. "He insulted me. He insulted my mother. There is evidence that he plotted against my father, and he'll definitely plot against me. Hecaetus will give him a choice. Take his own life or bare his neck to the executioner."

"Will the troops allow that?"

"Attalus is just a general. When Parmenio knows he'll be elevated to sole commander and the soldiers find out that there'll be an increase in pay, Attalus will be alone." Alexander sat back on the couch. "And you say the knife was Arridhaeus's?"

"Yes."

"And this great secret Antipater mentioned?" Alexander shook his head. "Simeon and I have been through my father's records. We can find nothing, though what you have told me comes as no surprise. Antipater was very jealous; like an old woman, he'd sit and brood. I always thought he was glad to see the back of Attalus."

Alexander got up and poured himself some wine, adding a generous spoonful of the water. He asked if Miriam wanted any, but she shook her head.

"Anyway," Alexander continued, "I've found nothing untoward in the records, except for the payments to Pausanias. Oh yes and one other thing." He came and sat down. "Strangely enough, my mother's creature, you know the necromancer Aristander? In the last few weeks of his life, my father began to patronize him even more than before."

"Before?"

"Well yes, according to the records, Aristander often received stipends from Philip. These are kept in my father's private accounts, little gifts, little tokens of affection. What a family!" Alexander smiled. "Mother definitely spied on Father; I think she even watched him make love to Eurydice. Father, through Aristander, spied on her. Everyone spying on each other, eh?" He narrowed his eyes. "I wonder whom he bribed to spy on me?"

Miriam moved uneasily on the couch. "Don't look at me like that," she whispered.

"Somebody did," Alexander laughed. "And I'm going to find out who. I'd like to discover this secret Antipater referred to, the one that changed my father. I wonder if Eurydice knows anything? I've been down to her quarters but I can't find her."

Miriam recalled Olympias sitting at that spinning wheel in her darkened chamber, Arridhaeus wandering in . . .

"Can you find her?" Alexander asked softly. "I am sure her maids will talk to you."

"What will you do?" Miriam asked. "Alexander, you won't kill the girl or her baby?"

Alexander looked into his wine cup. "No, I don't want their blood on my hands!" He glanced up. "But they are a problem, Miriam. Eurydice was Philip's queen and little Caranus will grow into a man one day."

Miriam fought to control the pitching of her stomach. She was glad she hadn't taken any of the wine.

"Tomorrow morning," Alexander continued, "Ptolemy and the others will be back." He tapped the maps. "Everything in Aegae is settled. These revolts, I must show my enemies that I am king of Macedon. The Thessalians have risen in revolt and seized the mountain passes to the north. They will provide as good an object lesson as any. Miriam, I want you and Simeon to come with me. No, no." He shook his head. "Don't refuse, you'll be safer with me. Well, until these matters are settled and treachery has revealed its true face." He started sorting through the papers. "I think you'd better find Eurydice." His voice fell to a whisper, "I feel uncomfortable. Mother is not leaving her room and I want to know what is happening?"

Once she had left Alexander, Miriam almost ran along the corridors, hammering on the door to Olympias's quarters. Aristander opened it and ushered her into the antechamber.

"The queen is busy," he declared softly.

"You look pale, Aristander." Miriam seized his hand. "And your fingers are ice cold."

He tried to push her out.

"The queen is busy." He cocked his head and Miriam heard Olympias singing, a low, doleful chant.

"Let me through!"

Aristander still stood his ground.

"Let me through!" Miriam bluffed. "Or perhaps I may have to tell Olympias of your frequent meetings with her late husband!"

Aristander's face went paler. There was a strange rattling at the back of his throat as he fought for breath. Miriam thought he was about to have a seizure.

"You know," he said, "about Nechtanebo? You know about Nech—?"

"Yes, yes, I do," Miriam lied. "Now let me through!"

Aristander caught wildly at her arm.

"You won't say anything, will you? Please!" He clasped his hands together.

Miriam looked at him. Now was not the time or place, she thought, but never had she seen a man so agitated, so deeply frightened. She slipped into the queen's room. The spinning wheel stood by itself; the door to the chamber beyond was half open. Miriam hurried across and pushed this aside and then stepped back in horror. It was a square, boxlike room with gray-slabbed walls; a metal grille, high up, provided some light. Pitch torches, giving off an inky smoke, spluttered in the breeze. Olympias sat on a carved, wooden throne. On the floor around her writhed snakes, slipping and sliding over her feet, moving sinuously so it seemed as if the floor itself was rippling. Olympias had her hair down covering her face, which was painted a thick white with great black lines under her eyes. Miriam was not sure what she had glimpsed: a pair of dangling feet, a corpse hanging from one of the beams. Miriam seized Aristander's rod, which stood in the corner, and reopened the door. She swished the rod from side to side, fearful lest any of the snakes approach her. She glanced up. The woman's corpse, swinging from a hempen rope, swayed slightly to and fro. Head slightly twisted, long black hair covering her face, Miriam recognized Philip's former wife Eurydice. The corpse turned, the beautiful olive skin was now mottled, the eyes popping, jaws slack. Olympias seemed unaware of Miriam's presence but gazed at the corpse, smiling and muttering softly to herself. Now and again she would break into that wild, chilling chant. Miriam closed the door and thrust the rod back into the agitated Aristander's hand.

"Where's the child?" she rasped, pushing the necromancer back out of these hate-filled chambers.

The necromancer fled into the anteroom, closing the door behind him. He leaned with his back against it, gasping for air.

"Where's the child?" Miriam repeated.

The sorcerer shook his head. "I don't know," he gasped. "Olympias invited the girl and the child here yesterday morning. The child must be dead!"

"And Eurydice?"

"Olympias put that noose on the beam. She locked the

girl in and then released the snakes. The girl was given a choice: either hang herself or die from a venomous bite. I had no hand in it," he pleaded. "The first I knew of it was when the queen took me in to show me, as she put it, 'the sights.' "

"And Caranus?" Miriam urged.

"The child would have died. You've seen the graveyard beyond the palace, the old cemetery? That's where Olympias hides her victims."

Miriam found she was trembling as the full shock of what she had seen made itself felt.

"I need to talk to you," she kept her voice steady, "about Nechtanebo. I will come back."

Miriam fled down the passageway. A guard tried to stop her but she quickly sidestepped and threw herself into the room where Alexander sat poring over maps. Antipater and two other officers were with him. One rose, half-drawing his sword.

"Leave her be!" Alexander snapped. He took one look at Miriam's pallid face. "It's Eurydice, isn't it?"

"Olympias!" Miriam gasped. She sat down clutching her stomach. "Olympias has her."

"Antipater," Alexander ordered, "take six guards, don't hurt Mother! Eurydice's dead?"

Miriam nodded.

"Take her corpse." Alexander rose. He snapped his fingers and the officers left. For a while Alexander just walked up and down the chamber.

"And the baby?"

"Gone," Miriam replied, "the poor soul's gone."

She watched Alexander's face. Was that a look of relief in his eyes? Had his mother carried out a task he had preferred not to? Miriam swallowed hard and watched this man, the hero of her heart. In the short while since Philip's death

Alexander had changed, had become harder, more ruthless. She gestured at the maps.

"You have chosen your enemy?"

"Yes," he said, "the Thessalians are holding the pass at Tempe. I am going to teach them a lesson, short and sharp, so all Greece will know." He clapped his hands and sat down. "I also need the Thessalian cavalry. They accepted my father as chieftain. I want to show them that I am a better man than Philip."

"Philip never killed children!"

"So? Who does?"

Miriam bit back her words. She wondered how much insulting of Olympias Alexander would actually accept. "Swear to me, Alexander, you had no hand in that child's death!"

He threw her a look.

"Neither the child nor the mother," he riposted. "Nor did I urge or encourage Olympias. Believe me, Philip's death or no, Eurydice signed her death warrant as soon as she gave birth to that child."

Miriam glanced away. Did Philip fear Olympias so much; was he planning to kill his former wife? Was she Pausanias's intended victim? Was that why Philip had left those assassins in the palace the morning he died, Hecaetus's assassins? For her own reasons, Miriam decided not to speak about the terror she'd glimpsed in Aristander's eyes.

"Who is Nechtanebo?" she asked.

"Nechtanebo." Alexander grinned. "You sound like Aristotle in one of our history lessons. He was an Egyptian pharaoh, some years before I was born. Driven out by the Persians, he fled for a while to Macedon. Why do you ask?"

Miriam shrugged. "I just heard something," she stammered. "Listen," she hurried on, eager to change the subject, "on the day your father died, everybody in Aegae seemed to be intent on murder. We know Cephalus the Cretan archer managed to take his bow and quiver into the amphitheater, yes?"

Alexander nodded his head in agreement.

"But he must have stayed somewhere?"

"Certainly not in the palace," Alexander interrupted. "But I agree," he added quickly, "Cephalus would stay in the city. There are enough shops and taverns in Aegae. It won't take long to find out. Antipater can make a few enquiries." Alexander tapped the maps excitedly. "By tomorrow, Miriam, our friends will have rejoined us."

Alexander was becoming absorbed in his maps so she rose to leave, Alexander absentmindedly telling her to take care.

Miriam went to look for Simeon, but he was busy with other clerks and scribes. He moaned that his fingers were beginning to ache from so much writing. Miriam returned to her own chamber. She was still shocked at what she had seen in Olympias's chambers. Yet, she reasoned, Olympias was always a killer. People who crossed her met violent deaths and it was well known in the palace how her husband and son quickly and quietly covered up the results of her homicidal rages.

Miriam lay down on the bed. She stared across at a Samian earthenware jug and the frieze painted around its base, showing a man chasing a clown who had apparently stolen a ewer of wine. Miriam tried to make sense of the tangled politics surrounding Philip's death. So far one line was clear. A wide circle of conspirators, including the Persians, Demosthenes, Attalus, and the Lyncestrians, had been active. They had plotted to kill Philip and Alexander. Miriam chewed her lip. Athens and Persia would be delighted to see Macedon tear itself apart, but why should Attalus, whose niece was married to the king, want Philip's death? Did he see himself as a kingmaker? The relationship between Pausanias and Philip, however, was much more mysterious. Pausanias loved Philip. Pausanias, in his own devious way, loved Olympias and had no real grudge against Alexander. Yet, when Pausanias struck, it wasn't against Attalus or Eurydice, but against Philip. And yet, why should Philip encourage his own murderer? And why use Arridhaeus's knife? Who was the person in the vineyard? Someone else Philip had put there? Miriam wished she could speak to Hecaetus, that so-called royal messenger. Philip was supposed to have told him to stay in the palace, yet what was he hoping to do here?

Miriam rolled over on her back and screwed up her eyes at the sunlight pouring through the window above her. And if Pausanias had escaped, where would he flee? Many cities in Greece would welcome Philip's assassin: Thebes, Athens, not to mention Sparta, which persistently refused to acknowledge Philip's overlordship. Pausanias had been given two horses. Was, therefore, the intended journey a long one? And how could she find out? Miriam drifted into sleep. She heard a knock on the door, but it was only Simeon; she drowsily replied that, no, she didn't want to eat. When she awoke it was growing dark; there was a great deal of noise in the courtyard below and, from her window, Miriam saw that Alexander's companions had arrived earlier than expected: Ptolemy, as usual, dancing from one foot to another and Niarchos jingling the money pouch in his belt while tall, dark-haired Hephaestion looked longingly at the door. Alexander appeared. He and Hephaestion met and embraced. Miriam resisted the tug of jealousy. Both men stood apart laughing, clapping their hands, and they again embraced before Alexander turned to greet the others. Simeon arrived and drew Niarchos into conversation. Miriam watched them all stroll back into the palace. She washed her hands and face and went down to the stables to search out Philobetas. She found the groom tending a mare lying in one of the great oaken stables; he was gently stroking her swollen stomach.

"Too much fresh grass," he explained, as Miriam walked in. "She ate too greedily, too fast." He smiled up at her. "I haven't been troubled since you visited me last, so I know I'm not to blame."

"Of course not." Miriam crouched down and allowed the mare to nuzzle at her hand.

"Will she be all right?"

"Of course," Philobetas replied, "as long as she doesn't eat or drink any more and her stomach's massaged. The swelling will go down." He glanced nervously over his shoulder at the stable door. "You have more questions?"

"Just one. Let us say Pausanias reached the horses? What would have happened then?"

"I suppose he would have fled."

"But where to?"

Philobetas shook his head.

"I know," Miriam replied, "you are a groom, you carry out orders, but Philip must have given you instructions."

"Not really. I was to guide Pausanias out of Aegae by back lanes and then into the countryside."

"And then?"

"I was to leave him at the crossroads, you know, near Apollo's shrine."

"And which direction do you think he was going to take?"

Philobetas grimaced. "The king mentioned something about the horses being good, a long journey to the southwest."

Miriam got to her feet. "Thank you, Philobetas. I won't bother you again."

Miriam left the stables. If the groom was correct, and

Pausanias had been allowed to escape, it was almost certain that he intended to flee to Philip's former enemy, the city of Thebes. Miriam was hardly in the palace when a page came running up. He was a black-eyed, curly-headed youth with a cheeky smile who introduced himself as Meleager.

"I am to lead you to the Golden Lyre in the Agora," he explained. "Cephalus stayed there."

"Then, in which case, you'd better start now."

The evening was warm, the shops and wine booths all still open. People were out on the streets, either servants coming from the palace or townspeople returning to their homes. They paused before entering the Agora, as a girl and a young boy led a flock of sheep across the path. The Golden Lyre was a wine shop and bakery with clean, tiled floors and large, open windows overlooking a cobbled yard on one side, and on the other, a well-laid-out garden with flowery arbors, an ideal place for a lover's tryst. The wine keeper was lean and furtive eyed.

"Yes, I remember Cephalus," he mumbled. "He hired a chamber, oh, two, three nights ago. He didn't come back so I let it to someone else."

"And his possessions?"

The wine keeper looked Miriam over from head to toe.

"Don't be so crude!" Meleager broke in. He waved his staff bearing the emblem of the royal household. "She's the Jewess, a friend of the king while Cephalus was not." Meleager tapped the staff against the man's shoulder. "So none of your rudeness or I'll bring some of the lads here!"

"I'll do better," Miriam added, "I'll bring General Antipater."

The wine keeper's lower lip began to quiver. "But—"

"Don't add lying to thievery," Miriam retorted. "A man comes here and stays two or three nights. He leaves. We know he carried a bow and a quiver. He must have arrived on a horse. Where's that? His harness, saddlebag, other possessions?"

"You'd best come with me," the fellow sighed.

He led them through the kitchen to a small storeroom; he took out a bunch of keys, unlocked the door, and brought out two bulging, leather bags.

"I collected everything up and put them in here." He threw them on the floor. "If he didn't come back, then I thought they'd be mine."

"Well they are not." Meleager picked them up and slung them over his shoulder. Making an obscene gesture at the wine keeper, he led Miriam out of the shop. He walked in front, swinging his bottom, whistling and tapping with his stick for people to stand aside. "That's the only way to deal with such people!" He called out over his shoulder.

"How did you know where to go?" Miriam caught up with him.

"Oh, it's quite easy," Meleager pouted back, his eyelashes were so long any maid would have envied them. He fluttered these in a mock show of innocence. I'm one of Philip's boys," he murmured.

"Yes I can see why." Miriam smiled back.

"That's what he called us, the king, 'Philip's boys.' His little puppies he'd send scampering here and there. When I heard that old, one-eyed goat Antipater was searching for where Cephalus had lodged, I immediately put my hand up. You see, I took Cephalus there. An archer, wasn't he? He had a horse, no one knows where that is now; also a bow, a quiver of arrows, and these bags."

Miriam grabbed his arm and dragged him to a halt.

"You took Cephalus to the tavern?"

"Yes, of course I did," he pouted. "And stop pinching my arm. Philip told me to take him there."

Miriam groaned.

"What I remember," Meleager continued, "was Philip coming out of the courtyard where I and the other lads were sunning ourselves. 'Meleager my boy!'" he shouts, 'Go down to the palace gates; you'll see a Cretan, an archer, there with a horse.' He didn't give me his name. 'Find him lodgings at the Golden Lyre.' So I did."

"Did Cephalus speak to you?"

"No, except he wanted to take me upstairs to his room and see how pretty my bottom was. I gave him the same farewell I did the wine keeper."

Miriam walked on. She couldn't understand this. Pausanias's actions were mysterious enough, but now Cephalus? What had Philip been planning? At the palace she thanked Meleager and took the saddlebags to her own chamber. They contained some coins, a dagger with the handle shaped in the form of a pretty boy, arrowheads, some cord, a comb and brush, and a dirt-stained letter. Miriam read this. It was from Attalus to Philip saying that, at his request, he was sending the Cretan archer Cephalus back to Macedon. Miriam sat on the bed and put her face in her hands. She heard the door open.

"Simeon, Simeon, this is a puzzle worse than I thought."

"All life is a puzzle!"

Miriam looked up quickly. Aristander stood there.

"It's dark," he declared. "The queen is sleeping. I gave her a potion."

"Nechtanebo?"

"Yes," Aristander replied. "I have come to talk about Nechtanebo. . . ."

CHAPTER 10

MIRIAM AND ARISTANDER slipped out of the palace, across some disused land, and into the sprawling, derelict cemetery. Although she had visited Aegae on a number of occasions, Miriam, like others, always avoided this place. Legend had it that Aegae was an ancient town even when Achilles sailed for Troy and that this spot was accursed. No one was buried here now except for felons, beggars, and the unknown. The cemetery sprawled over the brow of a small hill, its tombstones and plinths thrusting up like black pegs against the evening sky. Bushes, brambles, and other weeds choked pathways; moss had eaten deeply into the stones.

A place of no order and little harmony. Now and again some animal would scuttle through the undergrowth, or a bird, wings spread, float lazily over them. It reminded Miriam of the battlefield of Chaeronea; she and Simeon had been there when Philip and Alexander had crushed the combined might of Athens and Thebes. The graveyard was a dark, somber place where ghosts walked, and those not yet in Hades still clung to the last vestiges of life. Miriam glanced sideways at Aristander. He, too, seemed frightened. His sharp nose and wispy beard gave his face the look of a cunning satyr. He walked with his stick, but the limp he practiced had now disappeared. Miriam cursed her own stupidity; she should have carried a knife, some defence, for what would happen if Aristander meant her ill? Was he on some errand from that witch queen of his? Full of vengeance that Eurydice's corpse had been taken down?

"Where are we going?" she snapped.

Aristander stopped, head bowed, and when he walked to sit on a lichen-covered tomb, the limp had returned. He sat there and sighed, bony shoulders sagging, tapping his stick between his feet. Miriam sat on a stone opposite. Aristander glanced up at the sky.

"I know a little of your faith," he began. "They say your God moves like the wind; that he is not to be worshipped in stone statues or images?"

"I doubt if my God is in Macedon," Miriam replied, "though not because he lacks the power."

Aristander smiled. "I know what you mean, girl. This is a wicked, bloodthirsty place and yet such a contrast, eh? Philip was a great killer but also a man of great mercy. Alexander's no different. He will wage war, Miriam, eternal war. He will march to the brim of the world and back."

"Why?" Miriam asked curiously.

"To prove himself. To show that he is the son of a god, greater than Philip. What's that line from the *Iliad*? 'The son has a duty to show himself a greater man than his father.' "

"And Olympias?"

"When I first met her," Aristander replied, "she was a person, Miriam, in whom light and dark dwelled together. When she smiled, when she decided to exert her charm, she was irresistible, a good friend, a generous patron, loyal and courageous." He glanced up at the emerging moon. "The Persians believe the world is divided between the lord of light and the lord of darkness, and that these two are constantly at war. Each person must make a choice between them." Aristander scratched his scrawny neck. "In the beginning Olympias was like that. What ever happens, she is Alexander's mother. You should pray for two things, Miriam: either that Alexander turns to the light or that he dies before his soul becomes the home of darkness." He paused like a teacher waiting for his pupil to absorb a lesson.

Miriam accepted that Aristander was telling the truth, a perceptive insight into Alexander, a restless young man with a hunger for fame and a burning ambition.

"Olympias is now full of darkness," Aristander continued. He started as a bird screamed overhead. "If she knew what I was telling you, I would not live." He glanced around. "Just like the rest."

"So, why are you telling me?"

"Every man has his price, Miriam, just like a jug of wine in the marketplace."

"And what is yours?"

"Alexander likes you, Jewess. The soldiers call you his 'Little Mouse.' " His head came forward. "I like you, too, and that's not flattery. I trust you. I want one favor and one favor only. When Alexander marches, he must take me with him. I must not remain much longer with Olympias."

"Are you so frightened?"

"I am not frightened, woman, I am terrified. Olympias can hide in that chamber, squatting over that damned spinning wheel and brood for hours. On other occasions she'll sit on that wooden throne and stare at me."

"But there's something else, isn't there?" Miriam asked.

"Yes, yes, there is." Aristander rubbed his face. "Olympias

broods over every insult, every slight. Now, she's full of vengeance, exulting in the death of her enemies. She fusses over her son, but soon Alexander will be gone, and when he goes and all becomes quiet, Olympias will return to her brooding. Why did Philip reject her? Why did Philip divorce her? Why did Philip choose Eurydice and take her into his bed and give her a son?"

"And she'll hold you responsible for that?"

"She might start to guess the truth."

"Which is?"

"Twenty-two years ago," Aristander replied, "Philip met Olympias on Samothrace where both celebrated the rites of Dionysus." He pulled a face. "That wasn't her real name, you know. She was called Myrtale, a name to conjure up pleasant, shady trees, security, and peace. Philip gave her the name Olympias after his horse won at the Olympics. His queen took it eagerly. It sounds . . ."

"More majestic?"

"Yes," Aristander replied, "more imperious. Our Olympias had found her path in life. She was wife to the great Philip, queen of Macedon, and her husband was like soft wax in those lovely fingers. Yet, what Philip didn't know was that in Olympias there was a darkness, a burning ambition to control, to wield absolute power. What Olympias, in her turn, didn't realize was that, although Philip adored her, when he was on campaign, or when the fancy took him, he would have his boyfriends and girlfriends. Philip saw such affairs as nothing more than sunbeams to be enjoyed and forgotten."

"But Olympias was different?"

"Oh yes. She could never accept that Philip would even look at another woman, never mind bed her. In a short time her raging passion, her all-consuming love had turned to hate. I came with Olympias from Epirus. I had fought as a soldier, but a leg wound, how can I put it, led to a change in career. Olympias used me . . ."

"For what?"

"I acquired a knowledge of herbs, of the human mind, of astrology, of divination. Sometimes I predicted the future and sometimes I was right."

"Are you a seer?" Miriam asked.

"No, more an astute observer of human nature. I can predict what they will do."

"And now you apply this to yourself?"

"Yes, naturally." Aristander poked the ground with his cane. "Philip grew tired of Olympias's rages. He began to distance himself, and I grew frightened. Philip said he would eventually dispose of Olympias completely."

"Dispose of?" Miriam interrupted.

"That's what the king said, though he never opened his mind fully to me." Aristander swallowed hard. "It was then that I decided to act. If Olympias went, what hope could I expect? Philip played on that; he questioned me very closely about Olympias's conception of Alexander. You've heard the stories?"

Miriam nodded.

"Well, they are true!"

"What!" Miriam exclaimed.

"Twenty-one years ago," Aristander continued, "the Persians invaded Egypt. Nechtanebo was a pharoah, a strange man dedicated to the devotion of Ammon-Zeus. He was also a magician deeply skilled in all the ancient sorcery of Egypt." He held a hand up. "And I mean a real magician, a sorcerer who could turn water into fire, this cane into a writhing snake. His subjects actually believed he was a god incarnate. Nechtanebo used such sorcery against his enemies; the Persians used their Magi against him. Nechtanebo fled, first to the city of Tyre and then to Macedon. He was given shelter by Olympias. Now Nechtanebo's true magic was most powerful; he could actually change himself into a snake."

"Impossible," Miriam broke in.

Aristander scratched his neck. "I know, I know. But, Miriam, I saw this!"

"An illusion," Miriam countered.

"Perhaps."

"Of course it is," Miriam persisted. She walked across to confront him. "I have seen such magicians; they travel from beyond the Indus; they can disappear up ropes and, as you say, appear to change the very elements."

"Nechtanebo could change himself," Aristander insisted. "Anyway, I told all this to Philip. Unlike you, he didn't express disbelief. He told me how he'd grown suspicious of Olympias and Nechtanebo and one night spied on the queen. He saw a snake writhing over his queen, as if making love to her. What he knew and what I told him were proof enough. Philip believed Olympias had been unfaithful and that Alexander was the son of this magician."

"And Olympias herself?" Miriam asked.

"Oh, she claims Ammon-Zeus made love to her in the form of a snake and that she conceived a god incarnate."

Miriam turned and went back to her seat. She stared up at the stars now pinpricking the dark sky with light. An unreal world, she thought: men and women make love, beget children, and, if the truth be known, have a great deal of pleasure in doing so. Yet Olympias would have to be different from anyone else. Did Philip, she wondered, really believe such a story? Or that he had just been the victim of an illusion?

"But Philip never believed in anything supernatural," she declared.

"He would if he had the proof," Aristander retorted. "Describe Philip to me."

"Tough, squat, black curly hair, a rude, arrogant face, one-eyed—"

"One-eyed," Aristander broke in. "Philip told me how, when he asked the Pythian Oracle at Delphi about what he had seen, the priestess replied that, because he'd spied on a god, he would lose the sight of his eye. Shortly afterward he did."

Miriam folded her arms across her chest to hide her shiver. "Yes," she agreed, "Philip would have believed that."

"I told Philip what I knew," Aristander continued, "with the same understanding I have confided in you: when he crossed the Hellespont I would go with him."

Miriam studied this genial, treacherous, old man.

"And on the morning he died?"

"I warned Philip," Aristander declared, "I warned him to be careful. I told Olympias that both Philip and Alexander were in great peril."

"But, of course, people would say you were just being wise after the event?"

Aristander shrugged.

"On the morning Philip died," Miriam asked, "where was Olympias?"

Aristander now became agitated. He abruptly stood up and stared round, looking up at the trees as if the bats squeaking above them could listen to what he said and report back to the witch queen.

"What was going to happen?" Miriam asked. She gripped Aristander's clawlike hands, pressing the fingers against the slender, wooden cane. "What did Philip ask of you? Come on!" she urged. "When Philip was making his glorious and triumphant entry into the amphitheater, you were with Olympias. What was going to happen there?"

"I don't know," Aristander whispered. "All the king told me was to stay with the queen."

"And?"

"A messenger would come; he would demand an audience with Olympias, saying that he bore important messages from Philip to her."

"And what were you supposed to do?"

Aristander's eyes held hers. "Make sure this envoy gained admittance."

"Do you know who it was going to be?"

Aristander shook his head. "He would carry the royal seal; that's all I know."

"And Nechtanebo?"

"Ah," Aristander beckoned. "You'd best come with me."

He took her deeper into the cemetery, across the brow of the hill and down into a small grove of cypress trees. An oblong, stone tomb, with no markings on it, stood in the moonlit glade like some ancient altar. Aristander went to the other side. Miriam heard a click, a grinding noise, and then Aristander was urging her to come around. She found that the side of the tomb had been lowered. Aristander stood just inside, beckoning her forward; behind him was a glow of light, as if a fire burned there.

"Oil lamps," he whispered, following her gaze, "they are ever primed and easy to light."

Miriam squeezed through. Behind Aristander, steps swept down into the darkness: in niches on the walls glowed small oil lamps. Aristander sealed the tomb and, squeezing by her, went down, pausing every so often to light more lamps. At last they reached the bottom. Miriam was aware of cold darkness and space all around her. For a moment she panicked as Aristander disappeared into the gloom, and she wondered if he had led her there to trap her. There was no sign of an injury to his leg now. Aristander scurried around lighting more lamps or pitch torches fixed into the wall. The chamber glowed with light and Miriam found herself in a cavernous crypt with caskets all about.

"What are these?" she asked.

"Olympias's victims; the caskets are sealed." Aristander's face looked lugubrious in the flickering torchlight. "These are the lucky ones. Others are taken and hidden in shallow graves or ditches. She comes down here, you know." His voice sounded hollow. "She walks around, as if savoring past triumphs." Aristander tapped a casket with his cane. "Enemies whose bodies cannot be found lest the blood feud be invoked. To all intents and purposes men and women who just disappear. Philip never knew about this place and nor must Alexander." He shuffled closer. "I have your word, don't I? I have your word?" he repeated. "Soon Alexander will leave with an army. I must go with him."

"You have my word," Miriam declared, "what else is there?"

Aristander led her to a small doorway built into the wall. He drew back the bolts, and taking a torch they entered a smaller chamber. Again lamps were lit. The air was sweeter, more fragrant and, as the torchlight flared, Miriam gasped for it was a burial chamber. Artifacts hung on the walls. Most of these were of Egyptian origin: a face mask, a statue of Horus, of Anubis the dog god of the Nile, a flail and rod, an Egyptian wicker shield, a knife, headdress, and other items of armor or clothing. On the wall facing her was a mummy's casket fashioned out of black wood and bound with gold strips; the smiling head at the top was decorated with a snake headdress. Aristander went across, unlocked the casket, and pulled back the lid. The body inside was wrapped from head to toe in white bandages. Over the face was the serene, smiling mask of an Egyptian ruler. Around the neck hung a silver half-moon disc. Its arms were placed across the chest and into the stiff fingers a flail and rod had been pushed, the mark of an Egyptian prince.

"This is Nechtanebo," Aristander murmured. "Olympias comes here to worship him."

Miriam drew closer. She noticed the snake motif that decorated the inside of the casket. All around the body were sponges filled with aromatic herbs, frankincense, sandalwood, and myrrh.

"Nechtanebo died here," Miriam whispered. "How could Olympias arrange all this?"

"This is the palace of Aegae," Aristander replied. "Think now, Miriam. Alexander and his companions, you included, were locked away in the Gardens of Midas; Philip was constantly on campaign. This palace became Olympias's domain. It is riddled with secret passageways and trapdoors. The queen can do what she likes: entertain friends or despatch enemies. Philip should never have come here," he added. "It's a place of doom and I want to be away from it. Can you imagine what it's going to be like, Miriam, when the army leaves? No Philip, no threats, no Eurydice. Alexander has reinstated his mother to her former glory. Those who remain will feel the rod and flail. I don't wish to end up in one of these caskets or with my throat cut, my corpse buried out in the forest for the wolves and jackals to dig up."

Miriam stared around the chamber.

"But who did all this for her?"

Aristander chuckled. "This is Aegae," he replied. "Olympias left her household at Pella. When there are others around, Olympias keeps in the shadows. She has men and women who will carry out her every whim."

"And this," Miriam gestured at the casket, "is her dead lover? The possible father of Alexander?"

Aristander closed the casket and came back. "I said Nech-tanebo was a great magus. A very great magician. This is his body but his soul lives on."

"Nonsense!" Miriam retorted. Yet she felt uneasy.

"Haven't you heard of the transmigration of souls, Miriam? On the edge of the world are holy men who preach that our souls return in new bodies forty days after our death. Others make more startling claims that those who control the real power, the magic of life and death, can move to another body before they die. Nechtanebo," he hurried on as if wishing to be away, "fell ill. Philip was far away on his campaigns. Olympias hired every physician, but they could do nothing. Nechtanebo told Olympias and myself that he loved a young priest, some minor official in the ser-vice of Dionysus. The young man was brought to his cham-ber. Olympias ordered him to pray for Nechtanebo. One of his duties was to lay his full length on the sick man's bed." Aristander paused, gazing fearfully at the casket. "One morning Nechtanebo was found dead." He shook his head. "I found this difficult to believe, I still do. The young priest was still there, sitting cross-legged in the corner, lost in a trance just like Nechtanebo used to be. Olympias began to berate him, to threaten that his lack of power had caused Nechtanebo's death. The young priest smiled, opened his eyes, and began to speak. Olympias nearly fainted; it was the only time in her life I've seen her lose control. The body was the young priest's, but the voice, the eyes, the gestures were Nechtanebo's."

Miriam stared in disbelief.

"I saw it," Aristander murmured. "I saw with my own eyes what had happened: it was Nechtanebo in everything but appearance."

"And then what?"

"He stayed for two or three months but then told

Olympias he must leave. She was now very fearful of him. Her monthly courses had stopped. She knew she was with child." Aristander walked back toward the doorway, gesturing at Miriam to follow him. "In a way Olympias was relieved. She had dabbled in magic but had never seen such power before. Nechtanebo said he was going to the temple of Ammon-Zeus at Siwah in southern Egypt. One night he disappeared. Olympias swore me to secrecy." He opened the door to usher Miriam out. "And that's all I know."

Miriam was pleased when they left the tomb, Aristander carefully sealing the doors behind them. He then led her back across the cemetery and into the palace. Just before they entered, Aristander seized Miriam's hand; he made her swear, once again, to keep what he had told and shown her secret and to use her influence with Alexander.

"Tell him," he urged, "I can be of use to him." He smiled crookedly. "Every good general needs a soothsayer. If I stay here, I will die!"

Miriam promised. Aristander disappeared into the darkness. She went up into the atrium. As soon as she arrived, she could sense the change in atmosphere. The gloom and tension of previous days had disappeared. Torch and oil lamps had been lit. Guards stood about but were no longer fully armed as they had been in the days immediately following Philip's assassination. Servants and slaves had reappeared, going about their ordinary duties. Miriam heard laughter from the guardroom and sounds of greater revelry deeper in the palace. An officer of the watch told her that Alexander was celebrating with his companions. Miriam returned to her own room. She felt fearful after her meeting with Aristander as well as bemused by what she had discovered. She washed and changed, dabbing her face lightly with paint. She combed her hair, rubbing in some oil and holding it in place with an embroidered headband. She put on earrings, and a necklace Simeon had bought her. However, when she went to put on the arm clasps shaped in the form of a writhing serpent, she threw these back into a small treasure chest.

"Olympias and her snakes!" she muttered. "I'll never wear them again!"

Miriam found Alexander, Simeon, and the others in the great hall. The couches had been arranged in a square, the drinking cups had been circulated, and the boards were littered with food. Inside the tables two professional tumblers, young women, were dancing, their naked feet barely escaping the razor-edged swords that had been laid out. The tumblers, dressed only in diaphanous cloths, danced and cavorted to cheers of encouragement. Some women guests were there, kinsfolk of Alexander's companions, including Antipater's young wife; all were flush faced and bright eyed. At the far end, Alexander slouched, gazing dreamily at Hephaestion who, now in his cups, was, as usual, arguing with Ptolemy. Simeon, laughing uproariously at a story Niarchos was whispering to him, beckoned her over, making room beside him. Niarchos tried to rise but, he'd drunk so much, he simply flapped his hands, his sly, monkeylike face beaming with pleasure.

"I missed you, Miriam, you and Simeon. Believe me, it was cold where we were. Another few months and we would have been hiring out our swords." He leaned across Simeon. "But now the old bastard is dead and we've come into our own, eh?"

Miriam, as always, pinched the Cretan's nose between her fingers.

"You'll never be poor, Niarchos."

"I don't intend to be," he slurred, and pushed a wine cup into her hand. "Come on, you look as pale as a ghost! Everyone else is drunk, so why aren't you?" He broke off, toasting the tumblers with his cup, inviting the girls over, but the dancers were already Ptolemy's, who rose, arms extended, to embrace both.

"Where have you been?" Simeon whispered.

"On the king's business, and don't ask me what!" she hissed. "Macedonians are never as drunk as they pretend to be."

Ptolemy came down, a lazy smile on his face, an arm around each of the dancing girls. He pressed these to him and winked at Miriam.

"It's good to be back! Wine, soft flesh, silk sheets, not like camping out on a mountainside, eh Miriam?"

"Oh I don't know," she replied, "if it was a choice between you and the palace or myself on the mountainside . . ."

Ptolemy laughed and sauntered back to his seat, nuzzling each of the girls in turn.

Alexander was now chatting with Hephaestion, their faces almost touching. The king was talking quickly and quietly. Hephaestion turned and stared down at Miriam with dark, soulful eyes; his square-jawed face looked thinner, with furrows in each cheek above the neatly clipped beard and moustache. He raised his hand in salutation. Miriam replied, but Hephaestion was already back, deep in discussion with the king. Miriam watched them. Hephaestion was slightly older than Alexander. They had met when Philip had taken Alexander on a minor campaign. Hephaestion didn't know who he was and, standing with a group of officers, had begun to mock the 'mooncalf.' When Hephaestion found out who Alexander really was, he pulled out his sword and offered it to him.

"Don't report me to the king," he declared, "just kill me now!"

Alexander had taken the sword and thrust it back into

Hephaestion's scabbard. When the prince had left the army, Philip asked which of his staff officers he would like to take back to the Gardens of Midas. Alexander had chosen Hephaestion. They became as close as brothers. Miriam wondered if they were lovers. In a way, she recognized that she and Hephaestion had a great deal in common. They were blunt, didn't play games, and always tried to tell Alexander exactly what they thought. She, like Hephaestion, was totally loyal because, although she was reluctant to admit it, she loved Alexander and often wondered what would have happened if he, not Ptolemy, had tried to creep beneath her blankets. As if he knew she was thinking about him, Alexander turned and smiled dazzlingly down the hall at her. He picked up his wine cup and paid her the most fulsome tribute a Macedonian could, to toast a woman in public. Miriam flushed, returned the salute, and to hide her own discomfort, began to pick at some of the food around her. Now that the king had formally noticed her it would be rude to leave. Miriam was resigning herself to a long night's drinking when Alexander abruptly got to his feet. He clapped his hands, shouting for the hall to be cleared, except for Antipater and his companions. A servant came over and whispered that Simeon and Miriam should also remain.

The dancing girls, the musicians, the slaves, as well as the fire-eater and snake charmer who had vainly waited to be called, were all gently ushered out of the hall. The couches and tables were rearranged in a circle. Phalanx men, in full armor, came in to guard the doors. Alexander gestured at his companions to retake their seats—Hephaestion on his right, Ptolemy to his left. Niarchos, Antipater, and two other senior commanders with Simeon and herself completed the circle. Again the wine jug was circulated. Alexander raised his eyes heavenward and poured a small libation on the floor.

"You can drink as much as you want," he began, "but tomorrow at dawn we march south for Tempe. The Thessalians are holding the passes. I intend to teach them a lesson they'll never forget, and to accept their fealty, their gold, and their cavalry."

"And afterward?" Ptolemy asked.

"To Corinth. That's where Philip was hailed as captain general of Greece. What they did for him, they can do for me."

"The Athenians and Thebans have closed their gates," Antipater declared.

"When I take Tempe," Alexander retorted, not even bothering to glance at Antipater, "I'll be within striking distance of both Thebes and Athens; they'll get the message. Moreover, by the time I reach Corinth, Hecaetus will be back from Aegae, bringing Parmenio's allegiance."

"And Attalus's head!" Ptolemy joked.

"Other heads may yet fall," Alexander declared. "Mother is going back to Pella."

"Aristander," Miriam spoke up, her eyes holding Alexander's. "You should take Aristander with you. You'll need a soothsayer!"

Alexander sipped from his goblet and smiled over the rim at Miriam.

"He can go. Everyone in my household marches with me, women included." He tapped the side of his head. "Mother is in one of her moods. She will be co-regent with Antipater. She may decide to exercise her powers, so it's best. Simeon and Miriam," he said the names so fast he made it sound like the final lines of a poem, "have been entrusted with the task of discovering who turned Pausanias's mind against my father. I have taken an oath that Mother and I are innocent, as is everyone in this room, are they not?" He drank slowly, letting his words hang in the air. "Soon I'll know the truth." He stared down at the floor. "I dream about my father. I also wonder about that oracle issued at Delphi: 'The bull is wreathed for sacrifice. All is ready. The slayer is at hand.' "

"The gods can see the future," Niarchos gibed.

"Yes they can," Alexander replied, glancing at Miriam, "but, there again, sometimes they are given a little help." He lifted his wine cup. "Tomorrow, after dawn, we march to victory!"

CHAPTER 11

AFTER THE FEASTING, Miriam withdrew, spending the early hours packing her possessions and those of Simeon. They had not brought much from Pella so this was relatively easy. Simeon, who had also drunk moderately, collected his writing implements and took the saddlebags down to the great room near the stables where chamberlains and pages were preparing the baggage train. Outside the palace the night air was shattered by the sounds of troops marching to their muster points; only a small detachment of guards were being left to patrol the palace. Miriam snatched a few hours' sleep. She was awakened the next morning by the bustle and clatter outside in the passageways and courtyard. Miriam was used to this mode of traveling. The Macedonian court, although it had its palace in Pella, was constantly on the move to other palaces or toward the frontier in a sudden show of force against the Thessalians, Triballians, or Scythians—ever eager to probe Macedonian defences and test the metal of its princes.

Miriam kept well out of the way of the officious chamberlains and officers barking out orders. She learned from gossip that Olympias and the few members of her household had already left for Pella. Now that Philip was dead, his former queen was eager to exercise her authority and power. Miriam glimpsed Aristander. For the first time ever, she saw the seer smile in public. He raised his head and bowed ceremoniously toward her in gratitude that Miriam had her word. She wondered what would happen to that gloomy, eerie tomb? Would Olympias destroy it? Or, once Alexander and everyone else was out of the way, arrange for its contents to be placed in some permanent place outside Pella? Miriam had already decided it was best she keep Aristander's revelations a secret, even from Alexander. Sooner or later, Miriam reasoned, she would have to voice certain conclusions. Alexander would insist on that. Yet what could she say? As soon as she, in the words of Aristotle, formed a hypothesis, fresh information surfaced to destroy it. Perhaps Hecaetus, when he returned from Asia, might throw some fresh light on Attalus's role, if any, in Philip's murder. Miriam glimpsed a servant taking her theater costumes and masks down to the waiting carts. She sat on a ledge inside the atrium and smiled to herself. Everyone wore masks in this matter. Even Philip had not truly revealed his intentions. At the banquet the previous evening, watching Ptolemy and the rest, Miriam had wondered if Alexander's companions had played any role in Philip's destruction.

"Here she is, but you can't stay long!"

Miriam looked up; a page boy was beckoning forward an old man. He shuffled slowly, head peering out from his hood, like that of an inquisitive snail.

"He wants to see you," the page pompously announced to her. "He said it was a matter of urgency."

At first Miriam didn't know who it was. The page

flounced away, and the old man raised a hand, fingers all calloused.

"I saw you," he stammered. "I saw you about the room!"

Miriam got to her feet, shaking her head. The old man pulled back the hood.

"Of course!" she exclaimed, "the cobbler from Straight Street."

"It's about the contents of Pausanias's chest. Can I have them?" he gabbled. "I mean, the coins and clothes that the old man, the one you brought with you, the philosopher—"

"Ah yes, Hermanocrates."

"Well, that's what he calls himself. Anyway, he took most of the money, said it was his, but the rest he left."

"Of course you can take it," Miriam declared. "No one else is going to claim it."

The old man beamed. "My wife and I," he continued, "have talked about nothing else but your visit. Our lodger, Pausanias, he's the one who killed the king, isn't he? Fancy that, a member of his own guard! Well, my wife and I," he rattled on, "were much taken by you; I mean, you are very courteous, not like the rest. That page boy for example, he's asking to have his bottom smacked! If I were younger, I'd do it!"

Miriam guided the old man into an alcove well away from those milling around them.

"My wife and I have really thought—" the old man continued.

"About what?" Miriam asked.

"Oh, who came and went. And, do you know, we suddenly realized Pausanias had few friends. There was that old philosopher you mentioned but—"

"There was someone else, wasn't there?" Miriam interrupted.

"Yes, especially in the last few weeks. Someone who used to visit him late at night."

"A lover?" Miriam asked.

"I'm not too sure. He never came through the door, he always climbed up through a window at the back." The old man chewed on his gums. "I mean, there's nothing wrong with that, is there? Pausanias always paid. He was fairly quiet. We only knew this person had arrived because we could hear them talking, as well as the clink of cups. Afterward was silence; we then knew Pausanias's visitor had left by the same way."

Miriam recalled the room above the cobbler's shop. The window was high in the wall; it would take someone fairly young and vigorous to climb in and out.

"Now I'd forgotten something," the old cobbler continued. "When Pausanias left his room—and don't forget, sometimes he'd never use it, being on guard at the palace—he always closed the shutters on his window. However, that morning, he deliberately left them open, yet he told me to lock the door to his room and not open it."

"Why didn't you tell me this before?"

"I'd forgotten."

"Anything else," Miriam asked, "that you may have forgotten?"

The old man puckered his mouth and scratched his balding pate. "No, but I thought it was strange. I mean, why lock a door but keep the window open?"

Miriam thanked the old man, took him out to the steps, and watched him go. At least one puzzle had been resolved. She'd wondered how Pausanias could have fled without taking that small leather bag containing his money and his warrant. He had had someone else to help him, she reasoned—this mysterious friend who always came by night. He was going to crawl through the window, take the bag, and meet

Pausanias elsewhere. But who? Could it have been the same person who was waiting in the vineyard, ready to trip him up?

"Miriam." Simeon was hastening toward her. "Come on, all is ready. We are to be gone within the hour."

Miriam followed him out of the palace. It was already falling silent again, a house of ghosts. A few old soldiers lounged on guard but the rooms she passed had all been stripped; the cloths, tables, anything that might be needed, had been hoisted onto the carts and sent back to Pella. At the stables Miriam was given a choice, to ride in the cart with the other women or on horseback. As always, she chose the latter. She and Simeon left the stables, going out through the palace gates and into the great mustering ground. The royal army was already on the march, the carts being the last to follow and protected by cavalry. Miriam and Simeon mounted their horses and galloped along the flanks.

"Alexander means business," Simeon murmured, as they reined in to let a group of outriders gallop back to the rear of the column. "We are to march till we drop!"

"I won't complain," Miriam replied tartly.

"Good!" Simeon grinned. "Alexander has ordered that any one who can't stay up, must fall out and go back to join the old women in Pella."

Miriam didn't mind. She was tired, but found it pleasant to be away from the gloomy passageways and chambers of Aegae. The sky was clear, the heat not yet oppressive, and she felt a thrill of excitement as they passed regiment after regiment: Cretan archers, phalanx men, the light-armed infantry of Macedon's allies, the pennants, the gleam of the sun on armor, the shouts and cries of officers, all the gorgeous panoply of war. They found Alexander seated under a cypress tree eating dried figs and drinking watered wine. As usual, he was holding at least five conversations at once, listening carefully to what Hephaestion and Ptolemy were telling him, now and again breaking off to give some courier or officer an order. When he saw Miriam and Simeon, he beckoned them over.

"I didn't invite you to the sacrifices," he declared, turning to spit out what he was eating onto the grass. "I know you pray to your own God. Simeon, I'm glad you are here. Father always said you were the swiftest scribe." He gestured at Miriam to sit on the grass and threw a battered leather cushion for Simeon to rest on.

"Write out notes," he commanded. "Ptolemy here will take care of them. It's the same message to every commander, particularly those lazy bastards at the back looking after the baggage! The column must stay together, no stragglers. We are still in Macedon, but anyone who approaches must be regarded as an enemy. You've got that?"

Simeon, struggling to get out his quill and parchment, nodded.

"You've got that? Good!" Alexander smacked his thigh. "Anyway, you've got the gist of it! Remember, no one stops, keep together, any stranger is an enemy; be prepared to fight at a minute's notice!"

Simeon, with his back to the tree, began to transcribe the orders. Alexander beamed around, his face showing no signs of late-night drinking; his strange-colored eyes were alight with excitement.

"Aren't you glad you came, Miriam? I couldn't leave you, not with Mother, not in the mood she's in."

He turned and whispered something to Hephaestion, who glanced sourly at Miriam but got to his feet and walked away. Ptolemy and the others joined him. Alexander, rubbing a finger around his lips, watched them go.

"Did you notice, Miriam? They never mourned for Father, did they? Oh, they said they were sorry he was dead, that Father should never have trusted Pausanias, etc., etc." Alexander gestured with his hand. "But last night, I did wonder."

"That they had a hand in Philip's death?" Simeon spoke up.

"It's possible," Miriam mused. "They had no love for him, but they would scarcely approach a man like Pausanias."

"I know, I know. I'd just like to satisfy myself."

"What will you do?" Simeon asked, "if you discover they were involved?"

"Keep writing my messages, Simeon," Alexander retorted. He winked at Miriam. "What would I do?" He got to his feet and helped Miriam up. "I am not too sure. I want to know what Father was doing, what he was plotting." He pointed to the marching column. "I want to enjoy this." He murmured. "We have a good day's marching ahead of us. By tomorrow it will be hard knocks; I don't know what I will do." He spoke over his shoulder, then pointed at Miriam. "But I do want to know the truth. Anyway," he tightened his sword belt, "for the moment we march!"

Miriam was surprised by the rapid advance of the Macedonian army. Eventually they left the flat, open countryside striking southeast on to the border through the mountains that divided Macedon from Thessaly. At times the road was no more than a trackway going up through dark forests. All troops were put on the alert. The air grew colder, and slowly, yet perceptibly, the atmosphere changed. They were now in the border country, the hunting grounds of the barbarian, Scythian tribes, ever ready to spill over to loot and pillage the prosperous lowlands. By the third night out, they were camping out on an open plateau, the army dividing, the cavalry staying farther back, scouts being sent into the forest to ensure no night ambush was planned.

Alexander seemed determined to show his troops that he was as tough a soldier as Philip, exercising a ruthless, iron discipline. He seemed to be everywhere, riding up and down on his black warhorse Bucephalus, dressed in a white leather, pleated skirt, a bronze cuirass, and a back plate, though he wore no helmet. An ostentatious but very dangerous gesture. If an ambush was launched or a tribe made a sudden sortie, an unprotected head was poor defence against arrow, club, axe, or sword. Even at night Alexander only slept fitfully. He'd sprawl in a blanket before the fire, then suddenly rouse himself and, with a few picked men, go around and check the sentries or horse lines. Miriam caught the sense of danger. She found it difficult to sleep. One morning, in the early hours, she woke to find the necromancer Aristander, who had traveled in the carts, staring across the fire at her.

"What do you want?" she asked warily, shivering at the chilling howl of a wolf from the dark line of trees beyond the camp.

Aristander didn't look as confident as he had in that gloomy cemetery; he seemed jumpy as a fish out of water.

"Is that a wolf?" he asked nervously.

"We'll soon find out," Miriam replied. "But, what do you want?"

"It's years since I've been on campaign," Aristander replied. "I'm cold. My backside's sore, but I came to thank you."

Miriam had the fire to herself. Simeon was elsewhere. Alexander had insisted that she sleep in the center of the camp, well away from the men. She beckoned Aristander to sit beside her on a cloak.

"You must find this uncomfortable," Aristander declared, joining her.

"Not really," Miriam replied. "I was with Alexander and

the rest in the Gardens of Midas. Black Cleitus, our tutor, always insisted that we rough it. Sometimes the old bear didn't even let us have a blanket. He was a Spartan through and through."

"I know, I've seen him," Aristander replied. "He's up there with the vanguard. He doesn't seem to age. Thickheaded, close-cropped hair, and that black cloak he always insists on wearing."

"But you haven't come to talk about him, have you?"

"No, despite the discomfort," Aristander replied, "I am truly grateful, Miriam. Olympias is in one of her Medea moods—tight-lipped, narrow-eyed. She couldn't leave for Pella fast enough. I think she's going to settle grievances there."

"Didn't she object to losing her sorcerer?" Miriam teased.

"No, not really. She thinks I'll be her spy on Alexander, so she was quite happy. However, never mind her or what she plans. It's Philip I keep thinking about." He stared round the darkness. "I'm happier to be here than in some comfortable chamber at Pella. I'll let you get back to sleep. I've just been thinking about what we discussed. I tell you Olympias had no hand in her husband's murder but I keep thinking about Philip's order to me on the morning he was killed. I've had dreams about that."

"And?"

Aristander struggled to his feet. "May the gods receive Philip's shade. Nevertheless, I tell you this, daughter of Israel, I am sure that the morning Philip was murdered, he was actually planning to kill Olympias."

Then Aristander, his cloak clutched about him, walked off into the night.

Just after dawn the army assembled to march. As she ate a hasty meal—quick mouthfuls of cereal, bread, and watered wine—Miriam reflected on what Aristander had told her. In itself it wasn't important; Philip and Olympias had a mutual hatred. Nevertheless, Aristander's revelation, like everything she'd learned, made her feel like a spectator in a theater who had been given a poor seat and couldn't see the stage properly.

"I keep thinking Philip was the victim," she murmured to herself. She paused in collecting her possessions. Yes, she thought, that's only natural, or as Aristotle would say, logical. Philip was killed, hence he was the victim, the object—but that was wrong. Philip was a doer, a man of action, so I must change my perspective. What did Philip intend? What was he planning? What was he plotting?

"Will you ride in the cart today?" Alexander was standing over her.

"I don't want to," she replied. "I'll only end up with more bruises. . . ."

"You look peakish," Alexander declared.

"I just think I am wrong," she replied.

Alexander crouched down. He offered her his wine cup. She shook her head.

"Now is not the time for philosophy, Miriam!"

"It isn't philosophy, my king," she teased back. "I should be more pragmatic. If I want to know who really killed Philip, I must get into Philip's mind."

Alexander laughed, toasting her with his cup.

"If you can do that, Miriam, then you're sharper than I. I never ever knew what Philip was plotting." He sipped at the wine. "Especially in the days before he was killed."

"Why do you want to know, really?" Miriam asked.

"I told you. I want to clear myself of the accusation of patricide."

"But no one would dare accuse you of that?"

"Oh, not now," Alexander replied. "But look around you, Miriam, these Macedonian chieftains and generals. A time will come when they might want to dig up the dirt. And how do I know whether one of them, or more, is behind Philip's death? After all, if they can kill one king, why not another?" He got to his feet. "Listen, isn't it silent?"

Miriam picked up a bundle; the air was filled with the clatter of the camp, the neigh of horses, and the shouts of officers.

"It's anything but quiet!" she snapped, annoyed at Alexander for playing one of his games.

"No, I don't mean the camp," Alexander retorted. "It's the forest, Miriam. I was out there just before dawn. The enemy are near. They are watching us. So keep in the center of the column, that's an order!"

He spun on his heel and marched away. Simeon brought her horse, Perdiccas swaggering behind, his dark face full of merriment.

"What are you laughing at?" Miriam asked angrily.

"You should be back home." Perdiccas towered over her. He smelled of horse sweat and leather; his face was dirty, his eyes red rimmed. She noticed splashes of blood on his wrist guard.

"You've seen the enemy?" she asked.

"A scouting party, late last night," he replied. "If they capture someone like you, they'll eat you." He tapped her gently on the hand. "They like soft mice."

"And if they catch you," Miriam prodded him in the stomach, "they'll probably eat you as well and become even more full of hot air!"

She swung herself onto the horse as Perdiccas roared with laughter. He grasped the reins.

"Alexander says you are to march with our unit in the center of the phalanx. You'll be safe there, little mouse."

By the time the sun had fully risen, Alexander's army was snaking its way up the mountain pass. The enemy began to make its presence felt. A burly warrior with bright red hair, face and body daubed with paint, a gold torque around his neck, bracelets on his arms, slipped like a shadow out of the trees. He loped across the grass and killed one of the outriders before he was noticed. He took the man's head, did a wild dance, then disappeared back into the trees. The attack happened so swiftly not even the archers could notch arrows. Miriam watched round-eyed as they passed the severed corpse, blood gushing out, soaking the ground.

"That's the way of the Thessalians," Perdiccas commented. "Kill a man in single combat. I hope the silly bastards try it again."

They did so now and the army was ready. Five warriors burst out of the trees, hair streaming, colorful cloaks flapping out behind them like banners. They raced toward the right side of the column even as others came out of the trees on their left. All died before they even reached the Macedonian column, as the archers loosed a shower of arrows. On another occasion a larger group attacked, shattering the air with their war cries. At first Miriam was frightened, but she admired the ice-cold discipline of the Macedonian phalanx. Perdiccas rapped out an order; the hoplites turned to face the enemy, shields locked together, the long pikes or sarissas coming down like the quills of a porcupine awaiting an attacker. The Thessalians, frustrated, tried to break through, only to be skewered like pieces of meat. Those who survived withdrew; the sarissas came up, the column was reformed, and the march continued.

After a while they entered more open country. As they approached the great pass of Pydna, riders galloped along the column telling them to stop.

"The enemy are massing!" one shouted. "They are blocking the main pass with carts full of boulders. Alexander wants all officers to the front!"

Miriam followed Perdiccas along the column. The whole army had stopped. Alexander, Ptolemy, and the rest were clustered in a group at the side of the road just where it rose and swept up toward two great rocky outcrops. Although Miriam had no military knowledge, she realized the problem: The pass was blocked by huge carts full of boulders. Behind these massed the Thessalians, the sun shimmering on their armor.

"Well, what do we do?" Ptolemy asked. He turned to the short, wiry scout whose face was covered in cuts. "How many are there?"

"At least a thousand men and ten such carts. And, before you ask, Lord, there's no way around them."

Alexander walked ahead, staring up at the enemy. Miriam could tell he was tense and anxious. She closed her eyes and prayed he would not give way to panic.

"If we advance," Alexander called out over his shoulder, "they'll roll the carts down. If we mass in a show of force, they might still do so. We can't go around while, if we go back, we are finished. Ptolemy, bring up the guards regiment. Tell them to wear full armor; they are to advance against the pass now."

"What?" Ptolemy cried, "they'll be crushed!"

"No," Alexander replied, "I'll go with them." He turned and came back to his officers. "If the wagons hurtle down, the men must divide. Take shelter on either side. Let them go through where they can—"

"And those men who can't move?" Ptolemy snapped. "What do they do, fly?"

"Those men who can't move out of the way," Alexander replied quietly, "should lie down and lock their shields over their backs. Let the wagons go over their shields!"

His words were greeted by a hubbub of exclamation. Alexander made a slicing movement with his hands.

"That's my order! I'll go first!"

At the top of the pass a loud jeering broke out. Some of the Thessalians came out and stood before the carts. They pulled up their cloaks and waggled their bare backsides in derision at the enemy. Alexander, ignoring the taunts, ordered five hundred of the guards to mass, helmets on, visors down, shields slung over their backs, with their lances held out in front. Alexander donned a helmet, put a shield on his own back, and drew his sword. The guards' trumpeters brayed out a roar of defiance. The Thessalians stopped their mockery and stared in wonderment as the phalanx proceeded to advance slowly toward them. Miriam, standing with the officers, watched speechlessly as Alexander led the five hundred men up toward the mouth of the pass. She closed her eyes and prayed to her unnamed God. Alexander now seemed so vulnerable, like a boy playing a game. He didn't march but walked nonchalantly, sword by his side; then he stopped, the wind fanning the red plume of his helmet. He turned toward the guards, sword out, then bringing it around in an arc, pointed up to the Thessalians. They hurriedly withdrew behind their carts.

The road up to the mouth of the pass was now blocked by the Macedonian phalanx, men marching slowly behind their leader. The Macedonian trumpeters gave shrill brays of defiance. These were answered by the deep, long bellows of the Thessalian war horns, and then the carts slowly began to move. At first imperceptibly, but as they reached the incline, the foremost gathered speed, crashing down the rocky path toward the advancing Macedonians. Alexander rapped out an order. The phalanx was at least ten men across. The three on each side immediately flattened themselves against the cliffside while the four in the center fell face down onto the earth, Alexander with them. It looked as if some huge tortoise squatted on the mountain path road. Heads down, the phalanx men waited; the carts hit the shields, rumbling across. Miriam watched as a cartload of rocks and boulders hurtled by her. The Macedonians had put logs across the bottom of the road, and the cart smashed into these careering over onto its side. Other carts followed. The mountain path became hidden by billowing clouds of dust; then there were no more carts. The dust cleared. Miriam heard a great roar. Alexander was leading his phalanx men up to the mouth of the pass. He seemed uninjured, but on the road behind him at least two dozen men lay sprawled. Some twitched in agony, others lay as still as the rocks around them. Ptolemy, leading the reserve, ordered the trumpeters to sound the charge, and the rest of the Macedonian phalanxes, a huge sea of jostling men, filled the mountain pass road, streaming up toward the enemy.

Later in the day Miriam and the rest joined them. The plateau beyond the pass was now empty. The Thessalians had left a small guard to cover their retreat and these now lay dead, bodies stripped; already the scavengers of the air were flocking down to the feast. Despite their casualties, the officers were quick to congratulate Alexander on his generalship. Late that night the Macedonian dead were collected and placed in a great funeral pyre. Those Thessalians who had been taken prisoner had their throats cut and were thrown on top. Alexander himself lit the pyre and, as the flames roared up to the night sky, he led his Macedonians in a chorus of praise and thanksgiving to Zeus.

Afterward Alexander celebrated with his officers. They lounged in a circle, watching the funeral pyre die, impervious to the stench of blood and burning flesh mingled with the woodsmoke. Miriam only stayed for a while, but she could see that Alexander had achieved his aim. He had been faced with an impossible task and had resolved it by quick thinking, tremendous courage, and a speed that even surprised his own men.

The next morning the army continued its march southeast. Perdiccas explained that they were now taking the coast road through Methone and Pydna into Thessaly.

"If we don't take the pass at Tempe," he explained, "Macedon will be cut off from the rest of Greece. Thebes, Sparta, and Athens will be allowed to plot to their hearts' content. Demosthenes will sit around the supper table and gibe at the mooncalf unable to control even barbarian tribes. More important," Perdiccas scratched his beard, "we need the Thessalian cavalry, not to mention their gold!"

At last they entered the broad, sweeping vale of Tempe, which was blocked at the far end by a narrow pass between the mountains of Olympus and Ossa. Alexander ordered his troops to pitch camp and sent scouts along the coastal trackway where Ossa's precipitous side ran down to the Aegean. The scouts brought back doleful news: The pass of Tempe was heavily fortified by the Thessalian army. Alexander sent forward negotiators, demanding that they honor their treaties with his father, but his opponents sent back an insolent answer; they would wait and think about it.

"Aye," Ptolemy groaned, "and Ossa will slip into the sea before they come around to our way of thinking."

"If we advance," Niarchos spoke up, "we will be massacred. This is no mountain path and a few carts; the pass between Olympus and Ossa is at least two miles long. If we enter, the Thessalians will attack on three sides. Worse, they might let us in, close the door, and never allow us out!"

"If we sit here," Ptolemy argued, "the army will starve. If we retreat, the Thessalians will follow us and we'll be the laughingstock of Greece."

"There's no way around Olympus," Alexander declared,

shifting on his camp stool, "while Ossa is sheer cliff with the sea on one side." He grabbed makeshift maps he had ordered Simeon draw up. "So, what we need is a ladder."

"For what?" Ptolemy scoffed. "To climb the heights of Olympus? And, if we scale Ossa, the Thessalians will see what we are doing."

Alexander grinned and touched the tip of Ptolemy's nose.

"Ossa runs down to the sea, yes?"

"Aye and the tide sweeps in and out," Niarchos gibed. "And we all know what you think about swimming."

"You are a good swimmer," Alexander countered. "And thank you for volunteering, Niarchos. We have some engineers here, yes? You will take them on to the sea side of Ossa. I want you to cut steps up the cliff and build a ladder for the army to climb."

"Steps!" Niarchos blustered. "A ladder!"

"That's right." Alexander plucked up a rock. "See how it crumbles! The cliff face is as soft as this."

"You are just like Aristotle," Ptolemy grumbled.

"A good teacher," Alexander riposted. "Remember his dictum: Observe before you act. Mount Ossa has a soft, rocky surface. Niarchos, you can do it. Take your men at dusk; the Thessalians will never guess what we are planning."

Niarchos grabbed the rock and hurried out.

"How long do you think it will take?" Ptolemy asked.

"Three or four days," Alexander replied. "We'll leave the carts and cavalry here. I want to see the faces of those Thessalian chieftains when they wake up to find us deployed behind them."

His commanders and officers saw the funny side and laughed, relishing the clever strategy Alexander had devised. He gave a few more orders, deploying as many men as possible to help Niarchos. The officers left the tent. Miriam was about to follow when Alexander seized her arm.

"You remember your words about what Philip was planning?"

"Yes, of course!"

"One of those Thessalian captives we sacrificed last night told me before he died that Philip had asked them to murder certain envoys he would send to them."

"Whom?" Miranda asked.

"From what I know, the Lyncestrians!"

CHAPTER 12

THE THESSALIANS WERE taken completely by surprise. Niarchos and his engineers soon cut a stairway into the side of Mount Ossa, facing the sea. To create a diversion, the Macedonian cavalry and baggage carts looked as if they were retreating. The Thessalians thronged the pass, shouting abuse, brandishing their weapons. Meanwhile Alexander moved his phalanx men quietly and quickly up the rocky face and on to the cliff-side trackway, their movements concealed by a thick wedge of forest. Miriam, too, climbed the rock, though Perdiccas, teasing her as usual, insisted on going first; he tied a rope around her waist that, in turn, he secured to his wrist. Miriam had accomplished similar feats with other young men and women in the Gardens of Midas. She tied her skirt between her legs for modesty's sake, took a deep breath, and climbed, looking neither up nor down, left nor right. Before she knew it, Perdiccas was helping her over the cliffs. Niarchos had cut three sets of steps, each broad enough for a foot or hand, and carved in a symmetrical fashion to ease ascent. Only one soldier slipped, falling like a stone, his body bouncing against the rockface before thudding onto the shingle below. Others, who confessed they could not tolerate heights, were left below as a rear guard.

Once on the plateau, the army marched deep into the trees before Alexander gave the order to strike east. On a greasy plain, which swept down to the mouth of the pass, the Macedonian army now took up battle position; then, shaped like a bull's horn, with phalanx men in the center, it moved slowly toward the Thessalian encampment. Alexander's prediction proved correct. As soon as the Thessalians realized what had happened, they immediately sent envoys to sue for peace, declaring that they were ready to grant all of Alexander's conditions. A few days later bearded Sycthian chieftains in leather riding breeches, hair plaited over their shoulders, came out with gold and silver bowls and costly jewelry from their treasury as a tribute to the Macedonian king. Alexander met them in the center of an iron ring of phalanx men. A makeshift dais had been set up with a purple cloth thrown over a camp chair that now served as a throne. Miriam stood behind this with Ptolemy and the other officers. The Thessalian chieftains, overawed by Alexander, knelt before the throne. They offered him a tribute and renewed their treaties with Macedon. Alexander was thoroughly enjoying himself.

"Why are you so afraid?" he asked through an interpreter.

"We are only afraid of one thing," the principal chieftain replied.

Alexander grinned over his shoulder at his companions.

"And what is that?" he asked.

"We are only afraid of one thing," the chieftain repeated.

"And what is it?"

Alexander prepared to receive the supreme compliment, but the Thessalian pointed to the sky.

"That the heavens might fall on us!"

Alexander gazed speechlessly at them before glaring around at Ptolemy who'd begun to snigger. The Thessalians' faces remained impassive. Alexander sat wondering if he had been insulted or not, then he burst out laughing. He stepped down from the throne, lifted the Thessalian chieftian to his feet, and clasped his hand. Later there was feasting. An ox was roasted, Alexander toasted the Thessalian captains, received renewed promises of gold and silver for his treasury, and, above all, the superb Thessalian cavalry for his campaign.

Miriam was kept well out of sight, Alexander explaining that the Thessalians did not like women at their feasts. She stayed in a makeshift tent with some of the other women. Later that night, just as she was preparing for bed, Alexander, followed by two of his guards, came and asked for her. He took her by the arm and led her away, out to the fringes of the camp. For a while he stood staring at the pinpricks of torchlight and listening to the shouts and calls of the sentries.

"I must go back," he began, "otherwise the Thessalians will take offence." He sighed. "I keep thinking about what you said, Miriam, about Philip being a doer not a victim. I asked the Thessalian chieftain if he knew what my father had been planning. He gave the expected answer, that they were to provide him with gold and silver as well the Thessalian horsemen when he marched into the Hellespont. Only later," Alexander continued, "when the wine was flowing freely, did he confess to the other matter. My father had sent him a secret message that, before he marched on the Hellespont, he would send Macedonian envoys to treat with the Thessalian chieftains. These envoys were traitors. The Thessalians would provoke a fight and they had his permission to slay them out of hand."

"Did they know it was the Lyncestrians?" Miriam asked.

Alexander shook his head. "No, they did not. Only I know that. I found a reference to it among Philip's papers. Once his great celebrations were over, the Lyncestrian brothers were to be sent as envoys to Thessaly." Alexander faced Miriam squarely. "Philip was plotting something but, because I am too tired or, perhaps, too drunk, it escapes me."

He led Miriam back into the camp.

"And where to now?"

"Oh, we'll rest a day," Alexander responded, "then we march on Corinth. Once the rest of Greece learns what has happened here, there'll be no further problems."

He left Miriam near her tent and walked back to where the celebrations continued. For a while Miriam sat outside, her cloak wrapped about her, half listening to the sounds of the camp.

"The key to this mystery," she murmured, "is Philip." She closed her eyes. Philip had brought Cephalus from Attalus; Philip had trusted Pausanias; Philip had made arrangements for Pausanias to escape; Philip had sent those killers to wait in the palace at Aegae; Philip carried treasonable letters from Demosthenes; Philip was arranging for the Lyncestrians to be slaughtered. Miriam heard a sound and looked up with a start; there's one piece missing she thought—Attalus. Once Hecaetus returned perhaps that piece would be fitted?

The next few days were taken up with turbulent preparations. The Thessalians withdrew from the pass. The rest of the Macedonian army joined Alexander's triumphant march to Corinth, his troops soon occupying that gleaming, white-porticoed city overlooking the sea. Simeon was busy as the king dictated letters and missives to the Hellenic League. In a sense these were not necessary. Alexander's brilliant generalship and consummate victory over the Thessalians had swept before him. All Greece now awoke to the fact that, though Philip was dead, someone just as subtle, ruthless, and skillful had taken his place. More important, a Macedonian army now controlled all the routes to southern Greece. The Macedonians not only occupied Corinth but were in close marching distance of Thebes, Athens, and Sparta. Only the Spartans held out. The rest of the cities, Athens included, had already sent envoys to Corinth to reaffirm their loyalties to Alexander, hail him as captain general, and promise their total support in his coming war against Persia.

Alexander and his generals kept their faces straight and accepted this homage. The Athenians, however, were forced to wait. Alexander met them in the city council chamber of Corinth. The principal envoy Pasocles, a close friend of Demosthenes, was obviously nervous. He swaggered in with his cloak thrown over his shoulder. He extended his hands, bowed, and saluted Alexander seated before him. The Macedonian, however, totally ignored him, engrossed in whispered conversation with Hephaestion seated on his left. Alexander then turned and spoke to Ptolemy on his right. The Athenian envoy became nervous; he shuffled from foot to foot, wetting his lips, and he jumped as the guards slammed the doors behind him and stood, swords drawn.

Miriam was with Simeon where he sat, to one side, at the scribe's table.

"This could go on for hours," she murmured.

"I hope it doesn't," Simeon replied. "Pasocles looks as if he's going to either faint or wet himself."

Alexander stopped whispering to Ptolemy and, pulling at his lower lip, stared at the floor.

"Where is Demosthenes?" He brought his head up and glared at the Athenian envoy. "Demosthenes controls the Athenian mob. Demosthenes told the council that he had a vision that my father had died, that Greece had been spared a great despotism. Demosthenes should have come here to explain himself."

"Demosthenes is only one man," the Athenian envoy stammered. "Athens cannot be held responsible for what he says."

"Can't it? Can't it?" Alexander repeated. "I will decide, sir, who and what is responsible. I have evidence, however," he continued remorselessly. He held up a hand, jabbing a finger at the Athenian, "that Demosthenes knew that my father was dead long before anyone else did! That Demosthenes called my father a despot! That he dismissed me as a mooncalf!"

The Athenian shrugged. "Great King, all I can reply is that Athens is loyal, Demosthenes has fled."

"Fled?" Ptolemy interrupted, "fled where?"

Again a shrug of the shoulders. "He has gone. We are not accountable for what Demosthenes has done. Athens is loyal to Macedon. Athens will join in the holy war against Persia."

Alexander cocked his head and tapped his sandals against the floor. Miriam felt a secret thrill of excitement. This was a moment of triumph. The great city of Athens, which had lampooned Alexander as a mooncalf, a mere stripling, now trembled before him. Alexander got to his feet and approached the Athenian envoy who stepped back, but Alexander put his arm around the man's shoulder and led him across to a small alcove that looked out over the bay. They walked so close anyone would think they were lovers. Alexander whispered into Pasocles' ear. The Athenian stopped and stared round. Alexander patted him on the shoulder and walked on. Every one else stared at each other in stupefaction. Alexander and the envoy stood on the balcony. The Athenian was now talking volubly, chatting as if he were Alexander's close friend. Alexander would nod and, now and again, lean down to sniff some of the bowls of wild flowers the Corinthians had placed there. After a while the Athenian fell silent. Alexander patted him on the shoulder, clasped his hand, and snapped his fingers for the guard to open the door.

"Athens is our friend," Alexander announced, arms extended, a boyish smile on his face. "The Athenians swear eternal friendship."

"They did the same for your father!" Ptolemy yelled.

"I have sent a message back," Alexander riposted. "If Athens rebels again, if the city lifts its hand against me and mine, I will burn it to the ground! I will sow the site with salt as a warning to all Greece!"

The king leaned across and whispered to Simeon; he then stalked out of the council chamber, beckoning at Miriam to follow him.

Alexander's personal chamber lay behind the council room. Its marble floor was covered by an exquisite mosaic showing Theseus fighting the minotaur. On the walls was a freshly executed painting of Achilles swearing vengeance over his friend Patroclus, Corinth's attempt to flatter Alexander with such a blatant reference to his famed ancestor. Miriam sat on a stool. Alexander crossed to a small alcove with a statue of Apollo attired as a hunter; a small fire burned before the shrine. Alexander sprinkled some incense on the flames, pulled his cloak over his head, and for a while stood hands out, shoulders bowed, lost in prayer.

"Apollo the god of truth." He turned and came back to sit on the edge of a table, looking down at Miriam. "I've just sent a messenger," he declared, "back to Pella, summoning Antipater here."

"Why?" Miriam exclaimed.

"Because Attalus was not the traitor on the Macedonian council."

"It was Antipater?" Miriam asked.

"Yes the "A" stood for Antipater, not Attalus. I think we have made a dreadful mistake. But, there again, perhaps Macedon, without Attalus, will be a safer place?"

"What will you do?" Miriam asked.

"I'll wait to see what Antipater has to say. I am sure he has a good explanation for what the Athenian envoy told me. I am certainly very keen to hear it."

"Has Hecaetus returned?" Miriam asked.

"Soon," Alexander replied, "but I have one further place to call. I must visit Delphi, to consult the oracle as Philip did."

"To know the future?" Miriam teased.

"Yes to know the future," Alexander replied. "Before she left for Pella, Mother came to my bedroom. She had her hair groomed, her face exquisitely painted. She sat on the edge of my bed as if I were a child and she were the great Olympias. She grasped my hand and told me she had a secret."

Miriam stiffened.

"She said I was not Philip's son, that she had been visited by Ammon-Zeus and that I would find the truth and proof of this in his temple at the Oasis of Siwah on the Nile." He smiled at Miriam. "But you don't believe that, do you? Your faith won't allow a god to conceive in a woman's womb."

"We are God's image," Miriam replied. "Alexander, your greatness will depend on you, not on Olympias, or Philip, or the Oasis of Siwah; nor will you find the future at Delphi."

"I am not interested in the future." Alexander scratched the side of his face. "I keep remembering the oracle Delphi issued when Philip asked what would happen when he advanced against Persia."

" 'The bull is wreathed for sacrifice. All is ready. The slayer is at hand.' " Miriam repeated the prophecy.

"We'll be there by tomorrow afternoon." Alexander

opened the door. "When we return Hecaetus and Antipater will have arrived."

Miriam left and wandered along the porticoed corridor back to her own quarters. One of the women, Ptolemy's mistress, came running up, saying that the baths in the gymnasium were now empty and would she like to join them?

Miriam agreed and spent the rest of the day splashing or lying on thick woollen cloths beside the pool like the rest of the women. They were all eager to wash off the aches and dust of the campaign, and to be pampered by the slaves and servants of the council of Corinth. A masseuse carefully rubbed aromatic oil into Miriam's body, another clipped and rearranged her hair. Miriam made herself relax, listening to the chatter of the women, the tittle-tattle, the gossip and scandal. She only hoped Simeon would not come searching for her: her brother had definite ideas about such places, and they often argued about what a proper Jewess should and should not do. In a sense Miriam had won the argument years ago, but every so often Simeon would return like a dog to a bone.

Miriam slipped back to her own chamber. She felt hot and drowsy so she slept for a while. It was dark when she awoke; through the square, open window she could glimpse the night sky and hear the faint cries of the guards and the distant sounds of the palace. She sensed that someone else was in the chamber. Miriam pulled herself up on the bed; a faint glimmer of light showed that someone was holding an oil lamp, just to the right of the door.

"Do not be frightened, Jewess." The voice was soft and silky. "I mean you no harm."

The oil lamp was put down on a table. Miriam could make out an indistinct shape.

"Hecaetus," she declared. "I recognized your voice. I've never seen you, but how could I forget our last meeting?"

A soft laugh answered her.

"They say you are brave, Jewess."

"Who does?"

"Those in the palace. They say you are one of the few women that Alexander is not frightened of. He is frightened of women, isn't he?"

"You are not supposed to be here," Miriam replied tartly. "You are supposed to be still journeying from the Hellespont."

"I have been there and returned," Hecaetus replied, "but officially I will not be back until tomorrow." Again the laugh.

"Why the secrecy?" Miriam asked.

"I am the king's weapon. If the hand lets go of the weapon, the weapon falls but the hand remains. Oh, I do like to be long-winded. I just had to make sure it was safe."

"What do you mean, safe?"

"Oh come, come, my little Jewess. Remember, I have just returned from the Hellespont!"

"What happened there?"

"I can't possibly tell you now. As you have said, I am not supposed to be here. Yet it's all terribly puzzling, isn't it?"

"What do you mean?"

"In a while. First, I've come to clear the air. I'm sorry about the murder of that chamberlain, but he bumped into me in the dark coming out of Pausanias's room. I had no choice; he was going to scream for the guard, and I had no real excuse for being there."

"So, why were you?"

"Like you, I was curious. I wanted to find out what was happening. Everything seemed to be a maze, a muddle."

"For you, Hecaetus?" Miriam mocked, "the king's weapon, his silent shadow?"

"No, I won't lose my temper," came the serene reply. "I

said I was the king's weapon not the king's mind," he added tetchily. "That one-eyed fox, Philip, has us all on the run. It's like a play, isn't it? Everyone was given their role, their part, their lines. Philip was the playwright but then he was killed and no one knows what the plot was."

"What was yours?" Miriam asked.

"Philip had become very secretive. In the weeks before his death, as he was planning his great celebration, he began to act in a secretive, cryptic way. One thing was on his mind, his invasion of Persia—that, and the little honeypot he had married, Eurydice. I hear she's dead, poor thing!"

"Olympias always settles her accounts!"

"Ah yes," came the chuckling reply. "Olympias, an unloosed, raging tiger. I don't think I'll be going back to Pella for some time."

"What did you know about Pausanias?" Miriam asked.

"Nothing," the reply was petulant. "But that's not the real reason for my visit. I'll exchange information if I have your word that I am your friend, not your enemy. I mean no danger to you or your brother, that secretive little scribe."

"So you're more of an ally?" Miriam replied.

"To begin with," Hecaetus humored her. "But let me explain. I know nothing about Pausanias. To me, he was just one of Philip's bum boys, a sulky young man; if I had been Philip, I'd have taken his head long ago. I don't want to lie," he continued, "but my orders on the morning Philip was killed were quite simple. Contrary to popular rumor, I did not go with my companions to the palace. Four of my boys went there. Why, I don't know. Philip said he would send a message. I was to stay in the amphitheater."

"And?" Miriam asked.

"I was to look out for a Cretan archer called Cephalus. Philip suspected him of being an assassin. Now, you know Cretans; they carry these horn bows, short but powerful. I was to watch Cephalus. If he did anything untoward, such as notch an arrow to his bow, I was to kill him immediately and slip away to Philip for further orders. Now the first part of my task was easy. Cephalus was a clumsy killer. He tried to hide that leather bag under a cloak, but," Hecaetus added smugly, "I glimpsed it, and you can always tell a Cretan from the rest. I sat close behind him, a dagger in the folds of my robe. It was a splendid morning, wasn't it? Every so often I would check on my little friend to make sure he was behaving himself. Then the sun fell from heaven. I heard cries from the gate that the king had been killed. Everyone left the amphitheater. Cephalus, however, remained. I wondered what to do. Join my lads back at the palace? Or carry out the King's last order? Cephalus remained in the amphitheater and so did I. Do you know, I even wondered if Philip was playing one of his tricks, whether he was really dead or not. I decided to act. I killed Cephalus in the gateway and slipped back to the palace. I was genuinely confused and, I admit, a little resentful. I went down to Pausanias's chamber but I could find nothing. I hid in the shadows and that chamberlain just blundered into me. The rest you know."

"And Attalus?" Miriam asked.

"I can't tell you, not yet. I will hide for one more day before making my presence felt."

"You are safe," Miriam replied. "The king has no grievance against you. These lads of yours," she continued, "the ones waiting at the palace?"

"I don't know," Hecaetus replied. "Like everyone else, they were surprised by the king's death. The message never arrived."

The oil lamp was picked up.

"Good-bye, little Jewess, when we meet again, remember, you do not recognize me."

"Wait!" Miriam called. She could feel the uncertainty

coming from the figure now standing a few yards from her.

"What is it, Miriam?" He said her name softly as if she were his lover.

"You are right," she flattered, "Philip was the author of a play, but no one will know what was in his mind. So, what do you think, Hecaetus? Come, if we are allies. And if you wish my friendship?"

"I am glad you've said that," the voice replied. "Do I have your word, Miriam Bartimaeus, by your unknown God, that you are no threat to me?"

"I am no threat," she replied. "I swear!"

Miriam was pleased to see this mysterious man retake his seat.

"I do not know what was in Philip's mind when he died. Miriam, you saw the king as good-humored, generous, magnanimous, yes?"

"I and my brother were recipients of his munificence." Miriam replied.

"Philip was two people," Hecaetus continued. "The flamboyant soldier, the man who loved women, wine, young boys. He was courageous as a lion, but Philip had a dark side. You were safe, Miriam, because you were never a threat. Look at our young king bent on achieving greatness; he feared his father; what he's forgotten is how much much Philip feared him."

"What?" Miriam exclaimed.

"Philip feared Alexander," Hecaetus said defiantly. "Now and again he would sit with me; it was always the same story. How on the night of Alexander's birth, the temple of Artemis had been burned down. Whether it was or not," he added casually, "I don't know. Philip made careful searches. According to one gossip, the Persian magi saw the destruction of Artemis's temple as a prophecy of what would happen to the Persian throne and nation. There were the other stories: Olympias dreaming she had been penetrated by a thunderbolt so that fire had seeped out of her womb. You know Philip consulted Delphi on his son's birth? He received an answer that, in future, he should pay great honor and reverence to Ammun-Zeus, whose shrine lies at the Oasis of Siwah."

Miriam's hand went to her lips, fearful lest she betray what she knew.

"Oh yes," Hecaetus continued, "Philip was terrified of Alexander. And when Philip was frightened, that dark side emerged. Look at Philip's past. He waded to the throne of Macedon through a sea of blood, his own brothers, even his mother. Nothing ever stood in his path." Hecaetus scraped back the stool and stood up. "I thought of this on my journey to Attalus and back. It's a wonder," he joked, "Alexander ever reached the age of twenty! Good-bye, little Jewess!"

Miriam heard no further sound. She waited a while, then got up. She lit an oil lamp and opened the door; the gallery outside was quiet. She went back and lay on her bed. Hecaetus's words about Philip being a dramatist preparing a play had intrigued her. Once again she listed the characters and the events surrounding the king's murder. First, Olympias: she hated Philip, Philip hated her. He had divorced and virtually banished her from court. A dangerous woman seething with hatred and a desire for revenge. What had Philip intended for Olympias? Why had Philip inveigled her seer Aristander to his side? Instructing the necromancer how, on the morning of his great triumph at the amphitheater, he was to open the door to his messenger. Why were Hecaetus's men left in the palace? What message would they have received? How powerful was Olympias? A princess of Epirus, which lay on Macedon's strategic western border, but Philip had invited its king, Molossus, to court, and married him off to his daughter Cleopatra, loading him with gifts and honors. The Lyncestrians, blood kin to Philip with a claim to the Macedonian throne? Philip had apparently decided to send these on an embassy to Thessaly from which they would never return. They had seized the moment of Philip's death to make their bid, and they could have been successful but, like many others, they had underestimated Alexander. Attalus, uncle of Eurydice, Philip's new love, joint commander in chief of the forces in Aegae? He had been suspected of being in correspondence with Demosthenes, part of a wide conspiracy to kill Philip, weaken Macedon, and, in return, receive gold from Persia through Demosthenes. However, Attalus's guilt was now highly suspect. In fact he may have been completely innocent of any treason or involvement in the king's death. Cephalus? At first he seemed to have been a paid assassin sent by Attalus and financed by Demosthenes to kill the king. Now all the evidence indicated that Philip himself had brought Cephalus to Aegae. If Hecaetus was telling the truth, Cephalus was no real danger. He was simply brought to Aegae like some sacrificial goat to be killed as soon as he tried to string his bow. Pausanias? Now there was the real mystery. A man who had sought justice from Philip but received promotion instead. How had he gotten hold of Arridhaeus's knife? Why had Philip arranged the escape of his own assassin? Providing him with horses? A free pass? Miriam rubbed her eyes.

"Philip! Philip!" she muttered.

If she could only understand what had gone on in Philip's mind. And there was something else. Pausanias had killed Philip and fully intended to escape. True, it never ever goes according to plan. Perhaps Pausanias had not expected Perdiccas and his companions to pursue him so closely. Pausanias had fled into the vineyard; if he hadn't stumbled, he would have reached his horse and ridden away. But that leather bag held at the cobbler's house? It held the money and documentation; Pausanias would have needed those. So, what was missing from this puzzle? Miriam got up and swung her legs off the bed, resting her chin in her hands.

"It must be," she muttered. "It must be."

Pausanias had an accomplice, somebody who had agreed to collect that leather bag and meet him in the vineyard. But this secret friend had betrayed him. Instead of collecting a leather bag he had gone to the vineyard; yes, it must have been he who arranged for Pausanias to trip. The royal guards had caught up and that had been the end of Pausanias.

Miriam rubbed her face. But Philip? Philip had not intended to die. Of course, he hadn't planned to die. Miriam smiled and clapped her hands. Hecaetus had said it was a piece of theater. He'd also wondered if Philip was playing one of his tricks. Had something gone terribly wrong? Had Philip encouraged Pausanias to launch a murderous attack upon him?

Miriam got to her feet and paced up and down the room. Philip was full of tricks. Had he encouraged Pausanias in a pretended attack on him? And the same with Cephalus? Those letters from Demosthenes found on Philip's corpse. Would these have been found on Cephalus's body? Philip would then have had the excuse to strike against Athens and, if Pausanias had fled to Thebes, that city too could be held to account. And the Lyncestrians? Philip could send them to Thessaly and arrange for their execution. He could later claim this was a just punishment for their treasonable activities as well as give him a reason to threaten Thessaly if and when he wished. But why? Miriam paused in her pacing. Philip wished to march against Persia; he wanted to leave no opposition at home. If he could get rid of the Lyncestrians, bludgeon Thebes, Athens, and Thessaly into terrified submission, depose his plotting queen Olympias, exile Alexander's friends and keep Alexander closely under scrutiny, Philip would be safe. But what had gone wrong? Was it a mere accident? Had Pausanias stumbled? Or Philip pressed too hard against the knife?

Miriam went to the window and looked out. The sky was already lightening. She heard shouts and the clatter of horses below and realized the royal grooms were preparing for Alexander's imminent departure for Delphi. What would the king find there, she mused? Some solution to this mystery? Or had she found it already? One of Philip's tricks that had gone terribly wrong? If she could only discover Pausanias's secret friend and ally. Miriam went and sat on the edge of the bed; she pulled her sandal toward her and stared down at it. She picked it up and examined the sole curiously. She had missed something. A memory began to nag.

"What was it?" she whispered.

Something she had seen on the day Philip had been killed? Something that had intrigued her but she had then forgotten about? She sighed and slipped her sandals on.

CHAPTER 13

MIRIAM DID NOT go to Delphi. Alexander invited her to the council chamber and explained.

"Just a group of us," he declared. "We'll ride by fast horses. I want you to stay here. If Antipater comes, soothe him. Lull his suspicions. I'll be back within a day."

Miriam was disappointed. She had only been to Delphi once and had looked forward to visiting the shrine with its great marble porticoes, painted walls, sacred way, and the strange, blood-tingling music of its priests.

"You are a woman," Simeon explained, as they walked through the gardens after Alexander had left. "They won't allow a woman into the shrine, and Alexander expects difficulties."

"What difficulties?"

"It's nearly autumn; Apollo leaves the shrine and travels into the west." Simeon shrugged. "Or so they say. Anyway, Pythia will give no oracle, and Alexander will be rebuffed." He paused. "Well, we have our task here, entertaining that old fox Antipater."

As it was, Alexander returned before Antipater arrived. The king rode back into Corinth celebrating "his victory over the Pythia." She had refused to prophesy. She claimed Apollo had left. Accordingly, Alexander must wait before she sat upon the sacred rock, breathed in the dream-enhancing smoke, and peered into the tripod that would reveal the future.

"That didn't stop our king," Simeon exclaimed. "He marched into the temple, seized the priestess, and dragged her out of the shrine. 'Prophesy!' the king ordered. The priestess struggled, but Alexander held her fast. 'Prophesy!' he repeated. 'Alexander, let me go!' the priestess cried. 'You are invincible!' " Simeon paused, moving the pieces of papyrus around on his desk.

"And?" Miriam asked.

"Alexander let the priestess go: 'That's the only oracle I need,' he declared."

"And the other business?" Miriam asked.

Simeon glanced at her in puzzlement.

"Never mind," she declared, resolving to leave other questions till she met Alexander.

Miriam had come into the royal writing chamber, "to bother," as she put it, her brother. Simeon now went back to his copying. Miriam moved the scraps of papyrus around on the table until her brother clucked his tongue in annoyance and so she left.

A page boy met her, saying that the king was in the gymnasium and wished to see her immediately. Miriam went down there, across the sun-baked courtyard into a long, narrow room with a pool on the far side fed by a spring. Alexander had apparently been wrestling, then gone for a swim and, by the time Miriam joined him, he was dressed but still shaking the water from his hair, which he cleared from his forehead by placing a green headband around his brow.

Hephaestion, Ptolemy, and the others were there, some on the massage tables, others lounging about teasing each other. Alexander looked tired after his journey. He told his companions to wait and walked with Miriam up and down the cool collonade.

"Antipater hasn't arrived yet," he declared. "He's probably wary of what is going to happen but, if my spies are correct, he'll probably be here this afternoon. But come, we have someone else to meet."

He led her back to his chamber littered with maps, pieces of clothing, armor, and a small statue of Apollo that Alexander had bought at Delphi.

"I hear your journey was successful."

Alexander smiled over his shoulder. He poured himself some water from a jug surrounded by blocks of quickly melting ice.

"Do you want some?"

Miriam shook her head.

"You should drink that slowly," she advised. "Remember what Aristotle told us: Cold and heat don't mix."

Alexander sat on the couch opposite her.

"My companions don't like these little meetings." He smiled over his cup at her. "But, and I know you won't believe me, I haven't told them the reason and I won't until I know the truth. After all, one of them could be involved."

"I don't think so."

Alexander pulled a face. "You've reached that conclusion very quickly."

"Your companions were taken by surprise," she observed. "Philip exiled them quickly. They were hardly given time to pack, never mind plot!"

Alexander raised an eyebrow and put the cup of water on the table between them.

"The oracle was wrong," he began.

"What do you mean, the oracle was wrong? Which oracle?"

" 'The bull is wreathed for sacrifice. All is ready. The slayer is at hand.' I learned this after I seized the priestess and forced her to prophesy that I was invincible." Alexander grinned. "Insolent of me, wasn't it? But what else could I do? Anyway, I asked her about the oracle given to my father. She listened, then shook her head. 'I didn't say that,' the Pythia declared. 'I said the ram was wreathed for slaughter. All was ready. The slayer was at hand.' Now, isn't that strange; why did Philip change it?"

Alexander rose and stood by a window.

"I love Corinth," he declared, "the city, the sea, the land, the mountains. The air is so fresh!"

"As it is in Macedon."

"No, no, it's more civilized here. In Macedon you can smell the blood in the wind, that iron tang fills your mouth and turns your stomach."

"Did you fear your father?" Miriam asked suddenly.

"I worshipped him and I feared him," Alexander replied, "but I don't think he ever loved me. I could never tell what he was thinking. He always reminded me of, well, when I was a boy, of a day full of sunshine. However, as I grew older, I began to see the shadows. The more I got to know him, the longer and deeper those shadows grew. I'll never know what he really thought. He feared Olympias. Isn't that surprising?" Alexander turned around and came back. "He hated her but he truly feared her. I believe he married Eurydice not because of lust or love; he just wanted to show Olympias that he was no longer frightened of her."

"Did he fear you?"

Alexander looked at her in surprise.

"Fear me?" Alexander shook his head. "That thought has never occurred to me until recently. But, talking of Philip—"

Alexander walked to the door and opened it. A blond-haired, sallow-faced, foppishly dressed young man slipped like a shadow into the room. He was attired in a spotless white robe with a red frieze along the hem, his fingers were be-ringed, his face painted. Alexander waved him to a stool on Miriam's right. She studied this foppish, quietly moving man and realized this must be Hecaetus, Philip's killer, the king's weapon.

In the marketplace Miriam wouldn't have given him a second glance. His gaze met hers and she shivered; on second thought, she reflected, she would. His eyes were light, indistinct in color, like those of a fish and, in spite of the smiling lips, devoid of any light or life. He bowed imperceptibly as Alexander introduced her.

"I have heard of Miriam the Jewess," Hecaetus whispered. "One of your companions, Sire, from the Gardens of Midas. They say she has a sharp mind." Hecaetus turned his face slightly away from Alexander and winked. Miriam smiled back.

"What news?" Alexander began. "I know, I know," Alexander waved a hand. "I met you this morning but this time tell me in detail."

"Attalus is dead," Hecaetus replied. "I and my companions went across the Hellespont. After two days' travel we entered the Macedonian camp. Everything is in good order. The news of your father's death has already reached the army and a proper period of mourning has been carried out. I followed your instructions and met with Parmenio. I told him that you were in control of Macedon and its army, and how the council had accepted you as Philip's successor."

"And Parmenio?" Alexander asked.

"I also told him that you had confirmed him in his command and that he and his family in Macedon would receive further marks of preferment."

"In other words, he accepted the bribe?"

"Like a fish does a hook. I then confided that Attalus was a traitor. That you had proof of his correspondence with Demosthenes as well as the Persian court."

"And Parmenio accepted this?"

"Sire, he first rejected it as impossible; Attalus was Macedonian and one of your father's sworn hearth companions. I then put it to Parmenio, was he calling you a liar? Of course, Parmenio replied he was not and would accept your judgment. Later that same day, in the evening, we visited Attalus. He was nervous, even more so when a number of guards, handpicked by Parmenio, arrested him and took him outside the camp, well away from the troops. I put it to him that he was a traitor, that he had been corresponding with Demosthenes, and that he was involved in the plot against your father."

"And?" Alexander asked.

"He sat like a man hit by a thunderbolt. At first he thought I was joking. I told him in detail what had happened in Aegae, how sentence had been passed. He had three choices: he could come back with me to Pella and face Olympias, I could execute him now, or he could take his own life. At first Attalus raged. We had him in a tent closely guarded." Hecaetus stopped and stared out through the window.

Miriam watched, fascinated. Hecaetus seemed devoid of any emotion. He'd had a hand in the destruction of one of Philip's most powerful commanders, yet he sat coolly describing it as anyone else would a walk on a summer's evening.

"Continue," Alexander said.

"We let Attalus rage. He shouted and screamed. He called

you baseborn, not worthy of Philip. Then he calmed down. He asked if he could write a letter to you. I agreed, provided he did it immediately. He became more composed. He wrote the letter, sealed it, and handed it to me. Parmenio left the tent; he said he had no stomach for what was going to happen. Attalus asked if we would protect his family, that he was innocent of any charge and so were they. He drank a cup of wine and then arranged for some hemlock to be put in the second cup. He died quietly. I left his corpse for Parmenio and decided to leave immediately." Hecaetus coughed. "Attalus was popular with the troops. I didn't think it was safe for me to stay."

"And the letter?"

Hecaetus handed it over. Alexander broke the seal and read it quickly. He sat, tapping his foot. He studied the letter again, wiping tears from his eyes.

"Do you think he was innocent?" Alexander asked.

"Of involvement in Philip's death, yes."

"Of treason?"

Hecaetus smiled wryly. "That is more difficult, sire, to answer. There is treason and there is treason. If a plot succeeds it's no longer treason; it's only treason if it fails."

"I didn't know you liked riddles, Hecaetus."

The royal assassin bowed. "Sire, accept my apologies. Let me explain. Attalus was Philip's man, body and soul. His niece was married to the king. He was joint commander in chief of Philip's army in Asia. He would never plot with Demosthenes. He had nothing to gain and everything to lose." Hecaetus's fishlike eyes studied Alexander. "But I'm telling you what you know already, aren't I, sire?"

Alexander nodded.

"However," the assassin continued, "Attalus hated you. He hated your mother."

"I know that," Alexander interrupted. "He called me a

bastard and I threw my wine cup at him. Because of Attalus, my father drew his sword against me."

"Your father was drunk," Hecaetus explained soothingly.

"Father was never really drunk!" Alexander snapped.

"There was one other person he hated," Hecaetus added. "He said he wished he'd killed Antipater before he left Macedon. He had made one mistake in his life and that was it. He had forgotten how cunning the old, one-eyed bastard was."

"What else do you know?" Alexander asked.

"Of what, Sire?"

"Of my father's mind?"

Hecaetus's eyes moved quickly to Miriam.

"The day he died," Alexander continued. "Yes, yes, I know, you've told me. Some of your men were in the palace and you were left to take care of Cephalus. What else did my father ask you?"

Hecaetus tried to hide his agitation by moving the rings on his fingers. Miriam could see he was calculating how much the king knew.

"If you lie, Hecaetus," Alexander declared, "there is nothing for you here. What else did my father say?"

Hecaetus pointed at Miriam. "I was to ensure she and her brother left Macedon safely."

"When?" Alexander asked.

"The king didn't explain. He simply said that, when he gave the sign, Miriam Bartimaeus and her brother Simeon were to be given safe custody out of Macedon."

"Where to?"

"To his agent in Thebes, Lysippus the silver merchant."

"Thebes!" Miriam exclaimed.

"No," Alexander nodded. "A wise choice. Lysippus has the means, pack ponies, ships. Perhaps that's why Father was writing to him in the days before his death. I've seen the entries in the accounts." Alexander gripped Hecaetus's fingers and squeezed tightly; the assassin tried not to wince. "But you are forgetting something, are you not?"

"Yes, Sire. Philip said they were to be taken out safely and not to be killed like the rest!"

"Like the rest?" Alexander asked. "Who was my father referring to?"

Hecaetus shook his head. "Sire, I swear, I never knew!"

The king released his hand. "You may go, Hecaetus. Stay in the shadows like a good dog until I whistle again."

Once the assassin had closed the door behind him, Alexander handed Attalus's letter to Miriam.

"Read it aloud. Slowly, carefully, Miriam!"

" 'To Alexander King of Macedon. Attalus, Philip's general.' " Miriam looked up, Alexander shrugged. " 'Philip's general sends greetings and congratulations. The news of your great father's death reached the army before Philip's creature, Hecaetus, ever arrived here. I thought he'd brought news that I was to be confirmed in my command but the fates have decided otherwise. I am to die; I will do so by my own hand, not executed like a common criminal. I had no knowledge of Philip's plans or what was in his mind. If I had, he would not have been murdered and I would not be preparing for my own death. I beg you to look after members of my family; they, too, are innocent. Farewell, Attalus.' "

Miriam lowered the piece of papyrus.

"I wonder what he meant?" she said. "About knowing what was in Philip's mind? Attalus hints at something but doesn't say what." She paused at a knock on the door.

Alexander put a finger to his lips. "Someone has arrived who might be able to help." He raised his voice, "Come in, Antipater!"

The one-eyed veteran strode into the room in a show of

bravado to hide his nervousness. He sat down without bidding, resting a hand on his knees; he looked at Miriam from head to toe, then turned to Alexander.

"You sent for me!"

"Your king sent for you, Antipater!"

The general bowed.

"And how is dear Mother?"

"Dear Mother is as dear as always," Antipater growled. "I have to remind her she is co-regent, not queen and lord of all."

Alexander chuckled, but his eyes didn't smile.

"You hated Attalus, didn't you?"

"I couldn't stand him." The words were spat out. "In the beginning, Alexander, there were three: Philip, Parmenio, and myself until Attalus began to worm his way in."

"Were you and Father lovers? I mean, in your younger days?"

Antipater shook his head, though his lower lip began to tremble.

"But you would have liked to have been, wouldn't you?"

"I loved Philip." Antipater raised a hand. "I had no part in his death!"

"But you were part of his scheme?"

"Your father hated Demosthenes," Antipater declared, "and he feared Athens. He was going to lead his army across the Hellespont and he knew that, when he marched east, Demosthenes would stir up Athens like a hornets' nest. Anyone who invades Asia must fear the Athenian fleet. All it has to do is blockade the Hellespont and our communications are cut off. Philip was a soldier not a sailor."

"And so he was trying to lure Demosthenes out into the open?"

"Yes." Antipater smiled at Miriam. "Trust the little Jewess to use her noddle. Philip instructed me to enter into secret negotiations with Demosthenes, to draw him into the open as well as find out if there were other traitors in Macedon."

"And were there?"

"Yes, the Lyncestrians." Antipater shrugged. "But Philip knew that. They were like hunting foxes: they would seize any opportunity, as you found out."

"But you were hunting someone else, weren't you?" Miriam asked.

Antipater twisted his sandaled foot.

"You were hunting Alexander, weren't you?"

The old veteran nodded.

"But that's impossible!" Alexander sprang to his feet. "Can Father really think I would enter into treason with that prattle head in Athens?"

"Your father feared you," Antipater snapped. "There you have it. By all that's holy, Alexander, you are twenty years of age. You would not be the first to plot against his father. Philip thought there was a possibility."

"And?" Miriam asked.

"I found nothing," Antipater replied. "Nevertheless, Demosthenes rose to the bait, painting a picture of Antipater being ruler of Macedon or enriching myself on Persian gold. I played him along, on Philip's orders of course. Cephalus was brought from Asia by Philip, ostensibly to take part in a great archery contest, part of the royal celebrations. However, I gave him secret instructions that he was to shoot Philip at the King's crowning moment of glory. I promised him wealth and sanctuary. I also showed him Demosthenes' letter. Well, you know Cretans, they'd skin their mothers if you offered the right amount!"

"What proof do we have of this?" Alexander asked.

"You've all the proof in the world!" Antipater snapped.

He folded his arms. "You must have found Demosthenes' letter on the king?"

"Yes we did!"

"That would have been found upon Cephalus."

Alexander chewed the quick of his thumb.

"Of course!" he breathed, "you lured Demosthenes and the Persians into the open. You bring Cephalus into the amphitheater, the Cretan rises to his feet, arrow strung to his bow, but Hecaetus strikes and kills him. The Cretan falls. In the ensuing uproar his corpse is searched and letters are found upon him from Demosthenes of Athens."

"But how would they have explained away the 'A'?" Miriam asked.

Antipater shrugged. "Philip would have only published extracts."

"You knew all this, didn't you?" Miriam interrupted. "And you misled me? You put the blame on Attalus. You made him the scapegoat!"

"What else did Father plot?" Alexander broke in. "What other subtle schemes writhed and curled in that wily brain?"

"That's all he told me." Antipater held his hand up. "I was to write to Demosthenes and depict myself as a malcontent, eager for power in Macedon. I was to draw the Athenians out into the open."

"An abortive plot," Alexander declared. "And that would have given my father a pretext for what, Antipater? He must have discussed that with you?"

"Philip feared Athens. He'd have imposed harsh conditions: the surrender of Demosthenes, the loan of the fleet, hostages, and the destruction of the long walls."

"Of course!" Miriam exclaimed. "And Philip marched into Asia with a threat back home settled once and for all."

"And afterward?" Alexander asked.

"When Philip was assassinated," Antipater replied, "I didn't know what was happening. My world collapsed. The sun fell from the heavens. Who would want Philip dead? Demosthenes' assassin was in the amphitheater. Everybody was suspect: you, Olympias, Attalus. As the dust began to settle," he coughed, "I became frightened. I feared Attalus. Eurydice, his niece, had given birth to Philip's son and what if those letters were revealed? What proof would I have had that I acted on Philip's orders? Only the gods know what Demosthenes would have done!"

"He has a letter from you, hasn't he?"

Antipater nodded. "Nothing too treasonable or incriminating, but enough to make people think. Enough for them to point the finger and say Antipater was a traitor." His voice shook. "Even," he added, "that Antipater was Philip's assassin. On the day your father died, I wasn't being calculating and wily. I froze with fear." His fingers covered his blind eye. "I panicked. If the Lyncestrians won, what would happen to me? If Alexander won, what would happen to me?"

Miriam saw the old soldier's hands begin to tremble.

"I was terrified. Philip was dead. Philip and his madcap schemes. I don't have to say any more. I threw my lot in with you; I kept my word."

"But you decided to use the crisis to settle with Attalus?" Miriam asked.

Antipater nodded. "I knew you'd come tripping along asking questions, so I sowed the seeds. About Attalus knowing something secret from Philip's past." Antipater played with a tassle on his belt. "We all know the stories about Alexander's conception; Attalus fanned Philip's suspicions. He wanted Alexander put aside in favor of Eurydice's brat. After Philip's assassination, I seized the choice to turn the tables on Attalus. I depicted him as a potential assassin and traitor. Before you ask, Alexander, yes, I knew you'd rise to the bait. You and your mother hated Attalus. Because of him, Philip married Eurydice! Attalus was also the first to cast doubts on your legitimacy."

Miriam stared at this grizzled old warrior; how deftly he had played her. She quietly cursed her own arrogance. She wondered how many others had fed her the lies they wanted her to swallow.

"Did Demosthenes know it was you?" Miriam asked quickly.

"He guessed. I only used the letter "A." Philip instructed me on that."

"But Demosthenes is no fool?" Miriam asked. "He would need further proof—"

"That someone close to Philip was prepared to betray, even kill him?" Antipater finished the question.

"Yes," Miriam replied. "Antipater, Antipater, no more games, no more stumbling around in the dark! How many letters did you write?"

"Two."

"And what did they say?"

"Both were in a cipher. They talked of removing a rival."

"Oh, come, come!" Miriam went and stood over the old warrior. "Demosthenes would need more than that."

"I used the royal seal of Macedon."

Alexander clapped his hands. "And no greater proof there could be. Only a chosen few are allowed anywhere near that seal. Demosthenes must have been beside himself with delight."

"He asked for that," Antipater broke in. "He asked me to clarify and prove who I was. Or rather that I was close to Philip; otherwise the Persians would not accept.

"I can see that." Alexander rubbed his chin. "Demosthenes is in Athens, which, like the other cities, has accepted Philip as captain general of Greece. Philip intends to march against Persia. Demosthenes, however, suddenly receives a letter from someone close to Philip. The writer offers to betray, even kill Philip. Demosthenes asks for proof and you supply it. You give the first letter of your name. Demosthenes must have suspected who it was, especially when you confirmed your missive with the royal seal; that would be enough for him and those who supplied Persian gold. Philip would die. Macedon would be divided." Alexander tapped his chest. "And the mooncalf, I'd perish in the slaughter."

Antipater nodded.

"And the troops beyond the Hellespont on Persia's border?" Miriam asked.

Antipater snorted with disdain. "Demosthenes dismissed them as a body without a head. If civil war raged in Macedon, the army would have come straight home, probably hounded every inch of the way by Persian cavalry."

"Demosthenes must now be a very surprised man," Alexander taunted.

"Sire," Antipater emphasized the title. "Sire, everyone has underestimated your victory at Tempe." Antipater spread his hands. "Philip would have been proud."

"And the Lyncestrians?" Miriam asked.

Antipater pulled a face. "Philip would have taken care of them. They only struck at you because of the chaos."

"And Olympias?"

"I know nothing except Philip's hatred of his former queen."

"And Pausanias?"

"By Apollo!" Antipater murmured. "Again, I know nothing except the gossip. Pausanias's treachery came as a surprise. It destroyed Philip's plot. At first I thought Demosthenes was responsible." He shook his head. "But I couldn't see how." He looked askance at Alexander. "Then,

Sire, I thought of Olympias, even you." He chewed the corner of his lip. "When I saw Cephalus's corpse, I knew Hecaetus had been busy, but he's an assassin; he'd been given such an order, he'd carry it out." Antipater drew in his breath. "I was confused, but decided to use the crisis and strike at Attalus, shift the blame to him. I thanked the gods that his name began with the same letter as mine."

"And there is nothing else?" Miriam crouched next to this wily, old fox. "Antipater, there's nothing else is there?"

Antipater shook his head, but Miriam saw it: a quick lick of the lips, that blink of the good eye. You are lying, she thought. You may have told us what you know but not what you suspect.

Antipater patted her gently on the head and got to his feet.

"Sire, I am under suspicion?"

Alexander shook his head. "You may return to Pella. Give my love to Mother."

Antipater bowed, nodded to Miriam, and left. Miriam made to follow but Alexander told her to stay. A staff officer came in. Alexander took him out into the passageway and Miriam was left longer than she expected. She whiled away the time by sitting at the writing desk littered with small scraps of parchment. She picked up a quill and wrote down the first letters of the names of the principals: Olympias, Philip, Pausanias, Alexander, Antipater, Attalaus, Cephalus. Alexander came back into the room to say he would be even longer and would she stay? Miriam smiled and went back to her doodling.

Antipater and Hecaetus, she reasoned, have provided some insight into Philip's mind: He was determined to remove all opposition before he marched on Persia. Miriam moved the scrap of paper representing the dead king into the center of the table; on the left she placed all those whom

Philip considered his allies and, on the right, those who would be regarded as enemies or threats. She picked up another scrap bearing the final draft of a letter, and her stomach clenched. She closed her eyes and again blamed her own arrogance as well as Philip's skill as a consummate actor. She moved the scraps representing herself and her brother. Where should they go? Miriam stared up at the ivory cornices of the room. In her mind she went back to the amphitheater in Aegae: Philip, Molossus, and Alexander walking through the gateway. Pausanias's attack, his flight through the vineyard, his fall, the horses at the far end. Miriam looked down at the scraps of parchment; she was so absorbed that Alexander was standing beside her before she realized. She looked up.

"I know," she whispered. "I think I know the truth, but we must return to Aegae."

CHAPTER 14

THE JOURNEY BACK to Aegae took five days. Alexander was only too willing to return to deal with certain matters before returning to Pella for the final preparations in his expedition against Persia. The king was pleased by events of Corinth. The Greek states, with the exception of Sparta, had confirmed his title as captain general of Greece. Athens now posed no problem and Demosthenes was exiled.

"It's Thebes I worry about," Alexander told his officers the night before they entered Aegae. "Thebes has assured us of its loyalty, but we'll see."

Alexander made no reference to what Miriam had been doing. Some of his companions, however, particularly the sharp-witted Ptolemy, were becoming suspicious.

"Why not let the matter be?" He glanced sharply at Miriam, jealous of Alexander's trust in her. "Philip is dead, his body cremated; Alexander, you wear his crown and sit on his throne. What does it matter now?"

"It matters to me," Alexander retorted. "In the end I will know the truth."

When they arrived at Aegae, the army remained encamped outside the walls. Alexander, on the night of their return to the old palace, took Miriam out onto the portico overlooking the ground where his father's remains had been cremated.

"In a sense Ptolemy is correct," he declared. "There must be an end to all this."

"There soon will be," Miriam assured him. "This afternoon, I must go down to the amphitheater again."

Simeon, too, was becoming concerned by Miriam's absorption in the task.

"You don't keep me informed," he protested just before she left their quarters. "Both of us were assigned to this task."

"No, Simeon, I was, but perhaps you could have been more helpful!" And Miriam walked out before Simeon could prolong the quarrel.

She found the amphitheater deserted but signs of Philip's great triumph still remained. A tattered banner, pennants, some of the masks that had decorated the walls. The place was eerie, desolate, a dwelling place for ghosts. Miriam stood in the open gateway and stared down the road along which Philip had walked to his death. In her mind's eye she could see the three of them: Molossus, Philip, and Alexander. She pretended to be Pausanias. She drew an imaginary knife, walked forward, and struck quickly. She then hurried across to the deserted shrine of Dionysus, skirting the building and the olive grove. There were many paths she could have followed, small winding trackways, but she took the main thoroughfare, a broad, beaten trackway that led down to the end of the vineyard; its back gate still stood open. As she walked, Miriam tripped on some of the vine shoots and tendrils that snaked across the path. Sometimes they were long and thick as rope. She reached the place where Pausanias had stumbled. She picked up the vine shoot and, using it as a lead, walked in among the vines to the place where the person who'd tripped Pausanias had hidden. From where she stood Miriam could clearly see the trackway. In her imagination she watched Pausanias run toward it; he'd be looking up, staring at the horseman waiting at the far side of the gate. She picked up the vine shoot; on the trackway it rose at least five or six inches from the ground. A perfect trap. Miriam dropped the shoot and, instead of going back onto the trackway, made her way through the vineyard. It seemed to go on forever but she kept bearing left, following the narrow pathway laid out by the vine growers. Now and again she would be out in the open, and Miriam realized she was skirting Aegae and could glimpse the roof of the palace.

At last she reached a small gateway. Miriam went through it, crossed some wasteland, and found she was on the edge of the derelict cemetery where Aristander had taken her. This now lay silent under the afternoon sun, apart from the chirping of a bird and the hum of insects. She climbed the crumbling wall and found that she was blocked from the rest of the cemetery by a large, ancient boxlike tomb covered in thick moss and lichen. Miriam went around this. She stopped and looked down; her dress was covered in bits of green—soft and feathery lichen from the tomb she'd brushed by. Her sandals were much worse, dirty and stained with crushed grapes she'd trodden on. Miriam crouched to wipe them but the juice was ingrained on both the sole and the leather thongs.

"Of course!" she whispered, "vine growers never wear sandals. Their feet are always bare!"

Miriam got up and returned to the palace. She washed and changed and sent a page asking if Alexander would grant her an audience. An hour later she was ushered into the royal presence. Alexander was sitting, cross-legged, on the floor surrounded by maps and documents. Miriam had prepared her speech well. She had rehearsed it time and again on the journey back from Corinth.

"You are finished, aren't you?" Alexander asked, climbing to his feet.

"Yes, I think so."

Alexander's face took on a guarded look.

"Don't say there are going to be more accusations and executions."

Miriam shook her head.

"Well, we'd best do it comfortably."

Alexander ushered her to a couch. He took a small camp stool and sat opposite, crossing his arms.

"Miriam, we will not be disturbed."

"I want to talk about your father," Miriam began.

"Is he my father?" Alexander retorted. "Did Philip sire me?"

"I don't know," Miriam replied truthfully. "Alexander." She stroked the back of his hand softly. "I don't truly know and, to be honest, I don't think Philip knew; the same could be said for Olympias. What is more important is that Philip truly feared you. Despite his cynicism, Philip half-believed that you were the son of Ammon-Zeus, hence his detestation of the shrine at Siwah. He feared that you might prove greater than he, destined for a fame he would never have. Over the years Olympias baited him with this. Philip was proud of you, determined that you be his successor but, as you grew older and showed the promise of greatness, fear replaced the pride. Philip wanted to be the ruler of Greece as well as Greece's vengeance against the Persians. That was his great dream. He was probably terrified that you might take it from him."

"Yes I understand that," Alexander replied. "I once asked Father if he conquered the world what would be left for me?" He pulled a face. "Philip looked strangely at me. I had meant it as a joke; he probably thought I was serious."

"Philip was born into a bloody, violent family," Miriam continued. "He fought and killed his brothers, his mother, her lover, any rival to the throne of Macedon. Philip liked to act the bluff soldier, compassionate and generous, but the real Philip? I suppose he was a frightened boy, terrified that his toys would be taken away from him. Philip wanted to march on Persia but, behind him, he would leave a host of enemies: Olympias constantly plotting against him, Thebes and Athens seething with resentment, Demosthenes with his sharp, bitter tongue always ready to stir up opposition, the Lyncestrians, ever watchful, ever treacherous. What happens, Philip must have thought, if I cross to Persia and the whole of Greece rises in revolt behind me? Philip was cunning. Do you remember when he besieged Byzantium?"

"Oh yes," Alexander intervened. "I know the story well. Philip had to call the siege off. He later sent a message saying that the leader of the garrison had offered to betray the city to him. Philip got his revenge; the Byzantines executed the garrison commander."

"Yes," Miriam returned to her explanation, "that was our Philip, cunning and ruthless." She paused. "What I am going to say, Alexander, will hurt you."

"Continue," he insisted.

"Philip was preparing a bloodbath," Miriam declared. "He wanted to start again. He'd divorced and repudiated Olympias, taken a new wife and queen who had given him a baby son, the little and now lamented Caranus. Philip began to weave his plot. Olympias was a princess from Epirus, which adjoined Macedon. If Philip left for Persia, Olympias might flee back there and stir up resentment and rebellion."

"So Philip brings Molossus here and marries him to my half-sister Cleopatra?"

"Yes. Molossus is malleable. Philip would have had him as an ally while Olympias would be deprived of a power base."

"And me?" Alexander asked.

"Philip was also moving against you. He'd exiled your companions. More important, I suspect Philip was the source of the rumors that you were illegitimate and not a fitting successor to the throne of Macedon. Philip needed you isolated and vulnerable. He also sent you those mocking quotations because he wanted your resentment to become more public."

"In which case he was very successful," Alexander replied.

"That was only the beginning," Miriam continued. "Philip's scheme was much greater than that. The key to it was Pausanias, an unstable young man who had been raped by Attalus and his cronies. He'd gone to Philip for justice. Philip ordered Attalus to remain silent about the incident while Pausanias, a former lover, was promoted." Miriam paused, rubbing her face. "For some of this I have no proof. However, let's first deal with Pausanias: In the weeks preceding the assassination, stories about Pausanias's rape were common gossip."

"And who do you think was the source?"

"Why Philip himself." Miriam clicked her fingers. "I have no proof but it's a piece that fits in the puzzle. Now we know how Philip trapped Demosthenes. He used old Antipater for that. The Lyncestrians were marked down for a swift murder. True, Philip was the unsuspecting victim that morning. Perhaps it was just as well; he was planning a violent bloodbath and the spark for this was your death."

Alexander paled.

"I'm sorry," Miriam declared. "Philip was intent on your murder. Delphi sent that message, 'The ram is wreathed for the Slaughter.' Philip changed it deliberately to the bull so as to represent Persia; a ram is the personal sign of the god Ammon-Zeus."

"The Delphic Oracle was speaking about me, wasn't she?" Alexander gasped.

"Somehow or other," Miriam affirmed, "the Delphic Oracle, either by its own power or simple deduction, was sending Philip a warning. Philip was frightened that Olympias might detect something so he changed the ram to a bull. Philip had also taken Arridhaeus's knife, the one with the hilt shaped in the form of a charioteer, and given it to Pausanias. Pausanias would kill you; Arridhaeus would also be implicated."

"Philip intended to sweep the board, didn't he?" Alexander spoke as if to himself.

Miriam became alarmed at the sheen of sweat on his face.

"Yes he did," she replied briskly. "Pausanias would kill you and flee. Philip had directed him to Thebes."

"Which would give Philip a pretext for threatening that city."

"Of course," Miriam replied.

"But," Alexander rose and filled a wine cup that he didn't dilute with water. "If I was killed at the gateway, Philip, surely, would not have gone ahead into the amphitheater?"

"No, no," Miriam confessed. "That puzzled me at first. However, we are looking at the sequence of events as we saw them, not as Philip intended. This is what would have happened. Philip and you would have entered the amphitheater, taking your seats on the dais. Philip would not want that disturbed. During the ceremony, Cephalus would make his move. Hecaetus would kill him. You, your father, and Molossus would leave the amphitheater. Pausanias would strike, stab you, and flee. Cephalus's body would be searched. Philip would produce letters from Demosthenes.

Athens would be blamed for that. Pausanias, because he fled to Thebes, would also invoke the royal wrath and give Philip further grievances. Meanwhile Philip had planned other deaths, in particular Olympia's!"

Alexander just shook his head.

"I'm afraid so," Miriam insisted. "Why else did Philip invite his rejected and divorced wife and queen to Aegae? Once you were dead, Philip would have sent a message to the assassins in the palace and Olympias would have died. She had to, can't you see Alexander? Philip couldn't march on Persia and leave little Eurydice and Caranus to your mother's mercy. Arridhaeus, too, would have been swept up in Philip's bloody cleansing of his palace."

"But Arridhaeus is a half-wit!"

"He can still be used," Miriam insisted. "As a figurehead, for rebellion, a possible puppet on the throne. No, within a matter of days, Philip would have removed Olympias, Alexander, Arridhaeus, the Lyncestrians, not to mention having grievances against both Athens and Thebes. I think that old fox, Antipater, knew something was about to happen. There was always the danger of Macedon slipping into chaos, hence his words to Arridhaeus about being king." Miriam shivered. "Do you know it could have happened, a bloodbath in which only the half-wit escaped."

"Philip intended to remove us all!" Alexander shook his head.

"It stands to reason," Miriam insisted. "There would be no one left in Greece to threaten Philip once he marched, no bothersome son, no malicious ex-wife, no Lyncestrian mischiefmakers, no opposition from Thebes or Athens."

"But how could Philip explain this to all of Greece?"

"He wouldn't have to. You were already isolated, Alexander. Rumors were rife that you were illegitimate. Your companions were exiled. You must never forget the night you and Attalus quarreled; Philip drew his sword against you. Now, that was a clumsy mistake but this—" Miriam emphasized the points with her fingers. "There are many in Greece who would like to see Athens and Thebes humbled. The Lyncestrians were troublemakers. And who loves Olympias? Philip would declare that she was part of a conspiracy."

"What conspiracy?"

"Against his wife, his new child, his kingdom. And you were a part of this conspiracy." Miriam drew in a deep breath. "Let us imagine Philip had been successful. Philip would have had the best of both worlds; you were dead and Philip could now blacken your memory. A mad man had slain you but this was only the judgment of the gods on an impious man who may or may not have been his son. This is the explanation Philip would have given. He would have portrayed you as discontented and rebellious, a dabbler in treason!"

"Treason!" Alexander exclaimed.

"Demosthenes' letters!" Miriam replied.

Alexander's hand flew to his mouth.

"Look at them again," Miriam offered. "They are addressed to someone whose name begins with "A," who could identify himself with the royal seal of Macedon. It wouldn't be far-fetched for Philip to claim that Demosthenes was writing to you!"

"But Demosthenes dismissed me as a mooncalf."

"That's right," Miriam replied. "Some weakling, deeply jealous of his father. Old Antipater suspected what your father may have been plotting."

"And Pausanias would have allowed himself to be so easily managed?"

"Alexander, we are dealing with a volatile, unstable, young man. It would be easy to turn his mind."

"And how would Philip have done that?"

"He circulated the gossip about Pausanias being raped by Attalus's cronies but informed Pausanias that you were the source. After all, Pausanias had come to you for help. . . ."

"And I refused. I never liked him. I sent him packing. Yet, would Pausanias accept that? After all, he was one of Mother's coterie."

"That's a two-edged sword," Miriam replied. "Philip could use that against Pausanias, depicting you as jealous not only of Philip but of Pausanias's relationship with Olympias. As I have said, Pausanias was unstable, bordering on insane—a man who had been raped, who had not received justice, and who now began to fear the laughter and smirks of every soldier in the Macedonian army. Philip would have exploited this, given him Arridhaeus's dagger, told him when to strike. Pausanias knew he was in some danger; that's why he told those guards, led by Perdiccas, to keep a special eye on the king. Pausanias simply wanted a little time, a period of confusion, to make his escape."

"But." Alexander put the wine cup down. "Would Pausanias really believe he would be allowed to escape? Wouldn't he be able to tell Thebes and all of Greece that Philip was behind his own son's murder? Would Thebes, a great city, really harbor a man like Pausanias and bring down upon it the wrath of Macedon?"

"You're forgetting Lysippus, Macedon's agent in Thebes; Philip was as you told me and Hecaetus, writing to him in the days before his death. Philip thought Pausanias unstable enough to accept any assurances. I'm sure Lysippus had his instructions, or would receive them, and kill Pausanias before he became an embarrassment." Miriam smiled thinly. "And Thebes would still be held to account."

"A drama worthy of Euripides," Alexander declared bleakly.

Miriam sighed. "Ah yes but, as in a play, nothing ever goes according to plan. Perdiccas was more quick-witted than the rest. Pausanias fled and tripped. Perdiccas was not involved in any plot. He's a member of the bodyguard and, like royal dogs, trained to kill. Pausanias slipped and he was slain immediately."

Alexander rose and paced up and down the room.

"Philip wanted to begin again, didn't he? A new wife, new son, new conquests. He was wiping out his past: Olympias, myself, Arridhaeus, as well as taking care of his opponents, the Lyncestrians, Athens, and Thebes. Yes, I can just imagine how Philip would have fooled everybody. His son had been murdered but was Alexander really his son? Would a true son plot against his father or communicate with Demosthenes? Then he'd have cast his net further. Olympias would have been involved. True, no one likes Mother. Who would miss her? Her brother Molossus of Epirus would be firmly in Philip's camp. I can just imagine Philip, more in sorrow than in anger, threatening Athens to deliver up Demosthenes, using my death as further pretext against Persia. Of course, Pausanias would be stupid enough to think the Thebans would harbor him. Lysippus would have taken care of him but Philip would still use Pausanias to beat them over the head. My companions in exile would also fall under suspicion: They would never dare to return to Macedon." He smiled thinly. "Only you and Simeon were to be spared. Philip knew that both of you might be caught up in a palace bloodbath. I wonder the reason for such mercy?"

"That was Philip," Miriam replied. "We posed no threat. What are we but two Jews, fine examples of his magnanimity?"

"Yes," Alexander conceded, "that was Philip's way."

"In the end," Miriam continued, "we come to Pausanias." She looked down at the floor.

"Why did he change his mind?" Alexander asked.

"Philip," Miriam replied. "Pausanias may have seen through Philip's trickery? Perhaps he truly blamed Philip for the rape or for not giving him justice against Attalus? He may have planned it or he may have changed his mind only a very short while before he plunged that dagger into Philip's chest?" Miriam spread her hands. "That is all I can tell you."

Alexander sat down. "I accept what you say. There were signs of it. The seer Aristander knew Olympias was in danger. He could see she was about to fall. He was right. Philip would never have allowed Olympias to remain alive if he left Greece. Antipater may have suspected. Attalus certainly did. But I?" Alexander beat his clenched fist against his knee. "I was so full of self-pity, I didn't realize the danger. Yet there are pieces missing from the puzzle. I thought you said Pausanias was tripped? How? He must have had an accomplice who turned against him?"

"That's still a mystery," Miriam replied. "I don't know. Possibly a lover, it may even have been his old tutor who'd panicked." She held Alexander's gaze; those strange eyes smiled.

"It was good of you, Miriam. Perdiccas calls you 'Little Mouse.' You searched out every little crumb, didn't you?"

"And what will you do with it?" Miriam asked.

"I shall not forget Demosthenes. I shall teach the man who calls himself king of kings not to plot against my house. I shall leave Antipater in Macedon so Mother can keep an eye on him." Alexander smiled to himself. "And, apart from you and Hephaestion, I'll never trust anyone again." He grasped Miriam's hand. "That's why Philip wanted you to leave. Once I died he knew there'd be no reason for you to stay. In the end it was like one of Euripides' plays. Philip grasped the knife, but it was turned on him, and all his cunning and all his glory couldn't save him." Alexander picked up a map from the floor. "I shall keep my generals busy. Miriam, stay close when we return to Pella. Mother is bound to become jealous of you."

Miriam left the room and walked into the corridor. Arridhaeus was there, walking up and down like a lost soul, hands flapping.

"I was left here," he moaned. "No one cares about me. Olympias didn't want me back at Pella and the king wouldn't take me to Corinth." He blinked his watery eyes. "I thought things would be better when Philip died, but they are not, are they?"

"You can return to Pella with me." Miriam squeezed his fingers. "And tonight, Arridhaeus, sit next to me when we dine. But I've got to go now."

Miriam walked out of the palace and down to the cobbler's shop in Straight Street. The old man beamed when he threw open the door.

"I'm sorry to trouble you again." Miriam slipped a coin into his hand. "Just a few last questions."

"I am going to miss all this," the old man chortled. "All the comings and goings of the great ones."

"Tell me again," Miriam said, stepping inside the musty, disused shop, "about Pausanias's friends."

"What he's left is now mine?" The old man raised his eyebrows.

"Of course it is," Miriam replied. "I just want to ask you to confirm what you told me before. Pausanias had two friends, one the old philosopher . . ."

"And the other one I never knew. Always came quietly, like a cat along an alleyway . . ."

"And did Pausanias ever talk about him?"

"No, not really except," he pulled the tufts of hair on his chin, "yes, except that he was his only true friend, that's all he said."

Miriam walked back up into the palace and her own chamber. She stood on the small balcony looking down. The guards below were laughing and joking with each other. The door opened behind her.

"So, we are going to Pella tomorrow, little sister?"

Miriam stepped back into the room. Simeon looked pleased, his face flushed.

"Why didn't you trust me?"

Simeon's smile faded.

"Why didn't you trust me?" Miriam came closer.

"About what?"

"Don't lie!" Miriam retorted. "You were one of Philip's clerks, weren't you, Simeon? You began to suspect what he was plotting. Were you Philip's spy on Alexander? Reporting back what he said? Is that why Hecaetus called you secretive? And why Philip was going to allow us to leave honorably?"

Simeon went pale and sat down on a stool.

"Does Alexander know? Have you told the king?"

"Everything except this," Miriam replied.

"How do you know?" Simeon asked.

"The night before Philip died," Miriam declared, "you said you felt ill. You were unable to go to the amphitheater the following morning. At the time I thought nothing of it but, on reflection, you were able to stage our play about Absalom and, in the chaos following Philip's death, you seemed sprightly enough. You weren't ill at all, were you? When everyone went to the amphitheater, you left the palace by a back door. You climbed the small stone wall, went across the cemetery into the vineyard. You pulled up a vine shoot, a perfect trip rope, when Pausanias fled along that path to where he thought you'd be waiting with his leather bag. You made him fall and the royal guards killed him. You then slipped back into the cemetery and returned to the palace. I found some moss and lichen among the vines from the old tomb you brushed by. I've never seen that before, lichen and moss, in a vineyard. Back in the palace," Miriam continued, "you changed your clothes but your sandals were stained with grape juice that is difficult to wash out so you burned those, didn't you, and wore a new pair? I wondered why, at such a time, you bothered with new sandals: You claimed Arridhaeus had used some paint and you'd stepped in it. Brother, Arridhaeus is messy but never once in the days before or after Philip was killed did I see his clothes stained with paint!"

Simeon wiped his mouth on the back of his hand.

"There were other small indications," Miriam continued. "The night I went to the cobbler's in Straight Street. You did not follow me up. You stayed outside. Why? Fearful lest you might be recognized?"

Simeon just stared at her.

"And, of course," she continued, "Arridhaeus's knife. He was constantly moaning about losing his 'Apollo.' At the time I didn't know what he meant, but you did. You, like everyone else, saw the knife used by Pausanias; never once did you explain how it was Arridhaeus's 'Apollo.'" Now, Arridhaeus is a half-wit. He never gave it to Pausanias; otherwise he would not have been moaning about losing it. You knew Philip had taken it and given it to the man he'd persuaded to kill his son."

Miriam sat down on the stool opposite her brother.

"Alexander told both of us to investigate this matter but you hung back, staying in the shadows, busy with this, busy with that. What really brought these matters to a head was when I visited you and picked up some of your writings. I very rarely see your work, Simeon. You were the scribe who wrote out the letters for Pausanias, weren't you? Philip thought he could trust you, his spy on Alexander, a Jew who could be sent packing."

"I will tell you," Simeon replied slowly. "Yes, I knew Pausanias." He shook his head. "No, I was not his lover, though I think he would have wanted that. I'll start from the beginning. Philip always trusted me as a scribe. I am a Jew, an outsider, totally dependent upon his generosity." Simeon looked up shamefacedly. "Yes, he used to question me about Alexander, tell me to keep an eye on both him and Arridhaeus. I was go-between, in his eyes an unknowing one, between himself and Pausanias. I met Pausanias shortly after he had been raped by Attalus and his kinsmen. Philip, well you know how he was, at first refused to see him. Pausanias spent most of his time hanging around or moping in his room."

"And you helped him?"

"He was distressed," Simeon replied. "So, one day, early in summer, I took Pausanias for a walk in the gardens. We shared a wineskin, some oatcakes. I asked Pausanias what was the matter. It was like slitting a water skin. Everything poured out—his anger, his humiliation, his anxiety, his growing fury at Philip's unwillingness to do anything. I interceded for him with Philip, who eventually placated him, bribing him with promotion. I was there when Philip, who treated me like a lapdog, solemnly promised that Attalus would do the same. After that Pausanias seemed happier, more settled. He wished to continue our friendship. I was not so keen. He would beg me to come down to the room he had above the cobbler's shop. I was frightened of being seen so I always entered and left by the window." Simeon wetted his lips. "I thought time would be the great healer. Indeed, I was becoming more concerned about Philip than anything else. He was growing more secretive. I could see he nursed a great anger against Olympias and Alexander. Then one evening Pausanias confessed everything."

"About the planned murder?"

Simeon nodded. "Philip had met him. He said that Alexander was laughing at Pausanias about his strange activities with Olympias. How Alexander, to wreak his own revenge, had mentioned to Attalus how Pausanias could be humiliated and Alexander was now spreading the gossip about the rape through the court."

"And Pausanias believed all that?"

"No, not really; he was mystified, puzzled. Alexander had not treated him favorably but he had never done anything untoward. He knew I was in Alexander's circle and asked if Philip was telling the truth. I told him he wasn't." Simeon held his sister's gaze. "Philip made a terrible mistake. He thought I was his creature but, like many others, he did not realize how deeply Alexander is loved."

"And you told Pausanias this?"

"Yes, I rejected Philip's story as a lie. I said that Philip himself must be the source of these stories and that the assassination of Alexander would be a great crime, heinous to the gods. However, Pausanias was bent on vengeance." Simeon spread his hands. "After that it was easy. It was not only my love of Alexander that made me do it. Philip acted in a callous, cynical way. True, it was I who wrote out that pass for Pausanias and I knew I was really writing out his death warrant. Pausanias showed me the knife Philip had given him. Poor Arridhaeus—he, too, would suffer. I didn't really suggest that Pausanias kill Philip: The thought occurred to him and I agreed."

"You mentioned other matters?"

"Sister, if Alexander had died, what would have happened to us? Given a little bit of silver and cast out to go back to a land and a people who no longer wanted us? Or would we really have been allowed to leave?" Simeon's mouth tightened. "I wanted Philip dead for your sake and for Alexander's. At the same time, I had to protect myself. Pausanias could not survive to tell what had happened. He told me that he would kill Philip when the king entered the amphitheater. He would flee through the vineyard. I would collect his leather bag from the cobbler's and meet him at the gateway just before he mounted his horse." Simeon shrugged. "The rest is as I described it. The night before Philip died, Pausanias and I walked down to that vineyard. I had been there on a few occasions. I knew exactly what to do. I wasn't nervous. I just hoped that they would kill Pausanias immediately. Even if he had survived, who would believe him? Pausanias would have to confess that he, and he alone, had killed Philip. As for any aftermath, I did not know what would happen. However, if Alexander was only a tenth of the man I thought he was, he would survive and overcome any difficulties. The Lyncestrians were not part of any plot. They were born troublemakers who'd brought their tribesmen up for the celebrations. Perhaps they suspected something might happen? Whatever, they exploited the chaos." He smiled thinly. "For a while I was frightened, but Alexander took care of them. I did feel guilty." Simeon got to his feet and walked to the edge of the balcony. "But what could I do, little sister? Tell Alexander what Philip was plotting? What could he have done? Persuaded Pausanias to flee?" He laughed. "Philip would have chosen someone else. All it meant was not collecting that leather bag, hiding in a vineyard, and pulling up a vine shoot."

"So, you had a hand in the death of Alexander's father?"

Simeon turned and grinned. "We know he wasn't Alexander's father, was he? Alexander is the son of a god!"

AUTHOR'S NOTE

THE SOURCES FOR the lives of Alexander, Philip, and Olympias are quite extensive and the events of 336 B.C., as described in this novel, are based on fact. Olympias and Philip did love each other passionately at the beginning. The legends about Alexander's birth and the involvement of pharaoh are contained in a number of manuscripts. Before Alexander left Pella for his years of conquest, Olympias told him to go to the shrine of Ammon-Zeus at Siwah in Egypt. Alexander did visit it; indeed some historians believe his body lies buried there and a current archaeological dig is now searching for his tomb at Siwah.

Olympias's mind undoubtedly became unhinged. She acquired a reputation as a killer. She may well have poisoned Arridhaeus when he was a child. She certainly murdered Eurydice and her baby in a most gruesome manner. Olympias also engaged in secret rites and held her own court. It is understandable that both Philip and Alexander feared her.

Philip comes across as a bluff, brilliant soldier yet that would be a superficial assessment. Philip was also a great killer: compassionate to those who did not threaten him, totally ruthless to any who did. Pausanias was raped by Attalus and yet promoted by Philip. No one has really explained why Pausanias killed Philip. Some people claim he was hired by Olympias, which is why she crowned his corpse with a wreath, but many historians reject that as unsatisfactory. Demosthenes and the new Persian king were conspiring against Philip at the time of his death. Indeed, Demosthenes seemed to know about Philip's murder within hours of it happening. In my view Philip may well have been plotting a bloodbath. Olympias had been divorced and rejected. Alexander's companions had been exiled, and the young prince silenced. There was a growing animosity between Philip and Alexander, and the story that Philip lunged at Alexander at a banquet over Attalus's insulting remarks is well documented. There was a palace revolt in the days following Philip's death when the generals, led by Antipater, sat, watched, and waited for the victor to emerge. As soon as Alexander vindicated himself, the Lyncestrians and Attalus died.

Alexander's character is very much as found in the historical documents: good looking, rather shy and girlish, with strange-colored eyes. They say people fell in love with him because of his charm and self-effacing manner. The soldiers adored him. His magnanimity is well known. He once came across a foot soldier carrying some plunder for the royal treasury; Alexander stopped the man and told him he could keep the lot. We know he suffered from panic attacks and could become highly anxious but, once committed to action, he was resolute and extremely courageous. His campaigns against the mountain tribes, as described in this novel, are based on fact. Alexander was a loyal friend, very shy of women, but with a mother like Olympias it's a wonder he even kept his sanity. He dealt with her through quiet humor.

He made her regent of Macedon, but she also had to share this with Antipater. They hated each other. Alexander's dry remark that "Olympias charged him excessive rent for the nine months in her womb" sums up the attitude of this great and appealing figure of history toward his mother, the witch queen.

There were Jews in Alexander's household. The Macedonian king was deeply interested in the Jewish religion. The status of women in the Macedonian household, as exemplified by Olympias and others, was well known. Women may not have had the same rights as those who fought in the army but Alexander's respect for women of any rank or nation is well documented.